I0720650

A Duke Once Lost

Jane Maguire

A Duke Once Lost

Copyright © 2024 Jane Maguire

All rights reserved. This book or any portion thereof may not be reproduced or used in any manner whatsoever without the express written permission of the author except for the use of brief quotations in a book review.
This is a work of fiction. Names, characters, and places are products of the author's imagination. Any resemblance to actual persons, living or dead, or actual events is entirely coincidental.

Cover design by Holly Perret
Edited by Nevvie Gane

ISBN: 978-1-7382727-0-9

www.janemaguireauthor.com

Also by Jane Maguire

The Inconveniently Wed series

Book 1: **Secrets and a Scandal**

Book 2: **Rumors and a Rake**

Book 3: **Longing for a Lady**

The Rockliffe Dynasty series

Book 1: **A Study in Desire**

Book 2: **A Duke Once Lost**

To my mom, for being <u>significantly</u> less intense than the Dowager Marchioness of Rockliffe. With all my love.

A Duke Once Lost

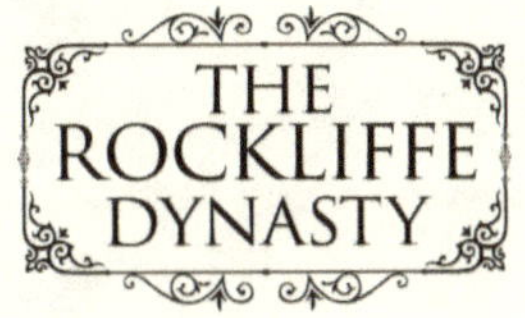

By Jane Maguire

Prologue

April 1795

The distance between Lady Amelia Prescott's bedchamber window and the ground below wasn't really *that* far. She peered out at the back garden, awash in the stark glow of moonlight, and reassessed her path.

Swing her legs over the windowsill. Grab ahold of the sturdy oak branch that stretched toward her like a helping hand. Let her feet find purchase on the branch below it and pivot inward, near the tree trunk, to gain stability. Drop down once, and twice more, until she was near enough to jump to the lush springtime grass dotted with tiny beads of dew. And then … freedom. The future.

Her heart pounded, but not from nerves. At least, not the type that inundated her like a cold, choking weight, making the world close in around her until she could scarcely breathe. No, this feeling was light and fluttery, causing the world to burst open in brilliant shades of color. Hers for the taking.

There was no cause for fear. She'd practiced this clandestine exit several times over the past weeks, and for once, her thin, gangly legs proved a blessing instead of a curse. Besides, when she reached the ground, she would receive the ultimate reward. Her betrothed. Soon to be her husband.

He hadn't arrived yet, but she could already envision his polished black boots gliding noiselessly across the grass until he came to rest near the tree trunk beneath her window. Could see his dark eyes looking up at her, full of admiration and promise. His gloved hand reaching out, ready to take hold of her as soon as she descended from that final branch. Ready to lead her away from the back garden and into the waiting coach, which would barrel north as fast as possible. All the way to Gretna Green.

She bit down on her lip, purely from force of habit, as it began to twitch upward before she abruptly released it and let her smile break free. There was no need to hide her elation when she was alone in her bedchamber. Soon, there would be no need to conceal it anywhere else, either. She and Jonathan would cross the border, say their vows, and become blissfully happy newlyweds, able to reveal themselves to all of England. Or wherever they ended up.

No, they wouldn't have a lavish ceremony at St. George's to display their union to the ton, but what did that matter? Neither of them wanted the fuss and attention. And no, they didn't have her family's permission or blessing, but did that really matter, either? Her mother, the Dowager Marchioness of Rockliffe, wasn't a woman to be dissuaded from her opinions with coaxing or pleas. However, if she didn't learn of the marriage until after it had taken place, she would have no choice but to accept it.

Amelia nearly felt a small pang of guilt for the deception in which she was about to play a part. Nearly. But then again, why should she burden herself with the obligation to act primly and obediently when her siblings refused to do the same? Her oldest brother, Nicholas—the marquess himself—

had stormed around Beaumont Manor, their country seat, for all of Christmastide, saying for the second year in a row that he'd be damned if he traveled to Town for the upcoming Season. Instead, he'd retreated to his hunting box in Northamptonshire with his wife and young daughter, neglecting all his responsibilities in London as if he weren't the marquess after all. As for her middle brother, Samuel, he'd forsaken both the family and society entirely, opting to marry a woman who met with their mother's staunch disapproval and establish himself as a poet.

If anything, Amelia had just as much—*more*—reason to want to escape. It may be only her first Season, but she'd already had enough. So, when Jonathan had uttered those quiet words in the misty garden—*We could run away. To ... a cottage in the Lake District. Better yet, out of England entirely*—she'd answered with a resounding yes.

You need to be certain. He'd returned her assent with a grin that quickly gave way to a crease between his brows as his dark eyes turned solemn. *I don't have a title or property. I won't receive the inheritance from my mother's side for another two years. There are things I would like to give you that I cannot ...*

As if those things would change her mind. If anything, they made her want to become his wife even more. So they could go far away, somewhere no one else knew them, and start a quiet, simple life, just the two of them. Any funds he lacked, she would make up for with her dowry, for surely Nicholas wouldn't be cruel enough to withhold it. Together, they would have everything they needed. They would be happy.

Footsteps rustled through the grass, and her ears pricked, her heart skipping a beat. This was the moment, then. Time to drop down the valise she'd packed, heft herself onto the windowsill, and begin her descent.

She cringed at the loud creaking the window made as she

pushed it the rest of the way open—she thought she'd managed to sufficiently oil it—and couldn't help but suck in a breath at the noisiness of the body racing through the garden, drawing ever closer to her bedchamber. Jonathan usually took such care to move stealthily during these secret trysts, just in case someone else happened to be about. Anticipation must be making his footfalls rapid and careless.

Except the person who emerged from behind the dense row of hedges wasn't Jonathan. The moon's glaring light hit him the moment he stepped forward, revealing him as an unfamiliar stableboy.

Nonetheless, the boy barreled forward, following the path Jonathan was supposed to take to reach her, eagerly waving his arms. "Lady Amelia!"

She whipped her head backward to her bedchamber door, half-expecting to see her mother standing there, drawn by the clamor. The door, though, remained just as she'd left it—closed—and the corridor beyond stayed silent. She turned just as abruptly again, sticking her head out the window with a finger pressed to her lips, hoping her eyes conveyed just how desperately she required silence.

Undeterred, the boy continued racing along until he reached the tree trunk below her, calling up in a poor imitation of a whisper. "Lady Amelia, I have a letter for you. A gentleman bid me to deliver it at once."

She glanced behind her again, just in case, before turning her full attention back to the unexpected messenger several stories below.

A letter? Her stomach did a strange flip, the hopeful flutters in her chest becoming cloying. Any correspondence between her and Jonathan had been thus far delivered by Mary, her lady's maid, who'd been only too glad to assist with the endeavor thanks to the extra few shillings she garnered for her efforts. Not that this letter was even necessarily *from*

Jonathan, for he was supposed to be here, in person, any minute ... But at the same time, who else would take the trouble to send her a covert missive at midnight?

She leaned out the window a little farther, once more considering the steps to make it to the ground. However, her legs now felt unsteady, as if they may not have the precision needed to leap from branch to branch.

Fortunately, the boy spared her the trouble of contemplating it any longer and vaulted onto the lowest branch himself, scrambling up the oak tree until he rested upon the branch nearest her window. His long, skinny arm—not so different from her own—reached out, offering up his delivery. The letter lacked a seal, but the candlelight from her bedchamber showed her name was written across the folded page in a neat black scrawl.

Handwriting she would recognize anywhere.

She leaned over the remaining distance, snatching up the letter with a word of thanks and pulling herself back inside. Her fingers trembled, her mind racing with half-formed thoughts that didn't make sense.

She couldn't have waited another minute if her life depended on it. She tore open the paper, letting her weight rest against the window frame as the glow of her wall sconce brought the words to life.

My dear Amelia,

I've always prided myself on being a man of my word. However, upon closer reflection, I've come to realize that I cannot fulfill the promise I made to you, nor can we carry out our previously discussed arrangements. I was too hasty in asking such a thing of you, allowing my eagerness to overtake wisdom. The truth is, our plans lacked foresight and would not have led to our happiness in the end, once the thrill of it all wore off.

I'll always remember you fondly, but I feel the best way for us to move on from this error in judgment is to sever our relationship. I intend to take my leave from England at once with no plans to return and will not trouble you with additional correspondence.

I sincerely regret any distress this may cause you, but neither of us would benefit from embracing a future based on false hopes and rash decisions, and I cannot in good conscience continue pretending otherwise. I hope that you, too, can see the necessity of us parting ways, permanently, and trust that we will both find ourselves the better for it.

Farewell, Amelia, with all my good wishes for your continued health and prosperity.

Jonathan

A shiver racked her body. Not from the chilly spring air drifting in through her open window, but from the fragments of ice that had seized her heart and spread through her veins.

The words before her were hazy, almost like they came from a dream. Or rather, a nightmare. Yet she blinked and pinched her arm, and still, the piece of paper remained in her trembling fist, the ink refusing to fade away. *Farewell, Amelia …*

Farewell …

Her brain must be frozen, too, for it kept her numb, slow to process the implications of the word. Little by little, though, the ice was chipped away, and a dagger shot straight through her chest, digging in deeper with each passing second of clarity.

Now, the world did close in. She lived in one of the grandest homes in Mayfair, yet the silk-papered walls seemed to be shrinking, the plaster ceiling descending toward the rug, until soon, it would come to swallow her whole, and there'd be nothing left of the space at all.

Let it. She didn't care.

Everything surrounding her had become too intense, and she wanted it to go away. The sconce beside her flickered too brightly. Her heart thudded too painfully. The footsteps in the corridor echoed too loudly.

Footsteps.

Her body turned rigid, the ache momentarily subsiding as she went on high alert. It took mere seconds to discern that these weren't the quiet footfalls of a servant but steady, assured steps that approached her doorway without deference.

Suddenly, she couldn't move fast enough. One hand pulled at the fastening of her traveling cloak while the other grabbed hold of the hopeful little valise she'd left beside the window. She dashed across the room to her bed, dropping the valise to the floor and kicking it underneath. With one final tug, her cloak came free of her shoulders, and she gave it a kick as well, so that both pieces of evidence of her misguided escape attempt lay concealed in a heap beneath her bed.

Except ... Oh, except the damning piece of paper was still clutched in her fist, and outside her window, the stableboy-turned-messenger remained perched upon the tree branch, staring in with his mouth agape.

She nearly flew back across the room, mouthing a single word toward the open window. *Go.* She had no time to ensure he complied before she dashed to the fireplace where flames danced in the grate, guarding her bedchamber against the evening's chill.

She gave her wrist a small flick, but her fingers stiffened, refusing to release the letter. The last words she would ever receive from Jonathan. Even if they were words that had broken her heart.

A single knock tapped against her door, and she thrust her hand forward, forcing the paper to flutter down into the flames. Just in time, for the visitor didn't knock again before pushing the door open and stepping over the threshold.

"Amelia, what are you doing?"

She didn't need to turn around to realize her mother stood there, assessing her. She'd discerned her visitor's identity from the first footstep in the corridor.

Upon receiving no reply, her mother strode into the room, each step bringing her closer to the fireplace. "I thought you would be abed already, yet as I was passing by, I'm certain I heard noises."

"It was nothing. I couldn't sleep." Amelia's voice came out thin and clipped, but at least she accomplished words despite the sob that threatened to tear from her throat. At least her legs held her upright when she wanted nothing more than to drop to the floor in a pile of despair. At least she managed to turn and face her mother as she reached the edge of the mantelpiece while not allowing her features to crumple.

It was one thing to have her heart shattered and her secret dreams for the future dashed. But it was quite another to have her humiliation put on display. To have the details of her hidden betrothal and plans for elopement out in the open, only to make it clear how miserably she'd failed at her one attempt at rebellion.

"Why is the window open?" Her mother's shrewd gaze darted across the room, her pale eyes narrowing. Amelia should have known she'd never miss such a glaring detail.

"I ... thought I'd like a little fresh air before retiring. I'll close it now." She swallowed thickly, her throat feeling like it had been coated in ashes from the fireplace. Soon, she would lack the ability to speak entirely. Yet she had to keep up the facade just a little longer.

"Yes, do. The last thing you need is to catch a chill." Her mother's voice trailed after her as Amelia approached the window, her legs quivering beneath the practical wool skirts she'd selected for traveling.

The stableboy, in any case, had understood the message, for the outstretched branch was now empty, not disturbed by so much as a breath of wind. Just as it had been only minutes earlier when she'd been staring out, envisioning how she'd climb down into Jonathan's arms—

She slammed the window shut, her movements jerky and unrefined. Best not draw any further attention to the scene, for the boy still had to be out rustling in the grass somewhere. She wouldn't put it past her mother to notice even the minutest sound.

"You shouldn't be up this late. You look overtired." Her mother came up alongside her again, and Amelia tucked her arms across her chest to stop them from shaking. "I'll call for Mary to help you get ready for bed."

She shook her head. Her lady's maid always proved an agreeable enough companion, but having to maintain this ruse with another person, for a single second more than necessary, was beyond what she could endure. "There's no need to disturb her. I can manage on my own for tonight."

For a moment, the only sounds in the room were the fire crackling in the grate, swallowing up the remnants of the letter, and the blood rushing through her ears. Her mother was watching her again. Amelia's gaze remained on the black, cloudless sky outside the windowpane, but even so, she could feel the astute eyes boring into her.

She sucked in a breath, waiting. Feeling like the truth must be written all over her countenance, and her mother was about to demand an explanation, and she'd have no choice but to confess the whole sordid tale—

A hand reached out to rest atop her shoulder, giving it a subtle squeeze. "If you're certain." Her mother's tone contained an uncharacteristic note of gentleness. "Sleep well, Amelia."

The breath Amelia had been holding came out as a long, shuddering exhale. Her knees were wobbling again, her throat growing tighter, for that touch nearly led to her undoing.

She *nearly* sank to the floor and unleashed her burgeoning torrent of sorrow. Because yes, she may face no end of censure and ire, but it would *nearly* be worth it if she first had a shoulder to cry on.

However, her mother was already walking away, the stiff satin of her skirts swishing behind her as she retreated to the doorway.

Amelia could have stopped her with a single word. *Wait.*

But she didn't. She waited until the door clicked shut and the commanding footsteps faded into the corridor; only then did she let the first sob escape.

She pressed her face against the cold glass, peering frantically out into the night. Everything had happened so fast, yet she should have had the presence of mind to ask the stableboy to stay hidden somewhere. Then, she could have confirmed the identity of the gentleman who had given him the letter to deliver, found out when and where he'd received it, and asked if she could send a note in return. She dared to push the window open again, just a few inches, and give a quiet call to the ground below. The garden, though, was empty, and she received no response.

She spun away, half-running to her dainty escritoire at the opposite side of the room. She could still write a note—an inquiry. A plea. She could still scramble to the ground and see if the stableboy was at the Rockliffe House mews. Or she could have her horse saddled. Travel to the docks ...

It would never work, of course. She would never succeed in tracking Jonathan down in such short order when he could have gone anywhere. Even if she did, what good would it do?

The words of his letter were beyond clear. He viewed their betrothal as a mistake. He intended never to see her again.

The quill she'd taken up slipped from her fingers, and another sob tore from her throat. With it, the final remnant of strength she'd been clinging to fell away, and she dropped herself onto the velvet-cushioned seat before her, pressing her cheek against the tidy stack of paper on her escritoire.

She'd been such a fool, fancying herself wholeheartedly in love and thinking she'd found a man who felt the same way. Thinking she had the wherewithal to run away and start a new life, far from society, for if her brothers could do as they pleased and say damn the consequences, why couldn't she?

Yet, in all these imaginings, she'd forgotten herself. She wasn't large and commanding, born to be a marquess like Nicholas. Nor was she sinfully charming like Samuel. She was plain, silly Amelia Prescott. The girl of eighteen, who had a figure like a boy and stumbled over her own long, awkward legs. The girl who got dragged along in her family's scandals and could never smile brightly enough or talk prettily enough to negate them. She supposed she had a dowry to recommend her. But in the end, even that hadn't been enough for Jonathan.

For a long time, she let herself sit there and cry until her body turned raw and weary, and she became vaguely aware that the paper beneath her face would be ruined. Not that it mattered. She lifted her head, running her fingers over the damp pages.

Someday, perhaps she'd find comfort in letting the story of her heartache pour from her quill in a kind of diary. Her only confession. For sitting here at her escritoire, with her bedchamber a blur through her tears, she'd made up her mind on two points.

First, no one would ever find out what had passed between her and Jonathan. It would be her own private sorrow, concealed from the world. A secret she would take to her grave.

And second, she would never agree to another betrothal. Not without love, but not with it, either. She'd made an attempt, and never again would she engage in such frivolity.

Never again would she allow a man to lay claim to her heart.

1

The heat of the overcrowded ballroom had grown potent enough to cause hallucinations. What other explanation could there be for the fact that when Amelia happened to glance away from the couples spinning about the dance floor and toward the room's double doors, the person standing at the threshold was none other than Jonathan Astley?

The illusion didn't stop there. The figure, who peered into the room with the same dark eyes she would recognize anywhere, no matter how much time passed, was led forward by a footman to greet their hostess, Lady Englewood. And although chatter whirred around her and the orchestra continued to play, the footman's announcement still reached Amelia where she stood pressed against the wall a good distance away, trying to blend in with the wallpaper. *The Duke of Branscombe.*

A sharp gasp escaped her, and she turned her head downward, discreetly fanning her hand in front of her face for the tiny burst of cool air it would provide. She'd spent enough years attending this type of event that excess heat shouldn't cause her to become overwrought. It was just a momentary lapse, surely. Except when she looked up, Jonathan remained standing there, leaning toward Lady Englewood in a courteous bow. Very much not dead. And very much a duke.

"Amelia, are you well?"

It suddenly occurred to her that her mother, seated in a chair next to her, had ceased conversing with the lady to her other side. Instead, she gazed upward, arching a thin silver brow in Amelia's direction.

No. No, she was not well at all. Yet she quickly returned her hands to her sides and inclined her head, willing the heat in her face to go away. Forcing herself to look at her mother and absolutely *nowhere* else. "Yes, quite well. It's merely that I feel a little overheated. I believe I'll go to the retiring room and then fetch a glass of ratafia. Could I bring you anything?"

"Not at the moment. You run along." Fortunately, her mother didn't feel the need to question her further and turned back to her conversation with the Dowager Lady Chauncy.

Very fortunately, for a feeling was beginning to swell up in Amelia that she hadn't experienced for a long time. Walls closing in. The air growing too heavy.

She chanced another look toward the entrance as she took her first step away from the wall. Jonathan hadn't vanished. He occupied the same spot as before and was now engaged in conversation with their hostess. Which was good. Hopefully, his ability to chat so easily, making Lady Englewood's mouth curve upward with some comment he offered, meant he hadn't spotted her.

She took a few more deliberate steps forward, careful to avoid collisions with other guests as she observed the scene out of the corner of her eye. Lady Englewood was speaking now, the feather in her hair bobbing animatedly, and whatever the words, they caused Jonathan to laugh. Not a sound Amelia could hear, but his face lit up, and laughter echoed through her memory.

Her footsteps weren't cautious anymore. In fact, she practically ran as she dodged clusters of bodies, and if she didn't take care, she would do the very thing she sought to avoid and draw attention to herself. But she couldn't stop. She didn't want the retiring room or ratafia. She just needed to get away.

Another set of double doors stood at the opposite end of the room, leading to the terrace, and she burst through them, sucking in mouthfuls of the night air. In stark contrast to the stifling ballroom, the terrace was blanketed in icy early-spring drizzle, meaning no other guests had come out for a stroll.

Meaning it was perfect for her purposes.

She crossed over the slippery stones so she could lean against the balustrade and peer out into the dark, misty garden. It was so much easier to breathe out here, in this space devoid of people, where tiny raindrops hit her overheated cheeks. The ideal place to recover from shock.

The Duke of Branscombe. The name wouldn't stop turning through her mind.

For that matter, the name had been on all the ton's mind for the better part of a year, ever since Henry Astley, the duke's only son, had foolishly gotten himself killed in a duel, causing such a shock to his father that the duke's heart gave out that very day. The successor to the dukedom was the old duke's reclusive nephew and ward, everyone whispered. *Jonathan*. However, Jonathan had disappeared years ago, had perhaps perished at sea, and if the duke's solicitors could confirm the nephew's demise, they would then have to track down the next in line, whomever that may be.

Except apparently, Jonathan Astley had been found alive and well. In possession of a dukedom that drew him back to England.

She took a long breath, her eyes falling upon a stone bench

down in the grass that was surrounded by a row of leafless shrubs. That's where this had all started. Another stone bench in a garden outside a different ballroom, at one of the first balls she attended after making her debut. She'd needed to escape on that occasion, too, for a spot of fresh air after an endless whirl of activity. It had been even colder that night, with small snowflakes floating down from the sky, but still, she hadn't been alone. A figure—a man—had sat huddled upon the bench facing away from her, his shoulders sagging, his face turned to the ground.

The reason for his being there was none of her business. She knew from experience with her brothers that when something troubled them, it was best to stay clear, for they never stooped so low as to admit distress and actually *talk* about their feelings. Nonetheless, something drew her to this stranger who sat alone, perhaps feeling like the world weighed on him—a sentiment she could understand. And whatever that something was, it compelled her to tiptoe forward, down the terrace steps and over to the bench.

Nothing about it was proper. Even so, her hand had reached out toward his hunched shoulder, brushing against the back of his coat. *Are you all right?*

"Ah, Lady Amelia."

The memory vanished, catapulting her back to the present and the Englewoods' terrace. Every muscle seized at the unexpected male voice, and she remained frozen a moment before awkwardly spinning around. For a split second, she thought he'd come, that she'd conjured him ... But no, this voice didn't have the same measured tone as Jonathan's, and indeed, the gentleman standing behind her was only marginally familiar.

"Good evening ... Mr. Egerton." After forcing her spinning head to concentrate long enough to run through a lengthy list of acquaintances, she came up with what she *thought* was the right name for this young gentleman she'd crossed paths with a time or two at most.

Judging by the way he inclined his head with a slight smile, she must have chosen correctly. "I'm glad I found you." He crossed the terrace, coming to meet her by the balustrade. "I was hoping you might do me the honor of saving me a dance."

She pressed her lips together as an amusing picture cropped up in her mind. The too-tall spinster, gliding clumsily about the ballroom with Mr. Egerton, a gentleman who appeared barely out of school and was a good head shorter than her. The other guests would do no end of talking after witnessing that scene.

"I'm afraid I don't dance." She answered him with the only reply she ever gave. Most gentlemen of the ton realized that by now, but she could forgive Mr. Egerton for not knowing, given how fresh he must be to the social scene.

"I see." He continued peering at her with his large, pale eyes, unfazed by the rejection. "Well, it is rather stuffy in there, isn't it? Perhaps we could take a turn about the garden, then. I'm not one to be bothered by a little rain."

"I'm not sure that would be appropriate. We have no chaperone." She felt ridiculous, as a woman of nine and twenty who was decidedly on the shelf, bringing up such a point with him. However, the longer she racked her brain, the more that snippets of things she'd heard pertaining to his identity came to the surface. *Felix Egerton. The third son of the Earl of Stanfield. Sent down from Cambridge. An over-fondness for the card table. A rake.* In truth, she didn't *want* to walk with him.

"Quite right." He nodded, but instead of stepping away, he came a little closer. "However, I hope you have no objection to me taking the air with you on the terrace, where we're in full view of the ballroom doors."

He really didn't take a hint, did he? Her hope of regaining

her solitary refuge was quickly slipping away despite her best efforts at apathy. What else was she to do but accept his intrusion? After all, she'd become skilled at this type of scenario over the years. *Smile. Be pleasant. Ask questions. Listen attentively.* Even when her heart wasn't in it.

"Not at all." To her credit, she even managed to utter the words with a hint of warmth, which she supposed he deserved. Even if talk of him was somewhat unsavory, he'd done nothing specific to earn her censure.

On a positive note, having to share the terrace with Mr. Egerton was still far preferable to returning to the ballroom, where Jonathan would have begun mingling or was perhaps even joining in for the next dance. Not that his actions should matter to her, especially if he was going to start appearing at high society events from now on. However, while she could maybe grow accustomed to his presence in time, for tonight, any plans she had for seeking out acquaintances or nonchalantly observing the goings-on in the ballroom were lost.

She turned back to the shadowy view of the garden, tilting her chin upward so tiny beads of water could continue accumulating on her face. She should really think of some courteous comment or question for Mr. Egerton, but hopefully, he wouldn't mind if she took a moment of silence first.

His shoulder pressed against her arm, and his hand came down upon hers where it rested on the balustrade, squeezing her fingers through her thin silk glove.

"What are you doing?" She jerked away, snatching her hand back to her side. She may consider it her duty to behave decorously, but she *did* have limits.

He at least possessed enough modesty to flush in response, the reddish tinge of his skin visible even in the darkness. "Well, I ... dash it all, this is more complicated than I imagined! I was trying to display my deep and heartfelt affection for you."

An unladylike sound—somewhere in the area of a snort—

escaped her before she could contain it. "I'm flattered, Mr. Egerton, but I'm not sure where this is coming from. We hardly know one another."

"Nonetheless." His discomfiture vanished quickly, and he smoothed his coat before extending his hand to her with a ridiculous flourish. "Lady Amelia, you captured my admiration from the moment I first laid eyes on you. Make me the happiest of men and consent to becoming my wife."

Her jaw had to be near the ground, and her heart along with it. Had he been partaking too freely of the ratafia? Or perhaps something even more potent in the card room. Whatever the case, she had best put an end to this absurdity straightaway.

She took a step backward, folding her arms tightly across her chest. "Thank you, but I must decline."

He tilted his head, staring at her as though she'd answered in a foreign language. She would give him a cue to help him along, then. She narrowed her eyes and pursed her lips, doing her best imitation of her mother's notorious expression of disapproval.

Her efforts paid off, for his face paled, and he spun toward the garden, muttering under his breath. Not so softly she didn't detect the words, though. "They said nabbing a spinster would be easy."

"Excuse me?"

"The gents at the club." He turned back to her and pouted, his pretense of an amorous suitor forgotten. "They said that when it came to wooing someone who'd been on the shelf as long as you, I'd need nothing more than a few pretty words."

Her heart thudded dully within her chest. Did he mean to say he was doing this as a type of conquest? Or worse, as some sort of joke, and that she'd become a laughingstock at whatever gentlemen's club he frequented.

She stiffened her spine, refusing to let him see her tremble. "They were mistaken, Mr. Egerton, and I think you should go inside now."

He shrugged, his eyes taking on a hard glint that hadn't been there before. "Forget the pretty words part, then, because do you know what I think? You should marry me regardless."

"And why in heaven's name would I do that?" she snapped, her palms twitching at her sides. She was Lady Amelia Prescott: kind, gentle, and demure. Yet never had such a strong urge overtaken her to shove a gentleman into the nearest rosebush.

"Because it would be to our mutual benefit if we made an arrangement." He tapped the heels of his boots up and down against the wet terrace stones, his movements far too refined for those of a man in his cups. Which, in a way, made him all the more vile. "I'm not a total idiot. I had a backup plan, and it seems I must use it. So, tell me, Lady Amelia, are you familiar with the publisher Harding and Shipley? Or, more specifically, that magazine all the chits go wild for, *The Ladies' Spectator*? From my understanding, it contains some silly column offering advice pertaining to matters of the heart that's particularly popular. *My Dear Lady Lockheart*. Do you know it?"

Dread swept over her like a wave in a turbulent sea, threatening to pull her under. He had no reason to ask this. He shouldn't know ... He *couldn't* ...

She swallowed, attempting to push away the bitterness at the back of her throat. Praying the renewed heat in her face wouldn't show but knowing it already did. "What an absurd question. Of course, I know it. All the ladies know it. That has nothing to do with anything."

"On the contrary, I think it does, Lady Amelia." His lips formed a self-satisfied, calculating grin. "Or should I say, Lady Lockheart?"

"I don't know what you're talking about." She clenched her jaw and gave him another glare, trying to appear affronted. In truth, she probably looked more like a caged animal.

"I'm not sure if you've ever noticed that Harding and Shipley is located next to a gaming hell. Crocker's. You could be forgiven if you didn't, for it's only a small establishment, but I visit it often."

His smug smile wouldn't disappear, as meanwhile, her whole body grew tenser, her thoughts spinning wildly out of control. The fact he'd heard of Harding and Shipley and *The Ladies' Spectator* should mean nothing. It wasn't like she ever went there herself. She always took great care, leaving all deliveries in the hands of her lady's maid, Gwen, who'd proved herself an expert in discretion.

Except ... except that one day last month when, for the first time in more than ten years, Gwen had fallen ill at the exact time the column was due.

Amelia's stomach sank. She'd been so certain that she, too, had acted discreetly, showing up in Cheapside in a hackney while shielded by a plain, wide-brimmed bonnet. However, she had only to look at Mr. Egerton's face to realize she'd been mistaken.

"I'll admit that when I began digging around as to why Lady Amelia Prescott was frequenting such a place, I certainly didn't expect to discover *that*." His grin widened further. "In any case, I'm happy to keep it a secret between us, assuming you'll consent to becoming my wife."

"Why would you even want that? Me being an unappealing spinster and all, as you were kind enough to point out."

One of his sandy-colored eyebrows twitched. "Isn't that obvious? Your dowry, of course."

Yes, of course. Why had she even asked? For that's what it usually came down to.

"I'm a third son," he said, casting a mournful look toward the dark garden. "My father, reluctantly, offered to purchase me an army commission. The thing is, I don't want it, nor do I have any interest in some dull career in a church or barrister's office. Not if there's an easier solution."

"Being a magazine columnist isn't a crime, you know." She hated how small—how uncommanding—her voice came out when she spoke. However, she at least had to try with the last line of defense she had. She gave a little shrug as if the weight of the world *hadn't* come crashing down on her shoulders. "If I were to reject your proposal, and you were then to pass along this information to whomever will listen, it would hardly be the worst thing that could happen. In fact, I think I'd prefer it to entering a marriage under such callous circumstances." *Or any circumstances.*

"Maybe." He eyed her carefully, that note of smugness returning to his face. The confidence of a man who knew he had the upper hand. "While Lady Lockheart's tendency to advise young ladies against rushing into marriage may disgruntle some eager mamas, I suppose there's outwardly nothing too offensive about her. Nevertheless, I can't help but think that if you've taken the trouble to conceal your identity for more than ten years, there must be something about the secret you find worth keeping."

Oh ... blast! She forced herself to look at him in return, even as unwanted visions of the future raced through her head and made her blood go cold. Visions of headlines in the gossip columns once the truth of Lady Lockheart came out. Of her mother's staunch disapproval. Of all the eyes of the ton suddenly upon her, scrutinizing her ...

"I hope you won't object to me taking a little time to think about this." She tilted her chin downward, her face feeling as brittle as if it were made from porcelain. "A lady cannot be expected to rush her decision on something as significant as a betrothal."

"Very well, Lady Lockheart. I mean, Lady Amelia, of course." He chuckled softly at his own cleverness, impervious to the way her head pounded and her heart raced. In fact, he was drawing closer again, his arm coming down to join with hers where she held it rigidly near her side.

She stiffened as his hand clasped her once more, ready to wrench herself away and tell him to leave her alone until she made up her mind.

Something stopped her, though. A creak and rustle from across the terrace, cutting into the night's stillness. Mr. Egerton must have already noticed it, for he faced the terrace doors with a grin, keeping his hold securely upon her.

Someone else had stepped onto the terrace. Another man, a tall, broad-shouldered silhouette in the darkness. He moved through the mist, either unaware or unconcerned about disturbing a couple's private rendezvous, for he approached their spot near the balustrade, drawing closer and closer until the shrouded image of his face became a set of identifiable features.

Oh no.

Oh no, oh no, this could not *be happening.*

In her weaker moments, she'd allowed herself to briefly indulge in the fantasy of Jonathan returning to her. Of him suddenly appearing and gathering her in his arms, saying he'd made a terrible mistake and professing his undying love. Knowing in her heart, of course, that the love between them had been nothing more than an illusion, and he planned never to come back. That he might not even be alive.

Except now, he *was* here, standing before her on the Englewood House terrace. He looked her up and down, assessing her with the same dark-eyed gaze that had been branded into her memory. Under different circumstances, perhaps she could have remembered all her years of practicing careful manners and brushed it off, giving the appearance that she remained unaffected by the sight. However, it just so happened that Jonathan Astley, the new Duke of Branscombe, had shown up at the exact moment when the careful life she'd spent a decade building for herself had been snatched away by a nefarious blackmailer.

The air rushed from her lungs like she'd just taken a tumble from a galloping horse. With any luck, the ground beneath her would split open and drag her down so she no longer had to face what occurred on the terrace. It didn't, though, and with each passing second, it became apparent that she needed to do something other than stare in return.

She nearly gave him the cut direct. If the ground refused to consume her, wouldn't that be the easiest thing? After all, more than ten years had gone by. Surely, that was enough time for a person to forget an old ... *acquaintance* had even existed, and it would be improper for her to converse with a stranger. Perhaps that's all she was to him now, too: someone vaguely familiar but whom he no longer recognized.

She nearly walked away as if no tall, broad-shouldered figure had appeared on the terrace. Nearly, but then a voice, low and maybe a little unsteady, cut into the silence. "Amelia."

So, he hadn't forgotten, and just like that, the time to pretend otherwise had slipped by. Indeed, the look in his eyes spoke of nothing but recognition. That was, until his gaze shifted downward to Mr. Egerton—and lower still, to their joined arms—and something else seemed to cloud his features. It was as if his eyes became darker, and she would almost say the set of his mouth looked ... strained.

Her long-ago fantasy took the opportunity to wheedle its way back into her thoughts. Jonathan kneeling at her feet, his arms encircling her waist. *I'm so sorry, my love. Can you forgive me? I never wanted to leave. I've missed you.*

A terse grunt from Mr. Egerton alerted her that her nails had begun digging into his arm, and she gave her head a quick, subtle shake, forcing herself back to the present. What drivel. She was far from a naive girl of eighteen any longer, and the time for such imaginings had long since passed. No, she refused to waste a single second longer succumbing to useless, ridiculous thoughts. Which meant she had to get off this terrace as soon as possible.

Her world had crumbled before, and she'd always managed to hold herself together when it mattered. Tonight would be no different. She just had to endure a minute longer.

She attempted a downward motion with her legs, and thankfully, they cooperated, folding her into a stiff curtsey. She opened her mouth, and as it turned out, her voice cooperated as well, despite how her throat felt dry and thick. She even remembered the new, correct address. "Your Grace."

However, those few syllables brought her to a breaking point. The Englewood House terrace and gardens were vast—practically an abyss in the darkness—but the space closed in on her nonetheless, and the chilly air changed from refreshing to cloying.

She spun on her heels, no longer able to look upon the image of the past come back to taunt her. If only she'd been careful enough to pivot in a manner that didn't send her brushing roughly against Jonathan's side, giving her a fleeting hint of the hard, muscled arm beneath his coat.

But she couldn't afford to think about that.

She marched across the terrace, dragging the insidious Mr. Egerton—who still hadn't released his grip—along with her. Amidst Mr. Egerton's sound of affronted surprise, she could almost swear she heard her name uttered again as a faint echo through the night air.

She couldn't think about that, either. Her footsteps picked up speed, thumping gracelessly against the terrace stones as she approached the ballroom doors. Instead of acting sedate and unaffected, she put her inner turmoil on display, probably appearing like a woman half-deranged. But it didn't matter. Nothing mattered until she could escape the terrace, until she could breathe again.

They burst into the ballroom, hit by an onslaught of chatter, sticky heat, and candlelight. The very place from which she initially sought reprieve. Well, until the terrace became an even more dangerous location. However, the ballroom was still only marginally better, for there were eyes everywhere, along with Mr. Egerton's continued hold on her arm.

After being dragged unceremoniously alongside her, he managed to recover from the shock and plant his feet firmly in place just inside the doors, adhering them both to the spot. He turned to her, his gray eyes narrowing. "Who the devil was th—"

"Pardon me, Mr. Egerton, but I'm going to the ladies' retiring room. I'm afraid I have a headache." She wrenched her arm away, subtly enough—she hoped—not to cause a scene. At last, his grip slackened, setting her free. "I trust you understand and won't mind if we postpone making further arrangements until another day, once I've recovered."

She didn't wait for his reaction. Instead, she darted away, veering through the crowd in search of the quickest route out of the ballroom. Her eyes stayed glued to the floor, avoiding any chance of meeting acquaintances with whom she'd normally stop to chat. If anyone remarked upon her uncharacteristic rudeness, it would be secondary to what they'd say once her name became entangled in scandal. For a scandal was fast approaching, one way or another.

At last, she stumbled through another set of doors and reached the safe haven of the corridor, leaving the whirl of the ballroom behind. The ladies' retiring room was down a way and to the right. Amelia, however, went left until she came upon a darkened, vacant room—a study, it looked like—and slipped inside. She didn't truly require the retiring room. She just needed to be alone.

From here, the lively strains of music and conversation from the ballroom became muted, drowned out further by the blood rushing through her ears. How unfortunate that it did nothing to mute the voices from the terrace that shouted in her memory.

Her claim of a headache was no lie. She'd have to work up the courage to return to the ballroom—or better yet, find a servant who could deliver a message to the ballroom on her behalf—so her mother knew she needed to leave early. Sooner rather than later, for at the rate things were going, someone was likely to burst into the study at any moment and deliver another life-altering upset.

She required a minute. A minute to press her weight against the wall and try to stop shaking. A minute to see if she could compose herself enough to obtain a weak shadow of normalcy, at least for the carriage ride home.

She stood, waiting, but her chin wouldn't cease quivering. Her head wouldn't cease pounding with the knowledge that the quiet contentment she'd established in her life was about to shatter into pieces.

And her heart wouldn't stop painfully beating, having the audacity to remind her that, despite everything else that transpired, it suffered the renewed effects of a long-ago blow.

2

Perhaps the day would have gone differently had Jonathan Astley, the new Duke of Branscombe, not found himself fixated on memories of hair the perfect shade of reddish gold. On eyes of the purest blue. And on the willowy figure who'd stared at him last night as if she'd just encountered an apparition—not a welcome one—before marching away in revulsion with another gentleman upon her arm.

Perhaps, had the brief and perplexing and altogether jarring encounter at the Englewood ball not occurred, he could have awoken in the morning, spent a few hours reviewing the numerous papers that required his attention, and gone off to his first session in the House of Lords with more assuredness in his step. After all, he'd paid his fees and received his writ of summons. It was time for him to see to his new duties.

Regrettably, that wasn't how things transpired.

The most damnably frustrating part of it all was he really had tried to do everything right. Yes, he'd made up his mind many years ago that nothing remained for him in England and he had no cause to return. And yes, more ghosts from the past remained here than he cared to remember. Nevertheless, when the letter had reached him on the shores of Ceylon, informing him of the untimely deaths that led to his newfound status as the Duke of Branscombe, he hadn't bemoaned his fate. Instead, he'd set sail on the journey that was never supposed to take place, thinking, amidst the apprehension, that his father would say he'd been granted a gift. That this was a chance to do better. To right wrongs.

Images of that red-gold hair and those cerulean eyes were nothing new. They'd followed him across oceans and withstood the passage of time, becoming all the more frequent as *The Ariadne* lurched through the waves, drawing him ever closer to the English coast. Enough that as one of his first orders of business upon establishing himself at Branscombe House in London, he'd made discreet inquiries of his secretary as to the whereabouts of Lady Amelia Prescott. The revelation that she remained unmarried and divided her time between London and her family's estate in Kent had brought with it a simultaneous stab of regret and a pang that felt something like hopefulness.

Both sentiments he tried to quash. After all, he'd posed the question solely for informative purposes. So he could at least know what to expect should an encounter take place, for he didn't do well when caught off guard.

As it turned out, though, nothing could have prepared him for when the encounter *did* take place. He never could have accurately envisioned how much sharper the image of her would be—even in darkness—when she stood before him in reality and not just in his mind. Nor could he have imagined how it would feel to see her face etched with shock and coldness, not her sunny smile. To see her sequestered on the terrace with another.

However, the resulting pit in his stomach was yet another sensation he had to push away. He had no right to feel ... well, *anything* other than indifference, and the distraction of it wouldn't serve him well.

The House of Lords deserved his full attention, and he'd intended to give it. Unfortunately, his absentmindedness as he sat in his study, looking at ledgers without really reading them, meant he was late calling for the curricle to take him there. That set him off on the wrong foot and led to him rushing into the chamber several minutes after the appointed start time of a quarter to four.

Even then, he'd tried not to grow flustered, slipping into the back row of cross benches and trying to look like he belonged. Trying to restore focus. The session was important, after all. One of his first steps forward.

His uncle likely could have counted on one hand the number of times he'd attended Parliament, seeming almost to take pride in how he shirked his duty. Jonathan, on the other hand, attempted to sit attentively upon the wooden bench, listening to the speeches and debates and mentally penning the speeches that he, too, would someday deliver.

Only, as he sat there, little flashes of red-gold continued to trickle in. Memories of soft hands and even softer lips. Of a melodious laugh. Of letters.

By the time men began shuffling around him, making for the exit, it occurred to him that the session must have come to an end, and that for the greater part of it, he hadn't been attentive after all. He quickly stood, shaking the stiffness from his legs. But before he could begin to ponder the implications of his distractedness, an older gentleman of unknown name and title—for Jonathan had spent little time amongst society during his previous years in England—approached, giving him a polite nod. Which was a vast improvement on the curious looks—or, in some cases, downright sneers—he'd experienced upon walking in. "My condolences, Branscombe."

Jonathan returned the gesture. His uncle Tobias and

cousin Henry had created some bad blood between themselves and certain gentlemen of the ton, but little by little, Jonathan would seek to undo it. "Th-th-thank you."

He promptly froze, then snapped his jaw shut. He could almost believe the words had come from elsewhere. Yet the unknown lord looked solely at him, and the other voices surrounding them blended into an indistinct hum.

The other man blinked, giving one of his graying eyebrows a subtle lift. Or was Jonathan merely imagining things? In any case, the man continued speaking as if he hadn't noticed anything amiss. "I understand you've been away from England for quite some time. Must have been a shock to return under such circumstances."

Jonathan cleared his throat, giving himself an extra moment to prepare. "Y-yes." Damn it, why was this happening to him again? His hands clenched into fists, his body going tense. "If y-you'll ... excuse me."

He turned away, although not before noticing the man's face crease in bewilderment. And for good reason. God only knew what the man thought of the poor imitation of a duke he'd chanced to speak with.

Jonathan strode through the chamber with his eyes on the floor and heat flooding his neck and face, not stopping until he reached the street and was hit by a blast of bracing night air. The last thing he needed was for another peer to stop to offer condolences. Or worse, scorn. His throat felt too pinched for words, his tongue useless and heavy. Sensations he hadn't experienced in years.

However, the coldness of the nighttime breeze must have lulled him into a false sense of security, for after a few minutes standing in a shadowed alcove at the edge of the building, he found the fire in his skin abating and the speed of his breathing returning to normal. Enough that he could convince himself that his ineptness had merely been an isolated incident and perhaps he'd overreacted to it all.

Enough that instead of making a quiet retreat to Branscombe House—as he'd done the previous night when he slipped away early from the Englewood ball—he decided to carry on with his plans for the evening. Yes, he'd botched his time in the Lords. That didn't mean it would happen again or that he had to go home and cower.

By the time he emerged from his isolated corner, the other gentlemen had dispersed, either on foot or by carriage, leaving him to make the walk to St. James's Street alone. Just as well. The night was free of rain, and he could use the extra time to compose himself and prepare for what came next. And *not* to think of blue eyes locking with his, and long limbs, and the strands of silky red-gold he'd once held between his fingers ...

All too soon, he arrived before the brick and stone facade of Brooks's. For some reason, he seemed to be breathing heavily again, and not just from the brisk walk.

But what could he do but ignore it and push forward? Above all, he should be grateful that the gentlemen's club had consented to have him pass through its doors as a member. No thanks to his uncle's legacy. However, the fact that he'd taken the former duke's debts and seen them more than repaid—combined, perhaps, with blatant curiosity on the ton's part—had led to a membership vote at Brooks's in which Jonathan, surprisingly, hadn't been blackballed. A definite point in his favor, for the road to restoring the Branscombe dukedom would undoubtedly be a long one, and the club seemed an ideal starting point.

Taking a final breath of the crisp—if not altogether fresh—night air, he stepped inside, immediately surrounded by warmth and the scent of something cooking, rich and aromatic. Dinner might be just the thing once he got himself settled. He exchanged a few words with the steward who greeted patrons near the entrance, establishing his identity and getting his bearings in the unfamiliar space. Words that, fortunately, didn't get stuck or tangle in his throat.

After weighing his options, he decided to forgo the great subscription room—for beginning his foray into Brooks's with gambling might evoke memories of the former duke in others that would be better left to rest—and head to the small drawing room.

Keeping his top hat pulled low on his forehead, he sank into a wingback chair near the doorway, giving himself a moment to survey the scene. The room was buzzing with conversation, filled with gentlemen seated in clusters of chairs alongside tables filled with cards and crystal glasses. All of them strangers to him, or passing acquaintances at best. Yet now, he was their equal. There had to be at least one group who wouldn't mind if he came up and made an introduction.

Suddenly, a figure came rushing past him into the room, pausing briefly near Jonathan's chair before hurrying over to a table where a group of young gentlemen beckoned. "Over here, Stanfield!"

The man made an abrupt left turn to get to the appropriate table, pulling off his hat as he walked to reveal a shock of unruly black hair. Giving Jonathan a clear view of his profile.

Recognition hit him like a punch to the gut. At Eton, the man in question—then just a boy—had been referred to by his courtesy title, Viscount Ward. However, it had always been well known that he was the elderly Earl of Stanfield's oldest son. A son who was now, apparently, a peer in his own right. Jonathan, fortunately, hadn't caught sight of him during the session in the Lords. However, based on the timing of his arrival at the club, chances were he'd been there.

Jonathan's gaze snapped away from the unwelcome scene, instead drifting around the table of men who eagerly awaited their friend. No surprise, for Ward—*Stanfield*—had always been the ringleader. All at once, additional flares of recognition came, and the strangers at the table, five in total, became much more.

Nearly fifteen years had passed since Jonathan walked out of Eton for the last time. In some ways, a lifetime. But still, in the faces of these men, traces of the boys they'd once been remained. All carefree and boisterous, the sons of peers, landowners, or great military men. All still together as a group, just as they'd been at Eton, united by the confidence that could only come from privilege. The only one missing was Jonathan's cousin Henry.

Jonathan's vision suddenly went hazy and dark, for he was no longer at Brooks's but on the floor of an unlit dormitory. The sturdy toes of boots slammed repeatedly into his abdomen as above him, gleeful, mocking voices called out the familiar jeers.

"I thought Parliament was going to keep on the whole blasted night." Stanfield's animated voice traveled across the room above the other chatter, giving Jonathan an abrupt tug back to the present. Not that it was much of an improvement.

He glanced upward again, watching from beneath the brim of his hat as Stanfield accepted a snifter of brandy from an attentive waiter. "To add to it all, once the session finally adjourned, I had to stop in for a minute to see Felix, who's gotten himself in quite a snarl." Stanfield sighed dramatically, tipping the glass to his mouth and pouring the brandy down his throat. "But never mind. Another session's done for another day, and you won't *believe* whom I spotted in the House."

His companions made eager exclamations, and Stanfield gave one of his wide, malicious smiles—because some things never changed—drawing out the anticipation. All while Jonathan's skin prickled as if he'd just stepped outdoors into an icy winter wind, his stomach roiling as he awaited the announcement.

"The new Duke of B-B-B-B-Branscombe!" Stanfield practically shouted the name, no longer able to conceal the latest on-dit. Hearty strains of laughter rang out around the table, forming a cacophonous roar that pierced into Jonathan's skull. Stanfield took another mouthful of brandy, sending a trickle of amber liquid sloshing over the side of his glass as his hand shook from hilarity. "As if I needed something to make my days in Parliament even longer. Can you imagine what will happen if he thinks to say his piece? *I c-c-call your l-l-lordships' a-a-a-a-ttention—*"

He broke off, consumed by a fresh fit of laughter that had his companions following suit.

Jonathan no longer remembered all their names. From this distance, he no longer knew which voice, which grating chortle, belonged to each man, either. Nonetheless, he found himself frozen in place, half in the drawing room at Brooks's and half back at Eton, his head pounding with shouted words and his own broken ones.

"It's hard to believe Henry's really gone." A new voice spoke up, ridding itself of laughter and taking on a wistful note. Jonathan's gaze darted around the group until it fell upon the speaker, a lanky man with a head of closely shorn blond hair. The second son of a baronet, if memory served him correctly. Ambrose? Adam? He couldn't recall. However, a youthful version of the face peered down at him as another boot connected with his gut. A memory that would never vanish.

The man shook his head. "But if you saw his upstart cousin in the Lords, I guess that's all the proof we need. It's a bloody shame—"

"May I bring you anything, Your Grace?"

Jonathan's muscles seized at the sudden sound close to his

ear, and he tore his eyes away from the scene and jolted his head upward. A waiter looked down at him, his expression mild, ready to fetch whatever Jonathan desired. As if the Duke of Branscombe were just like any other peer, able to accept a snifter of brandy and spend the rest of the night mingling like he belonged.

Jonathan bolted upright so fast that the legs of his chair scraped along the floor. He turned brusquely, before the sound could draw attention to him and give the room a view of his face. Although maybe it was already too late.

He didn't wait to find out. He paused only long enough to give a single shake of his head, for his throat was tight and words, undoubtedly, beyond him. Then, he was out the door, striding through the entrance hall where he'd come in and back onto the street.

Once again, the night air greeted him, but this time, instead of revitalizing, it settled over his skin like a frigid weight. His blood, on the other hand, was on fire. He sucked in a breath and gave a rapid exhale, trying to find some sort of equilibrium between the two extremes. However, his efforts did nothing.

He plodded along the pavement, ignoring the passing hackneys in favor of a bracing walk home to Grafton Street. Yet with each footstep that slapped against the ground, his mind rattled, shouting one insistent word after another. *Misfit. Coward.*

His fingers clamped into fists so tight that his knuckles cracked. Perhaps he should have taken a page from his cousin Henry's book and called out Stanfield on the grounds of defamation.

He could nearly laugh at the thought if it wasn't so damn pitiful. For calling a man out required words, and words would only serve to make him a further source of mockery. *I ch-challenge y-y-you to a d-d-d-duel ...*

What was wrong with him? Eton, and all the other things that had gone so terribly awry during his previous time in England, was half a lifetime ago. Since then, he'd traveled the world. Found his voice. Hell, he'd crawled his way up until he amassed a bloody fortune. He'd become a goddamn duke. And still ...

Still, he could be reduced to a cowering schoolboy by some idle gentlemen's club gossip.

Just like he could sit in Parliament and become oblivious to the pressing matters of the nation, turning into a stammering mess because of dreamlike wisps of reddish gold.

He'd left London eleven years ago as nobody—a battered, broken shell—and returned as a duke, telling himself that the past no longer held any power. He'd marched right into the Duke of Branscombe's life determined to live up to the responsibilities of the title. Because that was the decent thing to do.

Because, apparently, he didn't know the difference between decency and idiocy.

Well, no more. His heavy footsteps turned the corner onto Grafton Street, carrying him to the polished front door of Branscombe House. The place he'd once damned and sworn he'd never return to. Maybe he'd been smarter back then.

He nodded a wordless greeting as the butler, Sawyer, welcomed him home, then took off to his study before Sawyer could say something that would require a response. Once safely shut away, he went straight to the end table containing the brandy decanter, unbending his stiff fingers to pour himself a glass. The drink he hadn't gotten to at Brooks's.

He took a long swallow, waiting for the liquid to ease the ache in his throat and the throbbing in his head. Which was perhaps an impossible feat. Yet he needed it to, enough for him to ring for Sawyer and make an intelligible request.

His things must be packed without delay. The carriage

made ready for the morning. Branscombe House closed up. For Jonathan was leaving.

He refilled his glass, his chest continuing to burn from brandy, outrage, humiliation ... and something that felt vaguely like a protest.

He wasn't running away. He *wasn't*.

Very well, maybe he was. But it wasn't as if he were fleeing to the country with no purpose but to hide. God knew there was plenty requiring his attention at Edgecote Hall, the Branscombe country seat in Northamptonshire. Far away from ballrooms and Brooks's.

He'd arrived in London filled with false hopes and good intentions, believing in the power of new beginnings. Underestimating the power of the past.

He wouldn't make that mistake again.

You can't stay away forever. A voice of reason managed to break through his thoughts, not yet dulled by the effects of brandy.

No, perhaps he couldn't. But he could stay away for a time. Long enough that the boyhood affliction he'd thought long since vanquished would truly disappear for good. Long enough that any leftover jeers from youth would roll off his shoulders.

Long enough that the red-gold of his dreams would fade, that if he happened upon the blue eyes again, they would no longer pierce him. Nor would he feel troubled by the sight of another man's hand upon her arm, or a waltz, or even a betrothal announcement in the papers.

Long enough to forget. Or if not that, to at least be unaffected.

3

Amelia hadn't intended to spend her first day out of the house after the Englewood ball disaster lying upon her sister-in-law's sofa, burrowed beneath two shawls, three blankets, and a rather hefty bulldog. Yet somehow, that's exactly what happened.

She wasn't proud of the fact that upon leaving the ball early, she'd immediately gone home and taken to her bed, remaining there for all the next day and another night besides. It gave her no satisfaction to lie bundled in her counterpane with the curtains drawn, every slight sound putting her on edge. However, her head truly had ached, and even once the pain eased, her mind whirled around as if trying to claw its way through a dizzying fog. Trying to gain purchase in a situation where, one way or another, she served only to lose.

Finally, after a second sleepless night, she'd risen with a plan. Not a particularly clever plan—such as, say, getting Felix Egerton banished from England before he could speak a word of gossip to anyone ever again, or turning back time so she never visited Harding and Shipley. But a plan nonetheless.

One that started with a visit to her brother Samuel's widow, Theo.

Making the trip between her bedchamber and the awaiting carriage, just outside the front door, had been the worst part. Her heart had thumped as she walked, half-expecting to find her irate mother in the entrance hall, holding a scandal sheet that contained the damning revelation about Lady Lockheart. Or to encounter Mr. Egerton approaching the house, ready to demand an answer to his proposal. Yet she'd made it to the carriage unscathed—discovering that her mother remained abed, the papers hadn't been delivered this morning, and no one passed by Rockliffe House but strangers—allowing her to breathe easier on the journey to Buckingham Street, where Theo had a home with her sons and new husband, not far from the printshop they owned.

Amelia had traveled there many times before as part of the regular visits she did with her nephews. If anything, the familiarity and safety of the place should have put her at ease. However, as she'd knocked upon their door, her legs gave a little lurch, and the resolve she'd spent the previous hours building up had begun to crumble.

A detail that must have shown upon her face, for when the door had flown open, revealing not Theo but two youthful faces, she'd been greeted with exclamations of both surprise and concern.

Aunt Amelia! What are you doing here? I thought we weren't meeting at the park until four.

Say, Aunt Amelia, are you quite well?

From there, everything had passed in a blur. She knew she'd *tried* to smile reassuringly and say she was fine, that she'd merely come for an early visit with their mother. She also knew, though, that her ever-clumsy feet had stumbled as she made her way inside, and suddenly, two small hands had joined with hers—a boy on each side—to drag her to the sitting room. There had been shouts, and postulations about agues and dropsy, and then, the appearance of Theo's new husband, Jeremy. Looking thoroughly perplexed, he'd grabbed his coat and made a hasty exit, uttering something on his way out about fetching Theo and how, in the meantime, the boys were in charge of seeing to their aunt.

Hence, the blankets and shawls, for her oldest nephew, Benedict, feared she may have caught a chill. And hence, the dozing bulldog on her legs, for the younger boy, Alexander, claimed there was no greater comfort than curling up with his cherished pet, Achilles.

"Do you think she needs a tonic?" Alex rose from his position by her feet, gazing questioningly at his older brother.

"Hmm." Ben ceased his task of adjusting the throw pillow beneath her head, instead reaching into his pocket to retrieve the spectacles he wore for reading. He perched them atop his nose, giving her an assessing look as thorough as that of an experienced physician. "Maybe. Or perhaps a compress."

"Thank you, boys, but that really isn't nec—"

"I'll go look in the medicine chest," Ben proclaimed, bolting from the room before she could fully form the protest.

Amelia shifted, struggling beneath her mountain of covers and dog to get herself seated. She wasn't really ill, after all. Anxious and heartsick, yes, but she'd come here because she had a plan, because she wanted to take charge and make things at least a trifle better—

"No, no, don't try to get up." In an instant, Alex was kneeling beside her, pressing a small but firm hand into her shoulder, encouraging her to remain prostrate. "You need to rest and stay calm. It's of vital importance."

She managed a real smile, then—a tiny one, anyway— letting herself sink a little deeper against the sofa cushions. This was the opposite of taking charge. Yet if her nephews insisted, who was she to argue? Besides, there was something comforting about lying here, tucked in and well-tended. As if the rest of the world couldn't touch her.

Seemingly satisfied that she'd obeyed his instructions, Alex released his hold on her, stretching his arm out to give Achilles a few scratches behind the ears. His face remained close to hers, though, his blue eyes watchful beneath the mop of russet curls that tumbled onto his forehead to border them.

It was uncanny, really, how closely he resembled his father. The same shade of unruly hair. The same brightness in his gaze. Samuel had been gone for well over a year, but if she squinted, it was almost as if he appeared before her again, youthful and carefree.

Samuel was the reason the whole Lady Lockheart disaster had begun in the first place. Well, no, that wasn't entirely correct. The original cause, of course, had been Jonathan. But what had transpired in the weeks following had all been her older brother's doing.

She could still picture that sunny June day, close to eleven years ago, when she'd sat upon a bench in Hyde Park, thumbing through the pages she'd spent the past week filling with her writing.

The Season had been about to draw to a close, and to celebrate the day of fine weather before everyone dispersed to their country estates, she'd been invited to partake in a picnic with other young members of the ton. She'd accepted the invitation because she always accepted. Because she had to take whatever opportunity she could to show herself, bright and smiling, not waylaid by the past or her family's scandals. Certainly not affected by a secret broken heart.

However, that didn't mean the effort never grew wearying, and while everyone had been engaged in a lively game of charades, she'd slipped away, needing a moment alone on that quiet bench.

Yet as she'd sat there, half imagining ideas for another ten pages and half thinking she should throw it all in the fire, a shadow appeared. A shadow, it turned out, that belonged to the estranged brother she hadn't seen in weeks, out for a stroll in the park.

From there, everything had happened so fast. She'd let out a cry of delight at the unexpected encounter. Jumped to her feet in excitement. And in the process, had carelessly sent the pages upon her lap fluttering to the ground.

She'd realized her mistake at once. Not fast enough, though, to retrieve the pages before Samuel bent down and secured them within his grasp. His eyes had fallen upon the top corner, and in his rich, expressive voice, he read the opening line aloud. *My Dear Lady Lockheart.* Causing her to cry out again—not with joy this time—and a wave of panic to take hold. The paper contained her secret words, not meant for anyone else.

Yet as he'd moved to hand the pages back, uttering a few words of apology with an easy but somewhat perplexed smile, the wave had faded. Given way to a sense of resignation and a feeling that she'd quite possibly overreacted. After all, it wasn't as if the make-believe letters, in which she'd chosen to act as both a lovelorn young miss and a wise matron replying with advice, revealed any real names. He'd never have cause to realize that she'd based the first letter on her own situation. As for the others, they were pure fiction, inspired by bits and pieces of relationship woes she overheard when she was out in society, looking for a distraction so she didn't have to think of her own troubles.

Besides, Samuel was a writer, too, who'd always enjoyed sharing his poetry with her during the days when he still lived in the family home. If anything, he should be proud his sister had taken after him in at least some small regard.

For better or worse, the sudden burst of affection for him had enticed her to leave the papers within his hands, muttering a few words about how they were only silly, fictitious letters, and he was welcome to read them if he wished.

But Samuel, after perusing the letters, didn't say they were silly at all. Instead, he'd smiled at her again with a look of unfiltered pride. Told her he could envision them in one of those periodicals Theo enjoyed reading. Told her he'd gotten to know some people in the publishing business, that if she liked, he could make inquiries on her behalf.

She could still remember the way her heart had seized at the suggestion. It wasn't the sort of decision that should be made in an instant. She'd never even considered the possibility …

But at that moment, a voice had begun echoing through the trees, significant because it belonged to one of the ladies from the picnic calling *her* name. She'd been gone far too long, and there was no more time.

And so, she'd left Samuel in possession of the letters with one condition. No matter what happened, her name could never be associated with them. She knew all too well what had happened during her previous attempt to keep secrets and rebel: her heart had shattered, and she'd nearly been ruined. However, she couldn't help but imagine having a little secret —something of her own—in the background. Something to break up her monotonous, lonely existence.

If it hadn't all happened so fast, she might have lost courage and demanded the letters back. But in the blink of an eye, her brother had left, gliding across the grass and mixing with the other nameless passersby on the nearby walking path. Thus bringing Amelia's brief, perplexing, and potentially life-altering encounter to an end.

True to his word, Samuel had drawn the right people to her writings. He'd garnered the attention of Harding and Shipley. Negotiated the deal to have her—Lady Lockheart— appear as a monthly feature in *The Ladies' Spectator*. He'd brought her to a place she couldn't have dreamed of, even if she did it all from the shadows, never revealing her identity.

Maybe matters would have turned out differently if they'd continued meeting in the park. For he was so unapologetically himself in what he strove for—scandals and consequences be damned—that his attitude may have rubbed off on her. It turned out, though, that the remainder of their communication had taken place through letters only, and after a while, even his messily scrawled notes had stopped. By that point, she'd been already well established in her role as Lady Lockheart and didn't require his help to continue. Nonetheless, she'd always felt the ache of his absence. One that had been made permanent with his death.

She swallowed down the lump in her throat, closing her eyes a moment against the onslaught of memories. What would Samuel say if he knew everything he'd set in motion for her was about to come crashing down?

Her eyes flew open again as something thudded against the floor, and she was met with the sight of Benedict bursting back into the room, his arms laden with bottles and jars.

"Sorry I took so long." He swooped down to retrieve an amber glass vial that had fallen to the carpet before hurrying over to drop the items on the end table next to the sofa. "I wasn't sure which medicine would be best, so I brought several different options."

"Let me see." Alex scrambled to his feet and darted to the end table beside his brother, leaning in close to examine the containers' labels. "We have fever powder, castor oil ... oh, these ones are called *female pills*—"

"I appreciate your efforts, but I'm not sure—" She struggled to push herself upright again, halting as her gaze fell upon the very person she'd come to see. Theo appeared in the doorway, surveying the scene with eyes wide from bewilderment.

Amelia opened her mouth, ready to utter a pleasant greeting. Instead, the words caught and her cheeks heated, for she must look like the sorriest sort of invalid—except she wasn't even sick.

If Theo found anything peculiar about the situation, she didn't voice it aloud. She merely turned to face Jeremy where he'd come up beside her, raising her eyebrows just a shade. "You said you planned to take the boys to the park for their lessons this morning, did you not? And that you were eager to get there straight away?"

"Yes. Yes, I did." He gave her a knowing nod, then emitted a whistle to draw the sleeping dog's attention and motioned to the boys—who were also his pupils, given his past as an Oxford fellow and tutor. "Come on, Ben, Alex. Achilles. I already have some books packed for the excursion."

Alex gave an eager glance out the window, which revealed a surprisingly cloudless sky beyond, before swiftly returning his attention to the scene at the sofa. "But Aunt Amelia's medicine—"

"That's quite all right." Theo rushed across the room, placing a hand on each boy's shoulder and gently steering them toward the door. "You've both been very thorough and attentive caregivers, I'm sure, but I can manage from here so you don't miss out on your lessons. Perhaps we can meet you in the park later if Aunt Amelia feels well enough. And then, if anyone's interested, maybe we can also go for ices."

The promise of a reward did the trick, for the boys uttered a few hasty words of farewell and scrambled after Jeremy, the still-drowsy bulldog trotting behind them.

Theo paused a moment, waiting as their footsteps clattered down the stairs, their enthusiastic voices fading away. Then, she was at Amelia's side, nestling herself onto the edge of the sofa. "Good gracious, what's happened? You must tell me everything."

Amelia gave one final push with her arms and at last managed to get herself sitting, swinging her legs so her feet rested properly against the floor. She shrugged, letting the mass of blankets and shawls fall away. As for executing her plan, she was doing a miserable job thus far, and it was time to get herself in order.

She folded her hands in her lap, flashing her well-practiced smile, even though the effort made her cheeks feel like they might fracture. "Nothing's happened. Nothing at all. I merely wished to pay a call. Good morning, Theo."

Theo's dark brows arched high on her forehead. "You arrive here unexpectedly, huddling on the sofa and looking as if you've seen a ghost, yet you say nothing has happened? Tell the truth, Amelia. I'm not blind."

Instinctively, Amelia's hand went to her head, where she realized her jaunty little bonnet had slipped to the side, and a tangled strand of hair had escaped her coiffure, falling limply over her shoulder. She'd known long before Theo's exclamation that she looked terrible. The mirror in her bedchamber—along with her lady's maid's pinched lips and curious eyes—had revealed as much as she'd gotten ready this morning. She'd hoped the dark circles ringing her eyes and the sickly white-gray cast to her skin might fade once she stepped out into the brisk springtime air on her way to Theo's. Apparently, her hopes were in vain.

But never mind. She was here now; it was just as well she carry on with her intended purpose, pallid face and ridiculous weak spell on the sofa notwithstanding.

"I'm well. It was only a misunderstanding." She intensified her efforts to appear pleasant, hoping her absurdly widened smile didn't instead have the effect of making her look mawkish. "I was just so eager to see you, for I've been thinking. I find the Season grows a trifle dull, and I'm ready for a repose. Why don't we go on holiday?"

"Holiday?" Theo turned the word over in her mouth, not seeming to understand.

"Yes, wouldn't that be nice? We could travel to the seaside. Or better yet, the Lake District. Have you ever gone? I know you've been busy lately and haven't had the opportunity to leave London in some time, so surely you could use a little break."

Amelia was rambling, the words tumbling out with artificial cheer, but she couldn't seem to stop herself. "The boys could come, too, of course, if you think it's all right for them to be away from their lessons for a time. Better yet, Jeremy could join us. That way, they could have lessons as we traveled, and the experience would be quite educational. After all the years we spent not knowing each other, I can imagine nothing more pleasant than having this time away together, and—"

"Amelia." Theo leaned toward her a little, her dark eyes gentle. "That's a lovely sentiment, but I'm afraid it's not possible right now. We're planning to print the first volume of Jeremy's latest novel next week, so we'd like to oversee matters at the printshop to ensure everything goes as it should. I also have another set of illustrated botany texts I need to finish painting by the end of the month, and in addition ..."

Her fingers brushed along her midsection, a slight smile crossing her lips. "I'm afraid I've been subject to bouts of morning malaise of late, which might make spending long hours in a carriage beyond my abilities. A disagreeable but not unexpected side effect, for it seems I'm increasing."

"You ... you are?" Suddenly, Theo's face appeared to be illuminated by a golden glow, and her grin widened enough that Amelia experienced a genuine smile of her own. "Oh, how wonderful! Congratulations. I'm so pleased."

For a moment, the abject misery floated away, making Theo's joy her joy, too. Theo had endured so many hardships —partially at the hands of the Prescott family—that she deserved happiness more than anyone. What a delight to know that in addition to a new husband who clearly adored her, she would soon have another child to fill her household with even more love.

Amelia's misery didn't wait long, though, to push itself back in. She was thrilled for Theo. She *was*. Enough that tears pricked the corners of her eyes, which abruptly became reminders of her own misfortune. And her poorly considered failure of a plan.

"Thank you. That's not to say I wouldn't enjoy a holiday when the timing is more opportune." Theo's hand left her abdomen, coming to rest gently atop Amelia's where it remained clenched in her lap. "However, I don't think a sudden desire for a holiday is what this is really about. So, I'll ask you again. What's happened? I *know* something is wrong. Please don't be afraid to tell me what it is."

Amelia blinked a few times until the excess moisture in her eyes retreated, then peered squarely at Theo's face, which had lost its elation and become drawn with concern. Over the years, she'd always had cause to wonder whether Samuel had shared the Lady Lockheart secret with the wife she'd never met. As they'd befriended each other, though, when Theo spent time living at Rockliffe House after Samuel's death, Theo had never given any indication she recognized Amelia as anything but a proper society lady.

Amelia didn't doubt Theo's trustworthiness. However, the thought of letting the whole story pour out, of undoing the years of secrecy ... she didn't have it in her. Not with every-thing else that transpired. As regrettable as it was, Theo would have to learn about Lady Lockheart at the same time as everyone else, whenever Mr. Egerton decided to blather the information. For, on one point, Amelia had staunchly made up her mind. She couldn't marry him.

"I need to leave London. Immediately." Her voice cracked

as she spoke, desperation creeping into the words. It was a poor explanation but the best one she could give.

"*Why?*"

Amelia shifted her eyes to the carpet. "My name is going to be involved in scandal. I cannot remain here as that happens."

"A scandal? Involving *you?*" Theo's tone turned incredulous. "Surely, it cannot be that bad—"

"I need to leave," she exclaimed, jumping to her feet in an awkward tangle of limbs. It may barely be spring, but the air in Theo's sitting room suddenly felt hot and oppressive. As did the air in the whole of London. She couldn't remain in the city and wait for what came next or she'd suffocate, yet her plans of an impromptu holiday had fallen apart before she'd fully formed them.

But what if ...

"I could still tell Mother that you and the boys are accompanying me on holiday, and she would never need to know that I'm actually going alone. I think she'd secretly be too pleased to pry, and I assume you would have no cause to visit Mayfair over the next while, so she shouldn't discover the truth." *For a time, anyway.*

"No, I certainly don't have plans to go near Rockliffe House." Theo pressed her lips into a firm line, the warmth in her eyes draining away. Last year, she and the dowager marchioness had experienced a falling out that started yet another period of estrangement, leaving Amelia as the only member of the Prescott family who still had communication with her and the boys. A fact that the dowager clearly regretted—even if she never outright admitted it—and left her strangely subdued when it came to matters regarding her grandsons and Theo. Which, in turn, made Amelia's claim of going on a trip with them the perfect alibi.

But while Theo's features softened, she maintained a slight

frown, clearly not convinced. "With that said, I still don't understand this urgent need to secretly depart London. Is it because you fear your mother's wrath? Because as far as I'm concerned, you shouldn't let that drive you away. Why should it matter so much what she thinks? What anyone thinks? And I hope you know that whatever the nature of this mysterious scandal, you'll always have my support. Our home may not be grand, but if you need a place to stay—"

"Thank you for your generosity, but no." Amelia shook her head, willing Theo to understand despite the lack of information she'd given her on the subject. "I really do need to depart London. Please, say I have your permission to at least pretend you've traveled with me."

"But where will you go? Have you ever done such a thing alone before?"

"I ..." They were valid questions, ones to which Amelia was lacking in satisfactory answers. Ideally, she would find a quiet country cottage, far from people who would blackmail or scorn her, and never surface in society again. Her income from more than a decade with Harding and Shipley remained largely untouched. Would that be enough to purchase a cottage? She was woefully unaware of how these things worked, for as a marquess's daughter, she'd always had everything done for her, handed to her. And no, she'd certainly never managed such an undertaking alone.

The cottage might have to come later, then, once she'd educated herself on the subject of property acquisition. But in the meantime, the Rockliffe marquessate brought with it numerous properties scattered throughout England. Some hardly used, maintained by only the barest staff. Nicholas, her eldest brother, had always favored Foxhill, the hunting box in Northamptonshire, when he wished to escape. As Nicholas was currently far away from England, perhaps it could become her retreat instead.

"I believe I'll go north," she said, managing a touch more confidence. Surely, it wouldn't be that difficult to find a stage-coach to take her there. And once she arrived, a few extra coins should entice the staff to keep her presence a secret.

"Amelia ..." Theo's face flickered, making her look as if she had a hundred different things to say. Ultimately, though, she let out a long sigh, rising to her feet to stand next to Amelia. "You must do whatever you think is best, and I won't interfere with your decision. I only hope you've fully thought matters through."

A small burst of relief shot through her, enough that she reached out to clasp Theo's hands. It was hardly a ringing endorsement of her plan, but it would suffice. Especially because the sooner she went home to pack a few effects and got underway, the better. "Thank you, Theo, again. For every-thing. I should really be going now, but I'll write once I'm settled, for I'll be eager for news of you and the boys."

Somewhere in the back of her mind, it occurred to her that leaving London permanently would mean not seeing them, or the baby to come, anymore. However, the notion flitted away before it could fully form, her thoughts returning to the one idea that had consumed her ever since the Englewood ball: *escape*.

They uttered farewells as Theo walked with her down the stairs and toward the entrance. Meanwhile, the steps she needed to take to implement this revised plan floated through her head. *Give my final column for The Ladies' Spectator to Gwen. Retrieve my stash of coins. Pack a valise. Hire a hack to take me to the stagecoach heading north.*

"I still don't think this is a good idea."

Theo's words, firm but gentle at the same time, managed to work their way into her awareness, providing a faint voice of reason amidst her inner to-do list. But by that point, Amelia was already out the door.

4

England was bloody cold. Jonathan adjusted his greatcoat, pulling the thick wool tighter against his torso as he watched rain beat against the carriage window, aided by the force of the blustering wind.

He'd never been one to mope dejectedly and feel sorry for himself, recognizing the futility of such an exercise. However, after spending years traveling to places filled with heat and sunshine, the dampness cut him to the bone, which, in turn, made him increasingly annoyed. Could nothing go right in this godforsaken country?

The day had started nicely enough, with sunrays peeking out from behind the clouds, suggesting there may even be some warmth come afternoon. But just as quickly, those weak rays had slipped away, returning the city to grayness and allowing the rain to set in with a vengeance. How fitting the transition had occurred right around the time the somewhat sheepish butler informed him that the ducal traveling coach had a wheel in need of repair and couldn't be made ready after all.

A muttered, half-formed curse crossed his lips at the

memory. But in the end, it didn't matter, did it? He'd solved the problem easily enough—amidst the butler's weak protests —by opting to take the older, smaller, less elaborate carriage typically used by the servants. In a way, the unassuming and unmarked vehicle would serve him better for the anonymity it provided, even if the seat felt like a rock and his legs were too long to bend comfortably within it. As for the weather? He'd be damned if he let that stop him, either. If the downpour kept up, the roads would likely become so rutted that they'd have no choice but to stop for the day. By that time, though, he would have already achieved what he sought: distance from London.

Now that they'd traversed the worst of the congestion in the heart of the city and made it onto a quieter stretch of road, he shifted against the under-stuffed seat cushion, ready to drift off and shut out the world for a time. Yet no sooner did he close his eyes than the carriage hit a dip with enough force to make his teeth rattle. Another oath escaped him as he leaned down to retrieve the contents of his traveling valise, which had sprung open with a jolt and gone crashing to the floor.

And now, the carriage was slowing considerably, adjusting its pace to little more than a crawl. So help him if this one, too, had sustained damage.

He returned to the window, surveying what little he could see of the carriage for signs of impairment. Except suddenly, none of that mattered, for lying on the side of the road was a crumpled, rain-soaked bundle. A tangle of fabric and limbs. A woman.

His hand shot upward to bang on the roof as a signal to stop, just in case the coachman had any doubts. Whatever had caused the scene, he couldn't say, but the bundle was so still. He didn't wait for the wheels to fully cease turning before pushing the door open and jumping to the ground. A blast of icy raindrops pelted him in the face, but he barely felt it, his attention focused on sprinting across the road.

At least he detected a few faint twitches as he approached. She was alive, then. But in an instant, any burgeoning sense of relief vanished. The woman remained curled in a ball beneath her cloak, her face turned away from him, pointed toward the ground. However, a strand of hair had escaped her bonnet, trailing down her back in a wet clump. Hair that, even when soaked and matted, stood out like a red-gold beacon. A light, even when the world was cast in shades of gray and black. The color of sunshine, and promise, and hope.

"Amelia." He was on the ground beside her in an instant, his blood feeling like it had turned to ice.

Her head snapped toward him, revealing eyes of bright, peerless blue. Thus confirming his worst fears. His mind hadn't merely played tricks on him, conjuring up an image of the person who wouldn't leave his thoughts. This woman was indeed Lady Amelia Prescott, reduced to a pile upon the muddy ground.

"Jonathan." She moved again—thank God for that—trying to push herself up with her elbows. As she did, her wide-eyed disbelief morphed into stony-faced recognition, and her cheeks flushed crimson. "That is, Your Grace."

The sound of the honorific, cold and distant on her lips, gave him a brief shock of discomfort, but it got swallowed by fear as his eyes traveled up and down her body, seeking visible marks of injury. "Can you tell me what's happened?" he managed to choke out, not meeting with any clues as horrific as blood or bruises but feeling his heart thud just the same.

"Oh, it's really nothing." She smoothed her skirts—as if that could somehow make them salvageable despite the mud caking the fabric—and ran a hand over her heated cheek, pushing away another escaped tendril of tangled red-gold. "I'm afraid I slipped as I was walking and lost my breath for a moment. I seem to have turned my ankle, too, but I don't believe it's broken, and I'm sure that after another minute of rest, I'll be able to get up and continue on my way. Please, don't let me delay you any further."

He blinked, and then blinked again. She'd both knocked the wind out of herself and hurt her ankle to the point that she lay crumpled on the ground in the driving rain, yet said this was *nothing*? Thought he should just leave her here and carry on with his day as though his heart hadn't nearly stopped at the sight?

In the next instant, he had her in his arms, careful not to jostle her ankles as he shifted her weight against his chest and rose to his feet. She emitted a yelp of protest, which mixed with a fresh gust of wind powerful enough to almost make him stagger. However, he planted his feet more firmly in the mud and let the protest go unanswered, marching across the sodden ground. Nothing—be it an indignant shriek in his ear or a full-blown hurricane—would stop him from reaching the shelter of his carriage.

The coachman had hopped down from his perch to hold the rattling door open for them, and Jonathan barreled inside, slowing for just an instant to ensure he deposited Amelia gently upon the seat. He spun around to utter a hurried set of instructions and slammed the door, barely having a chance to get seated himself before the coachman resumed his position and the carriage rolled back into motion. Which was exactly what Jonathan wanted. Speed.

He peered across the carriage's dim interior at Amelia, hoping she could find at least a small bit of comfort now that she was out of the elements and on her way to safety. Instead, she sat as rigidly as ever, the redness in her cheeks replaced by wanness. "Did I hear you order your coachman back to Mayfair?"

"Yes, I instructed him to travel to Rockliffe House as

quickly as possible," he said, feeling a flush of his own at the thought that if she pondered it hard enough, she may develop questions as to how he knew she still lived there. But given the circumstances, he had to cast that aside as insignificant, instead turning his focus to sounding as calm and reassuring as possible. "You'll be home in no time, and—"

"No. Absolutely not." Her hand flew to the ceiling, giving it a series of rapid bangs that had the carriage slowing once more.

While he'd made more mistakes concerning Lady Amelia Prescott than he wished to remember, he'd never imagined himself erring by coming to her aid when she was clearly in distress. Yet her panicked expression suggested he'd done just that.

In the next instant, her features softened, although the urgency never quite left her eyes. "That is, I ... I'm not going home. I was on my way out of London, and I see no reason that needs to change. If you'll kindly let me out, I'll resume my journey to St John Street to wait for the stagecoach, and you, too, can be on your way."

He sat in silence, able to do nothing more than look at her. Not because he was afraid he would stammer—for that rarely seemed to happen in her presence—but because now that his initial panic had worn off, questions about this situation were beginning to emerge at a far greater rate than answers. What was she doing on the northern outskirts of London carrying a small travel bag? By herself? In the rain? And why was the journey so pressing?

But rather than pose any of those questions, he led with a statement instead. "I may no longer be familiar with London, but to the best of my knowledge, St John Street is more than a mile back."

At once, the missing color returned to her cheeks, and then, she was the one stammering. "Oh. W-well ... It seems I took a wrong turn. No matter. I—I'm sure I can find where I need to go if you'll simply do as I asked and let me out."

"Can you even walk?" He glanced down toward her ankles, which she held stiffly beneath the clinging layers of her skirts.

"Of course." She started to move, unable to hide her sharp grimace as she transferred weight to her right foot.

That settled it, then. Not that he'd ever had any notion of setting her back out in the deluge, regardless. His hand went to the carriage's ceiling, balling into a fist—

"I said *no!*" She practically screamed the words, lunging toward him to pull down his arm and then falling back as another jolt of pain appeared to rush through her ankle. She gritted her teeth, her breath coming in shallow pants as she repositioned herself on the bench. "Please, Jon—Your Grace. I've already taken up enough of your time and won't impose on you further."

A knot formed in his chest. So, that's what this was. Her problem wasn't with accepting help, generally, but with accepting help from *him*. She didn't want to be around him. Didn't trust him, perhaps held resentment that time wouldn't erase. Which was fair, and no less than he deserved. But it was also damnably, painfully regrettable.

"It's not an imposition," he said quietly, feeling like a chasm had opened in the carriage, turning the inches between them into an impassable distance. "There's nothing about my journey to Northamptonshire that cannot withstand a delay. Let me take you home, where you can rest and receive the medical attention you need. If it makes the trip to Mayfair any more palatable, you can look out the window and pretend I'm not here. I won't take offense." His heart might take a hit, but that he would find a way to endure.

"You're going to Northamptonshire?" She perked up instantly, and maybe the chasm between them wasn't insurmountable after all, for instead of taking his suggestion and turning to the window, she made a slight movement toward him. "To the ducal seat?"

"Yes. To Edgecote Hall." As always, the name left a bitter aftertaste in his mouth. Yet the usual memories remained at bay, overshadowed by his increasing perplexity.

"*I'm* going to Northamptonshire. To my family's hunting box, Foxhill." She did look away from him, then, but rather than appear repulsed, she bit her lip, seemingly deep in thought.

The revelation brought with it even more questions. He didn't ask them, though; he simply observed the faint twitches of her brows and the gentle pull of her mouth, absorbing every detail. When she lifted her eyes to his again, the alarm in the crystalline blue depths had been replaced by unmistakable resolve. "You can take me there. If you refuse to let me out so I can find the stagecoach—and to be honest, I may not *quite* be up for walking—you can deliver me there yourself. Foxhill is south of Edgecote, I believe, so you wouldn't need to venture too far out of your way."

His fingers stiffened, digging into the threadbare velvet beside him, and he had to tense his jaw to keep it from dropping open. She *wanted* to remain in the carriage with him? Or, at the very least, had resigned herself to such a fate.

Once again, it would seem he'd misunderstood the situation. But what would a journey together even mean? Spending countless hours confined to a carriage with her at his side would be the worst torment. The greatest reward. Even if she never spoke another word to him again. Even if he spent the whole time gazing at her, at long limbs, delicate features, and strands of gold and copper. Thinking of all he'd once dreamed of. And of all he'd lost.

But none of that was relevant at the moment. Not when she was injured and in no condition for traveling, despite how she tried to insist otherwise. He took a breath, gathering his thoughts, preparing his words. "I'm not certain—"

"*No.*" That word again. She held up her hand, effectively cutting him off before he got started. "You said your journey to Northamptonshire wasn't urgent. Well, mine is. I *will* get there, one way or another."

He knew very well that a decade was enough time to change a person, but it was still difficult to believe that this voice of steel came from the Lady Amelia he'd once known. Then again, their time together had always been quiet and serene, full of affectionate words and whispered hopes. How would he know how she acted in a crisis? After the day when everything had come crashing down around him, he'd never seen her again. They'd each shouldered the resulting burdens alone.

"Amelia ..." He'd spent so many years away, getting his life in order, rising up, establishing control. Yet that control was now swiftly slipping away.

Her name on his lips effected a change in her. A slight quiver of her chin and flutter of her eyelashes, a momentary flash of hurt far deeper than that from an injured ankle. But in the next instant—so quickly he could almost believe he'd imagined what he'd just seen—the expression was gone, replaced by a stiffening of her jaw and narrowing of her eyes. She stared at him, the blue of her irises becoming icy. "You owe me, Jonathan."

The words dug into his chest like a knife, bringing mountains of memories flooding back in a matter of seconds. A decade was enough time to change a person. It wasn't long enough to make them forget. To erase the past. To undo his countless regrets.

Throughout the years, whenever the memories had gotten particularly bad—which tended to happen when he was at sea on a still, cloudless night, surrounded by an endless expanse of black ocean and sky, gazing up at the same moon and stars that shone over England—he'd told himself that she was better off for his absence. That perhaps her agreeing to his plans was nothing more than a girlhood fancy that she would have later come to regret. That she had likely found someone else far more suited to a marquess's daughter. That their brief time together had been so insignificant to her that she didn't even remember it.

Except she hadn't forgotten. Nor had she married some titled husband and gone off to a lavish country estate to produce a brood of bright-eyed, copper-haired children. She was alone, lost on a muddy road, rushing away from London for reasons she had yet to divulge. Still very much aware of all the ways he'd once wronged her.

And she was giving him a chance, at least in some small fashion, to make it right.

He should have known he could never refuse her anything. Even if he was fraught with reservations about it all.

He turned to the rain-streaked window as a violent wind gust shook the carriage, then back to Amelia and the right ankle that remained concealed beneath her skirts. "I'm not sure how much farther we'll be able to travel today if the rain keeps up. And when we do arrive at a coaching inn, we'll need to call for a doctor to see to your ankle—"

"That's fine," she said at once, her rigid shoulders loosening as she sank back against the seat. For just a moment, she squeezed her eyes shut, and when she opened them again, the hardness had drained away, leaving only bright, gentle blue. "That's all fine. Let's just journey as far as we can, shall we?"

Before he could think better of it, he opened the door and stuck his head out into the deluge, shouting instructions to the coachman. Instructions that got carried away on the wind but must have met the coachman's ears, for the coach rolled back into motion.

He resettled himself on the bench with a nod, unsure if his voice would continue working. Unsure if he'd done right or just made a mistake.

Amelia, on the other hand, appeared to have no such qualms, for she remained leaning back, looking more at ease than he'd seen her throughout this whole ordeal. She'd gotten what she wanted, after all.

Which she deserved. He didn't think otherwise for a second. He *did* owe her, and if she wanted to travel north, that's where he should take her. Only, why did it have to be now, while she was facing an injury and the rain seemed determined to stop her in her tracks? Why was she so insistent on escaping London?

His stomach churned at the thought that she could be in some trouble or danger. Would she trust him enough to talk about it if he asked her? If they were going to do this journey together—and they *were* doing it, because the coach kept lurching along, its wheels careening through the mud—he needed to know the truth of what was going on. He wanted no more secrets between them.

He cleared his throat, daring to lean in the slightest amount.

"I'm rather tired." She nudged her body over until her skirts became crushed against the door, and she let her head relax against the side of the carriage. "I trust you have no objection if I rest a while."

"Uh, n-no. Not at all." He straightened his body instantly, seeming to absorb all the tension she'd just shed. Already, her eyes were closed, making her message abundantly clear. She didn't wish to talk to him.

Later, then. He would get to the bottom of this later, once she'd slept and had a chance to recover from her ordeal. And after that ... who knew? There were so many other things he wanted to ask her, too. To tell her. The dilemma lay with whether he'd be wisest to voice them or leave them to remain in the past.

He was staring at her again. He couldn't help it. How could he do otherwise when a sight he thought he'd never see again had materialized and remained mere inches away from him? For better or worse, he'd be gazing at this sight for the next few days.

At the long, slender arms she'd folded around her chest, peeking out from beneath her traveling cloak. The clump of loose hair that had begun to dry, turning the copper-tinged blond more vibrant. The dusting of golden freckles across her nose, tiny lights in the coach's gray interior.

And the perfect fair lashes that swept against her milky skin, fluttering in a way that suggested she wasn't really sleeping.

5

The carriage made it little more than ten miles before the unrelenting rain forced them to stop. Even that short distance they'd done at a crawl, rolling carefully over the numerous ruts and dips in the road lest the horses stumble or the carriage be bowled over by wind.

Jonathan hadn't consulted his watch, but it had to have taken hours. An eternity, in some ways. A relentless stretch in which he did nothing but gaze at the rain or Amelia—mostly Amelia—noticing new details all the time. Like the faintest lines around the corners of her eyes that hadn't been there a decade before. The little cluster of freckles that spilled onto her left cheek. Traces of ink that bordered her fingernails.

As he'd observed her, it hit him that this was the same journey they'd nearly taken years ago. They would have traveled along the Great North Road, just as they did now, except instead of eventually veering off toward Northamptonshire, they'd have continued north, all the way to Scotland. A ring in his pocket. His heart full. The future awaiting.

The possibility of that youthful dream coming true had long since slipped away. Nonetheless, when the coaching inn finally came into view, signaling an end to their tedious and somewhat reckless journey for the day, his silent stretch of watching Amelia doze—or pretend to, in any case—also seemed to end far too soon.

However, the shudder she gave as the coach jerked to a halt provided a blatant reminder of why they needed to stop beyond just the weather. Despite what she might say about her ankle, the way her face contorted revealed that it was far from all right.

"We'll stay here for the night," he said when she opened her eyes, her expression returning to neutral, revealing no hint of pain. "We would have to rest the horses soon regardless, but given how the road conditions continue to deteriorate, it would be wisest if we wait until tomorrow to continue north."

He waited for her protest, for her to insist that it wasn't yet nightfall and they needed to keep going. Instead, she merely nodded with a stifled yawn, gathering up the small traveling bag she'd let fall to her side. Yet another clue that she'd merely been feigning sleep throughout the trip, for she was beginning to look exhausted.

He gave her no further opportunity for stoicism but gathered her into his arms in one fell swoop. He held her tight to his chest as the coachman opened the door for them, and they stumbled out into rain every bit as heavy as in London.

"Your Grace!" she yelped, her slender body wriggling against him, struggling to break free as he trudged over the muddy path that led to the inn. "This is quite unnec—"

"I think," he murmured, darting a quick glance around to ensure no one stood nearby, "that we'd best do away with titles for the time being. The last thing we need is to become the subject of gossip."

She made a small sound, almost like a laugh that had gone hollow. "Indeed." But while the word rang sharp, she stilled her body, no longer fighting his efforts to carry her.

Which was fortunate, as there was only so much he could handle of her arms moving near his neck like a rough caress, of her warm weight repeatedly pushing into his abdomen. He straightened, raising his face and looking at nothing but the courtyard ahead. He and Amelia both smelled strongly of mud and damp wool. But with her near him like this, he also caught a hint of something else. A sweet springtime fragrance, like the apple blossoms on the trees at his childhood home. She'd always smelled that way, hadn't she? Like something fresh but familiar all at the same time.

He clenched his jaw, willing his head to stay upward, away from things to which he had no right. For what had to be the hundredth time today, he returned to the mindset that this journey was a terrible idea.

Be that as it may, he finished traversing the courtyard and arrived at the inn's entrance, where a peeling wooden sign hung above his head, dripping fat splashes of water. *The Hound and Peacock.*

Perhaps the marks of disrepair didn't bode well for the inn's quality. However, at this point, they had little other choice.

The weathered door promptly flew open to grant them admittance, and he burst inside, where they were greeted by a blast of warmth from a fire, along with a short, slender man who had to be the innkeeper, eyeing them curiously through a pair of wire-rimmed spectacles. No doubt they looked like a pair of vagabonds, drenched and travel-stained.

"Call for a doctor." Jonathan shot a commanding glance at the man, finding himself too on edge for niceties. He had no plans to admit to being a duke, but nor could he leave any question that they warranted service. "My wife has injured her ankle."

At once, Amelia stiffened in his arms, and he inwardly cursed himself. Why had he said that? She was an unmarried lady traveling alone with a gentleman; it was inevitable that they'd need to invent some story to protect her reputation. However, if he possessed any sense whatsoever, the word he would have uttered was *sister*. His *sister* had injured her ankle and required a doctor.

"We'll also require a room for the night. Uh, two rooms." He was really making a mess of this, both his brain and tongue growing heavy and uncooperative. "And a bath, if that can be arranged."

There, he'd managed it all, even though the heat of the room had quickly turned uncomfortable, and the innkeeper continued regarding them with a frown. If it was any consolation, this part of the inn was otherwise deserted, keeping them free of prying eyes.

He shifted his arm just enough so he could reach into his greatcoat pocket and fetch some coins. Not that he wanted to give hints as to his status, but this much was necessary. The innkeeper's eyes widened as Jonathan held out the more-than-generous sum, his frown replaced by something far more amenable.

In a flash, the coins disappeared into the innkeeper's pocket, and the man held up a finger before scurrying away, disappearing through what appeared to be the kitchen door. His voice, along with several others, traveled back to them as indistinct murmurs.

When he returned a minute later, he was nearly smiling, apparently no longer bothered by the mud they trailed through the inn. "It seems luck is on your side, for the surgeon stepped into the barroom not a quarter hour ago. I've asked one of the serving girls to alert him that his services are required. More fortunate for you still, the weather has kept some of our usual crowd away, which means our two finest rooms are available so your lady can recover from her injury in comfort. If you'd like to follow me upstairs ... uh ..."

"Mr. Maxwell," Jonathan supplied in response to the innkeeper's questioning look, at least having the presence of mind to invent that much without fumbling.

His legs ached in protest as he began climbing the stairs, not yet recovered from his hours crammed into a carriage that wasn't quite large enough for him. However, he couldn't begrudge the ducal coach's broken wheel or the weather, either, for that matter. Not when the rain left the inn free of crowds, and his nondescript carriage made him and Amelia unremarkable to anyone who did happen to observe them.

"Here you are, then, Mr. and Mrs. Maxwell." The innkeeper paused by the first door at the top of the stairs, handing him two small keys. "This room and the one beside it are yours. If there's nothing else you require, I'll go down to make sure the surgeon's on his way, and I'll get the serving girls to bring up the tub. One of them can stay to assist you should you need it."

"That's lovely, thank you." Amelia—or Mrs. Maxwell, he should say—finally spoke, her voice weary but still unmistakably pleasant in that characteristic Lady Amelia way. In turn, he gave a brief nod of appreciation, then set the key into the lock. Now that he'd made all the necessary requests, he wanted nothing more than to get her away from any potential passersby and into the room, where she could rest.

He stepped into the lowly lit space and went straight for the bed in the back corner, setting her upon a dark green coverlet that had seen better days. Now that he took a moment to glance around, the same could be said about the whole room. It may be the finest The Hound and Peacock had to offer, but from the threadbare coverlet to the scuffed nightstand to the bedraggled wisp of a curtain that did a poor job shutting out the rainy bleakness, the space appeared worn, to say the least.

Not that he had cause for complaint. The room was still

far superior to many of the ship's quarters he'd occupied back in his early days at sea. It had a blazing hearth and a proper, if somewhat lumpy, bed, and a roof that didn't seem to leak.

As long as Amelia found it suitable, too. She'd spent her whole life as a marquess's daughter, and this had to be a far cry from the luxury to which she was accustomed. Then again, she'd once expressed a willingness to give it all up, back when they were young and foolish.

Whatever else may have changed over the years, her inclination to accept less-than-ideal conditions didn't seem to have altered. Indeed, she was so focused on carefully removing her cloak so as not to spread mud across the bed that she hardly appeared to notice the space surrounding them.

"Here, let me." He bent over her, helping to ease the wet wool away from her shoulders and taking it to spread out close to the fire. When he turned back, she'd brought her attention to her half-boots, trying to reach the laces without letting the mud-caked leather touch the coverlet. He rushed over to her again, kneeling beside the place where her legs dangled from the bed.

"That really isn't nec—"

"Please." He gave her a pointed look, cupping her left boot within his palm. *It wasn't necessary*, he knew. Beyond the use of his carriage, she wanted nothing from him. Yet if she wouldn't grant him at least the tiniest opportunities to help, he'd go mad from his own uselessness.

With a sigh, she straightened back up, giving her foot the slightest nudge against his palm. An easy concession, for she really did look tired, her eyes ringed with faint shadows.

With the weight of her boot still in one hand, he used the other to undo the laces, pulling them loose until her foot slipped free and he could move on to the other side, taking extra care on account of her injury. If he'd been smart, he would have done this for her hours ago, back when he'd first brought her into the carriage. He should have known the boot would pinch her ankle too tightly, should have insisted she take it off and rest her foot against the bench. For as he freed the second foot and guided it up onto the bed, the skin beneath her stocking felt hot and inflamed within his palm, the top of her boot having left an indent.

He *hated* that she'd gotten hurt. Hated that she was alone and away from home, and that he'd agreed to this harebrained plan, and that he didn't know the why of any of it. He hated that she didn't trust him enough to confide in him.

Hated that he didn't deserve her trust.

"Thank you, Your Grace." The slight wriggle of her leg reminded him that he'd completed his task and needed to release her foot from his grasp. She gave a polite nod, which turned into a tilt of her chin toward the door. "I'm certain I can manage from here, and I imagine you have needs of your own to attend to. Please, don't let me keep you any longer."

Her speech was nothing but courteous, yet an unspoken aloofness underlined each word. Again, she wanted to be rid of him, to keep him at a careful distance. And again, he didn't know how he was supposed to leave her. Not like this, in this well-worn room, where so much remained unsaid.

A knock pounded against the door. "Mrs. Maxwell?"

"That must be the doctor." She flashed him something that nearly resembled a smile, except the glint in her eyes spoke less of joy and more of relief. "You can leave knowing I'll be in good hands. I'll see you later?"

A blatant dismissal, if ever there was one. He pushed up from his knees, his joints stiff from the rough floorboards. He didn't want her to be alone for this. But if that's what she desired, who was he to argue?

He inclined his head in a silent farewell, then plodded across the room to open the door, revealing a man of middling years who carried a black medical bag. Jonathan took a moment to eye him up and down, ensuring there were no outward signs he'd overindulged in the barroom. Satisfied, he took another moment to utter a few instructions, hearing himself speak that word again: *Do whatever you can to alleviate my* wife's *discomfort.*

Then, there was nothing left but to drag his own muddy boots to the room next door. The inn's other finest room, which proved to be a mirror image of the one he'd just left. The walls were thin enough that Amelia's voice drifted through, and were he to lie down on the bed, he'd hear every word, for she'd be in her own bed directly on the other side.

He didn't do that, though. Instead, he searched for every source of distraction possible. Like removing his boots and greatcoat and positioning them in just the right spot before the fire. Having his valise and a pitcher of warm water brought up and scrubbing the fingerprints of dried mud from his neck. By that time, the doctor's voice had vanished, replaced by several unfamiliar feminine ones that were interspersed with the sound of water sloshing from buckets, filling up the tub. If Amelia was preparing for a bath, she certainly wouldn't welcome his presence now, either, despite his anxiousness to find out how she'd fared.

He snapped his gaze away from the shared wall, forcing his eyes back to the mirror above the washstand in front of him. He'd thrown off his cravat and let his shirt gape open in order to reach every mud-stained crevice, but still, small brown-gray splotches dotted the skin around his neck. He took the bar of soap he'd retrieved from his valise and plunged it into the tepid water, scrubbing himself with renewed vigor. Gradually, the spots faded, erasing the evidence of how he'd flung himself to the ground by Amelia on the side of the road.

However, that didn't make his skin stop prickling. Not from the rough motions of the soap and his fingertips, but from the other hands—*her* hands—that had pressed into his neck. Combative at first, pushing him away, before they turned soft and accepting, putting gentle pressure against the place just above his collar.

With that, another memory came, of a frosty garden from a long time ago, outside the ballroom that served as a veritable hell on earth. He'd snuck away to a solitary bench because while he'd tried to cooperate and do as his uncle bid him, everyone knew he was inept, fumbling, the last person in existence who should be relied on to improve the family's standing. He'd sat alone, gulping in mouthfuls of nighttime air, trying to restore his equilibrium enough to return to the crowd—for his speech always grew worse when he was anxious—but thinking he'd be better off slipping out the back gate and forgetting the whole endeavor.

His grandfather may have been a duke, but Jonathan was a failure, not meant for ballrooms, not meant for the ton, not meant for anything but his clerk's desk in the office of J. Watson, Solicitor—

And then, a hand had fallen upon his shoulder in the slightest, softest caress. *Are you all right?*

He sent a stream of water splashing over his face, washing the memory away with the mud. The towel that lay folded on the washstand was thin and abrasive, but he dragged it over himself until not a single speck or droplet remained. Only then did he return to his valise for another set of clothing, buttoning up and smoothing out a new waistcoat, tying intricate knots in a clean white cravat.

He'd either taken minutes or hours. Whatever the case, by the time he finished, nothing came through the wall but silence. Had she fallen asleep? He approached the door, cocking an ear in the direction of her room. Still nothing. She'd looked so weary when he left her that the last thing he should do was disturb her.

Letting out a long exhale, he turned around, sinking onto

a bed that was equally as lumpy as Amelia's. Not that he had any notion of sleeping.

He rifled through his valise, through the reports and correspondence he'd brought along that required his attention. If only he could concentrate on them.

In any case, the act of *attempting* to concentrate on them occupied his time. Enough that, while he was in the midst of what had to be his fiftieth reread of a letter from the Edgecote Hall land agent, a knock sounded against his door,

He brushed all his papers into a haphazard pile and was on his feet in an instant, hopefulness swelling in his chest. Yet when he threw open the door, the woman standing on the other side was a small, round-faced serving girl, bobbing into a curtsey. "I came to see if you'd like a tray sent up for your supper, sir."

Of course. Of course, it wouldn't be Amelia coming to his room. She could barely walk.

Yet as he pressed his hand against the doorframe, steadying himself against the jolt of disappointment, another idea took hold. "Have you already asked the same of Mrs. Maxwell? Is she awake?"

"She is, sir, and has asked for a tray."

That was a good sign. And if Amelia was awake, surely that meant he could see her.

He smoothed down his coat and stepped into the corridor. "I'll have one as well, please," he said, more an afterthought than anything. Despite the hours that had passed since breakfast, his mind wasn't on food but on the woman next door.

He waited until the serving girl scurried down the stairs before giving the door beside his a gentle tap. "Amelia?"

A pause. A moment when he considered that perhaps he was disturbing her after all, that he'd been too hasty. But then, the soft, familiar voice traveled through the wall. "Enter."

He let himself in, finding Amelia sitting on the bed just as he'd left her, except her hair now hung in a damp braid, she'd changed into a dressing gown, and her legs were stretched across the coverlet and tucked beneath a blanket. Much more the picture of ease, although a faint line appeared across her forehead as she took him in. "Jon—um, Your G—um, husband." She glanced into the dim corridor beyond him, biting down on her lip.

"It's all right. There's no one else about right now, so we can speak freely." Just in case, he closed the door behind him, wanting to approach her but thinking it wisest he remain near the room's threshold. "How was your visit with the doctor? I didn't wish to disturb you, but I've been eager to know."

"You have?" She eyed him for a moment longer, then straightened herself against the pillows and reached for the glass of water on her nightstand, taking a small sip. "It went well. He was able to confirm that my ankle isn't broken. Merely a sprain, and I should make a swift recovery if I take care to rest it for a few days. How fortunate that a journey by carriage requires nothing but rest."

She set her glass back down, nearly looking pleased, and a little of the weight he shouldered melted away. "I'm glad to hear it."

He really shouldn't stand by the door and stare. However, it was hard to look away from the red-gold braid that caught the firelight. The slender shoulders concealed by only a thin dressing gown. The empty space beside her on the bed that would make the perfect place for him to sit. To be close to her. To give voice to the many unsaid things between them.

"Thank you, Your Grace, for your assistance today and for coming to check on me." She pulled the blanket up to her shoulders, almost as if she knew he'd been thinking about them. "But please, don't let me keep you any longer."

There it was, as plain as day: another dismissal. Damn, but why had he allowed himself to stand there and get distracted?

He took a step forward, forcing down the tightness in his throat so he could make an attempt at salvaging what he'd botched. "If … if you'd like company for dinner …"

"Thank you, but that isn't necessary." She shook her head, as polite but distant as ever. "After the day we've had, you should go down to enjoy the dining room. I'll be fine here with my tray, and as soon as I've finished, I plan to sleep. With any luck, we can make an early start tomorrow."

That solidified it, then. A wall had gone up between them as assuredly as the one separating their rooms.

He spared the bed one more glance. Had the past gone differently, perhaps the first bed they ever shared would have been not so different from this one, at an inn in Scotland on their wedding night. A night they'd both anticipated as they exchanged kisses in secret corners of gardens, and the breathy noises she made sent fire running through his veins. *Waiting would make it sweeter*, he'd told himself during those moments when his body had become so tightly wound that it felt like it might snap. Because he'd be damned if he shirked honor as easily as his relations did, and the bliss would be so much greater once they'd said their vows and truly belonged to one another—

But what sense was there in thinking of that now?

He didn't argue. Arguing never got him anywhere but flustered and tongue-tied. But nor did he bid her a quick good night and immediately take his leave. Instead, he gazed down at her, the tall, slender figure bathed in firelight. Even if they weren't to have a conversation, he couldn't go without making at least one thing clear. "I'm sorry. For everything that transpired all those years ago. I—I never intended … never wanted …"

"There's no need." With a slight shake of her head, she stopped his speech in its tracks. "It all happened so long ago, it's hardly worth speaking of."

She even smiled at him as she spoke, a small, tight-lipped gesture. The expression didn't meet her eyes, though, which glimmered brightly. Almost as if they contained unshed tears.

"Good night, Your Grace." She nodded politely, her chin dipping against the scratchy gray blanket. A clear signal for him to leave.

He pictured himself sitting alongside the length of her body and saying it again, over and over. *I'm sorry*. For despite what she'd just said, how could he forget the way she'd looked at him in the carriage earlier, her eyes hard and desperate. *You owe me, Jonathan*.

He let out a breath, struggling beneath the new weight that settled upon his shoulders. "Good night, Amelia."

And because she said she was tired, and because she'd just claimed that past wounds meant nothing, he walked away, giving her the solitude she wanted. Even though everything about leaving felt wrong, and he didn't believe her on either count.

6

Perhaps all the "sleeping" Amelia had done on the first day of their journey was the cowardly way out. However, with the way events had spiraled out of control until she was in well over her head, she found doing otherwise had been beyond her capabilities.

Today would be different.

She peered out the carriage window at the passing countryside, at tree branches swaying in the breeze, displaying the slightest hints of springtime green. Unlike yesterday, when the world had been swathed in gray, the sun shone high in the sky, streaking golden light across the carriage and making quick work of drying the puddles outside. Almost like a recompense for the earlier storm.

She tilted her head so sunrays bathed her face, an action that would have earned her mother's censure for its associated risk of amplifying her freckles. But her mother wasn't here. And today, she wouldn't focus on the way she'd fled Rockliffe House with nothing but a poorly packed traveling bag, a note left behind for her mother explaining her holiday with Theo, and instructions for Gwen that she was to stay in London and deliver the column—likely Lady Lockheart's last—to Harding and Shipley in three days' time.

Today, she wouldn't think about how she'd accidentally told the hackney driver to let her out at the wrong location, and how she'd then grown so flustered looking for the stage-coach stop at St John Street that she'd tripped over her own feet and landed in the mud, only to have rescue come in the form of the Duke of Branscombe. Nor would she think of her panic. Her humiliation. And the way that, in a moment of desperation, she'd guilted him into taking her along to Northamptonshire.

She dared to turn her head from the window, enough that Jonathan—a large, stiff figure in this cramped, rather un-ducal carriage—came into view. When he'd deposited her upon the bench this morning, he'd taken the seat across from her and insisted she put her foot up, checking her boot to ensure the laces weren't too tight.

But she couldn't focus on that, either. For if she let herself remember how it felt to be cradled against the strong, unyielding surface of his chest, to have his fingers cup her injured ankle with the lightest touch, to hear him begin an apology that cut right to the deep-down place where she buried the aches time didn't erase ... well, she just couldn't. Not unless she wanted to risk another blow to her heart.

"It's lovely to see the sunshine." She curled her lips into a smile, forcing herself to meet his eyes and not look away. Perhaps her voice sounded too bright, and was she really attempting to talk with him about the weather? Yes, she supposed she was, because the topic of weather had the distinct advantage of being safe.

"Uh ... indeed." Jonathan tilted his head, his dark brows twitching upward a shade. She wouldn't blame him for finding her sudden commentary, after a day of near silence, odd. However, it was better she persevere than risk him beginning a conversation about something weightier.

"I believe I just spotted some daffodils." She pointed out the window as a patch of yellow amidst a grassy field streaked by. "I always enjoy seeing the first signs of spring."

Jonathan, however, barely nodded. He wasn't looking at daffodils but at her, his expression pensive. Which was exactly what she didn't want.

It was natural that he'd experience curiosity, have questions. She certainly did. Yet voicing them would only lead down a path better left untraveled. She didn't need to hear him say that the sentiments he'd once expressed hadn't been real after all. So much time had passed, and still, she didn't think she was strong enough to hear the ways in which he'd found something between them lacking, enough that it had enticed him to leave.

If they were going to speak, their conversation had to remain on trivial things. Nothing deeper. Comments that served no purpose but to pass the time until they arrived in Northamptonshire and once more went their separate ways. For good.

She pressed her face to the glass, scanning the countryside for something else to comment on. A felled tree or a grazing cow or ... *anything*. She was Lady Amelia Prescott, after all, always able to utter a pleasant word, even when her mind—her heart—was elsewhere.

However, the words that slipped out sounded more like an accusation. "Why are we slowing down?" For although the sun continued to blaze, the road before them remaining wide and clear, the carriage began to jerk erratically just as it had in the driving rain, its wheels rapidly decelerating.

She stared outside, surveying the road for some hint of

trouble, but nothing revealed itself. That didn't stop the carriage from shuddering to a halt, giving her ankle an uncomfortable jolt. She bit her lip to keep from crying out and alerting Jonathan. But Jonathan, she realized, was peering out the other window, his brow furrowed as he did his own assessment of the road.

A pair of boots thumped against the ground outside, and he threw open the door, revealing the sight of the coachman staggering toward them while doubled over, his skin a ghastly shade of gray-green.

"I don't feel so well, Your Grace." The thin, drooping man, who couldn't be much older than Jonathan himself, took a single moment to gaze at them with red-rimmed eyes, his face shining with a heavy coating of sweat. In the next instant, he was stumbling away, careening across the road and into a thick cluster of trees.

Amelia yanked her foot down from the seat, gripping the back of the bench to pull herself upright—

"No." Jonathan held out a hand, not quite touching her shoulder but encouraging her to remain seated nonetheless. "I'll check on him. You stay here."

"I—" She opened her mouth to protest but swiftly closed it. He had already leaped out of the carriage and begun sprinting after the coachman, darting over the road and around trees until he vanished into the wood.

She dragged herself across the bench until she sat by the open door, then stared at the empty expanse of scenic countryside, letting out a frustrated huff of breath. This dratted ankle was causing one problem after another and rendering her so infuriatingly useless.

Jonathan was right to tell her to stay, for running through the woods was currently beyond her capabilities. However, that meant she had nothing to do but remain behind and worry. The coachman, who had appeared in fine form yesterday, looked so severely ill. What if he'd contracted some horrible disease? Or worse, what if he'd caught a deadly chill after his hours spent out in the rain?

That would be her fault. She was the one who'd demanded they keep traveling north, that they couldn't go back to Mayfair. Yes, Jonathan had started the journey. But had she not been there, insisting on her need to get far away from London, maybe he would have done things differently.

She swallowed, the back of her throat feeling tight and bitter. She still wanted—*needed*—to go north more than anything. But for now, that plan would have to be put on hold. How far back was The Hound and Peacock? They couldn't have gone more than two or three miles. If she had to, could she guide the carriage back there, where she knew they had a proficient surgeon nearby? She'd driven her mother's gig several times in the country; this couldn't be that different—

A shadow wavered in the trees, coming closer until it became a broad-shouldered figure wearing a gray coat and breeches. Jonathan, stepping out of the wood, coming back to the road with brisk, severe strides. Her heart gave a small lurch, but the momentary relief at seeing him gave way to a fresh wave of unease. He was alone, the coachman nowhere to be seen.

"Is he terribly ill? Shall I go for help?" she shouted. She began to rise from the bench and abruptly stilled as her ankle gave a painful reminder of its inability to bear the weight of her jumping down from the carriage.

If her ankle hadn't stopped her, Jonathan would have, for the nearer he drew, the more she could see he had a face like thunder. He marched across the road, the carriage giving a slight shake as he propelled himself through the open door, dropping his body to the bench across from her with a thud.

"The only thing ailing him," he spat, picking a stray clump of grass off a coat noticeably more rumpled than when he'd left her, "is too much time spent in the barroom last night."

She blinked, absorbing this fresh development. She'd been so worried, so fearful that a man's life was in peril. But the coachman was simply ... facing the aftereffects of drink?

Jonathan glanced at his boots, which had become covered in a layer of muddy grass from the wood. With a frown, he tapped each one against the edge of the carriage, making the worst of the excess mud drop back to the ground outside. "Now that he has—uh—relieved himself of the contents of his stomach, I hope he'll begin to feel better soon and can resume his duties. In the meantime, I helped him to a shaded spot beneath some oaks, and he promptly fell asleep. It's probably best to let him rest a spell so we don't have a repeat performance of what just transpired."

"Of course." She nodded, but her insides were in knots, twisting in so many ways she didn't know how to feel. There was relief, obviously, from knowing they didn't have a crisis on their hands. At least, not the life-or-death type. Yet the longer she sat here, peering at a very disheveled Jonathan, the more she felt the discomfort of a different sort of calamity.

They'd stopped barely ahead of where they'd started that morning. Miles behind where they should be after this many hours of travel. Her plan to allow trivial conversation had seemed doable when she'd thought she needed only to maintain her polite but distant facade for a limited amount of time, with each word drawing them closer to Foxhill. But now, they'd come to a standstill, with no end to the journey in sight.

"We may as well get out." With a groan, he dropped his head back against the seat. He couldn't like this any more than she did. When he raised his head again, though, the tension in his features had drained away, and the look he gave her was mild. "I should bring the horses down to graze by the stream while we wait, and we're better off joining them than sitting on the side of the road. Let me assist you."

She froze, her body going rigid. A protest rose in her throat, just as it had each time circumstances slammed them together over the past day. No, it wasn't necessary for him to bring her into the wood; she would sit in the motionless carriage until the coachman and horses were ready to go again.

But while it had become increasingly apparent since yesterday that there were a great many things of which she was unaware, even she wasn't naive enough to think that waiting on the Great North Road, alone and immobile, proved a wise idea.

She glanced toward the trees, illuminated by sunlight almost as if in welcome, and gave a small nod. And no sooner did she make the gesture than she was in Jonathan's arms again, allowing him to scoop her up and exit the carriage.

It was a position of necessity, of course, because she couldn't handle uneven terrain with her ankle in its current condition, and Jonathan's sense of duty obliged him to assist.

That didn't mean she felt nothing. Her heart had once shattered, and then, it had hardened, and still, she couldn't stop the flutter of it each time he held her tight to his chest. She'd spent much of her life feeling too tall, too long-limbed, too out of place. Yet somehow, when she experienced his strong arms supporting her weight, carrying her as if she were a feather, she felt like she fit.

By the time they reached the wood, her hands were clenched into fists that made her knuckles turn white, and her neck ached from the effort of holding it stiff and upright. Anything to keep from draping her arms around his neck or nestling her head against his greatcoat.

"Will this suffice?"

His question snapped her attention away from the nondescript oak she'd been staring at, and she turned her head forward to where the wood had thinned out, giving way to a grassy clearing. Through it ran a meandering stream, its crystal water sparkling beneath the sunrays, and alongside that, there rested a lone felled tree trunk, waiting for them like a perfect bench.

"This is quite nice. Thank you." She loosened her taut fingers, giving her neck a shake as he brought her over to the trunk, setting her down atop its rough surface. Her body protested the lack of contact with him, while in her mind, she blew out a sigh of relief.

"Will you be all right here for a moment?" He straightened, his height casting a shadow across her skirts as she smoothed them into place. "I just need to fetch the horses and will return shortly."

She uttered her assent, watching his back as he hurried the short distance into the wood and toward the road, dodging the puddles that still hadn't dried in the shade.

Now, she could breathe a little. Take in a few mouthfuls of the springtime air and restore her equilibrium. At the edge of the trees, she caught sight of an unmoving lump—the incapacitated coachman—sprawled upon the ground, snoring lightly. Other than that, nothing made a sound beyond the trickling stream and the gentle rustle of grass. They were well and truly alone.

This delay was a disaster. But at the same time, it was so peaceful here, the space so clear and calm, that what she'd just told him rang true: it really *was* nice.

By the time he returned, she'd loosened her cloak and removed the boot from her injured ankle, going so far as to stretch her stockinged foot out in front of her and letting the grass tickle her toes. For a March day, it was pleasantly warm, the sun even more brilliant without the barrier of the carriage window.

Jonathan must think so, too, for in the midst of settling the horses at the edge of the wood, he shrugged off his coat, revealing the muscled contours of his arms beneath the crisp white shirt. She didn't mean to stare, but there was something captivating about watching his fluid movements that made it impossible to look away.

He gave one of the black geldings a final pat on the nose and turned, causing their eyes to lock for a split second before hers dove toward the ground. She should have known better than to gawk, should have been more discreet. Yet surprisingly, the sense of tranquility that had overtaken her didn't vanish with her misstep. Nor did it disappear while she continued to feel his eyes upon her, assessing the empty area on the tree trunk.

She looked up again, just for an instant, before tilting her chin to the space beside her. There was no harm in issuing the invitation, was there? Better that than keeping him standing while he gazed uncertainly from afar.

She didn't watch him this time, but she knew he accepted her offer by the way his boots swished over the grass until his shadow loomed next to her and his body settled onto the makeshift bench she'd offered. His proximity caused the crisp smells of springtime growth to mix with the same scent she noticed each time he held her. Something subtle but exotic, faintly reminiscent of cloves. Different from the mild shaving soap she used to detect during their early embraces. But while this new scent was different, it was also warm. Alluring.

She did look at him, then, taking in each detail up close in a way she hadn't yet allowed herself to do. The skin that, once white from an English winter, contained a faint cast of bronze. The ash-brown hair that had developed streaks of gold as if from repeated exposure to the sun. The jawline that had become squarer, the limbs that had filled out, making his tall frame look more solid.

But despite the changes, the brown eyes that met hers were unmistakably, painfully, wonderfully Jonathan's. Surrounded by a few fine lines now, but otherwise, no different from when he'd been a man of nineteen, sitting alone in the garden. And just like on that night, he looked like he had the weight of the world on his shoulders.

"I apologize." He tipped his face to the sky, and suddenly, she had an inexorable wish that he'd find the sunrays' warmth as restorative as she did. "I suppose I've always known this, but the longer I spend at Branscombe House, the more I realize that my uncle's servants had very little respect for him and, in turn, for their duties. Not that I can blame them."

She pressed her lips together, letting silence drift across the space once more. He'd spoken a little about the depravity of his uncle and cousin—always with a face like stone—back when they'd first met. While she'd spent the years following trying to avoid talk of the Astley family as much as possible, there were certain things she couldn't help but hear.

The degenerate duke, the ton had called the man, with a son just as bad. Both rakes of the worst kind, prone to engaging in all manner of vices while simultaneously shirking even the basest responsibilities. She'd even heard that, despite the prestige of his position, the former Duke of Branscombe, along with his heir, had been barred from certain social circles. Something about a bevy of unpaid debts, and there were even whispers of a scandal involving cheating at the card table.

Whatever disarray the duke had left behind belonged to Jonathan now. The dukedom was his to finish running to the ground. Or his to make better.

Despite all the years that had passed, and her broken heart and trust, she still didn't doubt that he would choose the latter.

She'd wanted no deep conversation between them. No closeness. But maybe, if she asked for just a little more of the truth behind all those missing years and his sudden reappearance, she would find closure. The edge of her curiosity would be satisfied, and the past would return to where it belonged.

After which, she could still walk away from this unscathed.

7

What a damn mess of a day. And it was only early yet.

Jonathan sat upon the jagged tree trunk with his face turned to the sun, letting it wash over him as his chest pushed in and out—the effect of both exertion and frustration.

If all had gone according to plan, he and Amelia would be in the carriage hurrying north right now, taking the much-improved weather conditions as an opportunity to make up time.

Not only that, but they might be speaking. Unlike yesterday, when her distaste for conversing with him had been abundantly clear, today, she'd begun making overtures. Just small, trivial points that, truth be told, had caught him off guard. However, the tiny hint of warmth—even if it was mixed with trepidation—had bored into him with more power than the sun.

It was a first step. If only she remained in a frame of mind to talk, then maybe he could have said the right things in return to persuade her to open up more deeply. To trust him with her troubles. To give him the opportunity to help fix them, if such a thing were possible. It was the least he could do for her.

Instead, he'd found himself bolting into unfamiliar woods after a poor excuse for a duke's coachman, dragging the ailing man about so he didn't pitch face-first into the stream. He'd then needed to do the man's job for him and tend to the horses, because the coachman apparently valued ale far more than the responsibilities of his position.

This was the former Duke of Branscombe's legacy. He'd been neglectful and dissolute, and he'd accumulated servants to match. God only knew what Jonathan would find at Edgecote Hall.

"When did it happen?"

The soft voice pulled his attention back from the sky, and he turned to find Amelia gazing at him, her eyes clear and inviting. Just like on that night in the garden, when his initial reaction to snap that he wanted to be alone had vanished in a heartbeat, the gentle blue giving him an instant sense of rightness.

"That is, your return to England," she said after a brief pause—a moment of silence that he spent digging through his brain to find the right words to match the situation. "I must not stay up-to-date on ton happenings as much as I should, for I didn't realize you were back."

He drew another mouthful of air into his lungs, his mind drifting back to a place nearly a world away. He could still feel the paper of the fateful letter as it rested within his clammy fingertips, could still remember blinking at the words as though they were made up of a foreign script. "Only a few weeks ago. It took months for news of my uncle's and cousin's passing to reach me, as I was in Ceylon at the time."

"I see." She didn't offer condolences. She understood enough about his past to know better than that. "So, it's true, then. You really did travel far from England. So far away that rumors circulated of your death."

Was it his imagination, or did her voice waver at that last part? He swallowed, wishing he were in possession of a flask to wash away the sudden dryness in his throat. "Yes. I went aboard an East Indiaman as a cabin boy. I was too old for the job, but they had me nonetheless." Back in the days when it was easier to pretend he was nobody, a man with no voice at all. Back when he'd tried to outsail his grief, but had a wave come and swept him overboard, he wouldn't have possessed the will to fight it. "I'd never been on a ship in my life, but I grew accustomed to it soon enough. I must have, anyway, for I've been on the ocean ever since."

"I see." She repeated the phrase, her expression growing wry. "I assume no longer as a cabin boy?"

"No." He made a sound in his throat, almost a laugh. "After nearly three years at sea, my fortune changed."

As if on cue, a sudden burst of wind swept over his face and made the branches behind them sway. Just a normal springtime breeze, but enough to bring him back to that night on the South China Sea when a storm tore at the ship's sails, and waves crashed upon the deck. Hardly anything had been discernible beyond the roar of wind and water, yet somehow, he'd detected the violent splash and then the shout.

While his sense of self-preservation may have been weak, he hadn't lost his sense of duty. A combination that had him diving into the turbulent waves.

"I was able to come to the captain's aid during a storm. His gratitude caused our relationship to strengthen." It had also caused Jonathan to open his mouth and speak, with a voice low and scratchy from disuse, for the first time in months. "After that, one thing led to another. Captain Maxwell had done extremely well for himself over the years and was looking to purchase more ships. I received some inheritance upon turning one-and-twenty and was in a position to invest. From there, Maxwell and Son Shipping Co was born."

"Maxwell." Her lips twitched as she repeated the name. "So, the name you provided at the inn wasn't just at random. Although why *and son*?"

"Captain Maxwell had no sons of his own, and I ..." He took another glance toward the stream, waiting for the painful sensation in his chest to pass. "With my own father gone, I no longer wanted to be an Astley." Not when the name was like a curse, a tie to the uncle he despised, a reminder of everything he'd wanted to escape.

"My adopting the name of Jon Maxwell suited us both. It solidified our business partnership, but it was more than that, too. Captain Maxwell couldn't have treated me any better had I been his true son, and I respected him as I would a father. After his death three years ago, I discovered that everything he owned—the ships—had been willed to me. I've spent the time since trying to do his legacy proud."

Amelia was still, her head tilted to the side in a way that displayed the milky column of her throat. "That's quite something. You've certainly done well for yourself." She spoke slowly as if still processing everything he'd told her. He could almost believe he'd heard a trace of pride in her words. But there was something else, too. Something that rang more like wistfulness.

He shifted against the tree trunk, his hand running over the decaying bark. Yes, he *had* done well. Far better than anything he could have dreamed the night he'd fled to the docks with nothing but the clothes on his back.

He'd sailed the world, always looking to acquire new ships, new trade deals. He'd made himself into someone unrecognizable, had amassed a fortune large enough that he'd never have to rely on his ailing dukedom for funds.

And still.

Still, it didn't erase his regrets. It didn't mean there was nothing about the past he wished he could undo.

"Amelia ..." He inched sideways until his legs nearly intersected with the edge of her cloak. Still not close enough, but he didn't dare go nearer and risk scaring her away. He had to make her listen. To make her *want* to listen.

I'm sorry, Amelia, for all the ways I wronged you. For my deception. I would do anything to win back your trust, to have you feel you can confide in me. I want to help you ...

Her body twitched, her lips rounding into an *o*, as a fat water droplet splashed against her nose. Then another. And another.

He jerked his head upward, where just minutes ago, he'd been appreciating the sunshine. The sun remained, a vivid orb above them, but raindrops fell nonetheless, intensifying out of nowhere. Water beaded in her hair, dripping down her face and forming dark streaks against the blue of her cloak, as meanwhile, wetness seeped into his own skin and clothing.

"We should go." She snatched up her boot, easing her foot into the damp leather. "It seems waiting in the carriage would be preferable, after all."

A beleaguered groan drifted out from the edge of the wood, and he turned to find the coachman struggling into a sitting position, blinking away the raindrops that had fallen in his eyes. Good. The man being semi-sentient would save Jonathan the trouble of dragging him back to the road.

All the same, he had to repress a groan of his own as he pushed himself to his feet, shrugging on his crumpled coat. Why wouldn't it bloody stop raining?

He'd sensed something shift in Amelia as they sat together on the tree trunk. A subtle thawing. A raptness as he spoke of his years abroad—a story he'd never told in full to anyone before—which sparked an ember of hope in him that maybe he could get her to speak to him as well, of more than just the scenery.

Only to have it doused by rain while the sun still shone in the sky like a false promise.

Wordlessly, he gathered her into his arms, pressing her close in an attempt to shield her from the worst of the downpour. If only he could undo the rain that had already soaked them both.

With any luck, this would be merely a passing shower, and once he got the horses hitched again, they could continue with their journey unhindered. This time, however, he'd have no choice but to ride outside on the box, ensuring the coachman didn't meet with further ... *difficulties.*

Amelia's head was beneath his chin, and he allowed himself a quick inhale, detecting, amidst the vibrant scents of drenched springtime greenery, the familiar hint of apple blossoms. She made a small movement, and for a moment, he felt certain she was going to tuck her cheek against his chest. He *wanted* her to, wanted her to rest directly above his beating heart, wanted to feel that closeness. A closeness that maybe, whenever they arrived at their inn for the night, they could resume.

He wanted her to, but then, just as quickly, her neck snapped upward, away from him, and her limbs adopted their characteristic tension.

Yes, they would have time at an inn tonight. More hours in the carriage tomorrow. Time to resume what they'd started on the tree trunk.

But by then, the moment may have already passed them by.

<h1 style="text-align:center">8</h1>

The accommodations at The Hound and Peacock had held unmistakable signs of disrepair, but they were downright luxurious compared to those at The Crooked Oak.

Amelia pulled her brush through her hair, watching as the light of her lone tallow candle flickered upon the raindrops trickling through the windowsill. No wonder the space smelled dank, with small black spots adorning patches of the whitewashed walls.

Not only that, but the force of the raging wind elicited a strange groaning from them, almost as if a creature inhabited the joists within and was trying to break free. Her mind traveled back to the storms she'd weathered as a child at her family's country seat, Beaumont Manor, where her brothers had crafted an elaborate story about the rattling windows being caused by a ghost in the attic. *Ghosts aren't real*, she'd insisted to them even then, and if anything, she should be more certain of that now. Yet on those nights when she'd lain alone in her little bed in the nursery, she'd always pulled the covers up tight to her chin and placed her pillow over her head as a makeshift shield, unable to shake the sense of foreboding. Not so different from the one rising in her now.

She shook the memory away, concentrating on working out a tangle near her scalp, the result of yet another drenching from a sky that wouldn't relent. This morning's sunshine had been a lie, giving way to a sun shower that then became a day as wet, dreary, and turbulent as the one before.

Had the weather been kind to them over the past two days, they could have arrived at Foxhill this very evening, bringing their ill-advised journey together to an end. Instead, the carriage had snaked along, taking them only another ten miles or so before it had pulled up to an inn, and Jonathan, soaked to the bone, had informed her of the need to stop for the night.

She'd known that another delay was imminent, but she couldn't begrudge it. Couldn't argue, even though shreds of frustration tugged at her insides. She'd needed only to look at Jonathan, his shoulders hunched and dripping as he pulled open the carriage door, and the ashen-faced coachman to realize that pausing the journey yet again was the only option.

All would be well. She'd repeated the phrase to herself over and over. As the malodorous innkeeper had shown them to rooms little bigger than closets. As she'd told Jonathan he could leave her and then flopped across a mattress that held all the comfort of a rock. As a tray had arrived, containing stale bread and a plate of some stringy, unidentifiable meat.

Yet, the fact was, they were farther north than yesterday. And as long as they could go at a pace fast enough that she'd be safely ensconced at Foxhill by the time the Lady Lockheart scandal broke, any discomforts along the way were secondary.

All would be well.

An especially fierce wind gust rattled the windowpane, causing an ominous creak and sending an extra burst of raindrops streaming inside.

Ghosts aren't real.

A shiver darted down her spine, and she hugged the thin silk of her dressing gown tight around her body. Had she been thinking more clearly, she would have packed warmer, less flimsy nightwear. Also, more than one spare dress, for the skirts of those she'd brought both contained mud stains that might never come clean.

Lessons learned, she supposed.

She returned her focus to making long strokes with her hairbrush, traveling from her head down to where the ends of her tresses fell in waves near her waist. It was silly, perhaps, to take such care when the rest of her looked a travel-stained fright. However, her hair had always been her one point of pride, the one part of her appearance that didn't feel lacking. Yes, it was maybe a touch too red to be considered the height of fashion, but it also contained notes of gold, and the strands were thick, a contrast to her too-thin body.

Besides, the repetitive motion was soothing.

Just as the flowing water of the stream today had been soothing. And the sunshine, while it lasted. And Jonathan, sitting beside her on the tree trunk in his shirtsleeves, revealing the mysteries of his past, smelling of spices and warmth—

Something darted across the floorboards. Darkness had already fallen, turning the contents of the room into indistinct shadows, but there was no mistaking the patter of tiny feet. Or the fur-covered body that fell under the glow of her candle for just an instant before scurrying under the bed.

Her hairbrush flew across the room as she bolted to her feet, biting down hard on her lip to quash the beginnings of a scream. Pain surged through her swollen ankle, but she ignored it, grabbing onto the bedpost for support. That was one advantage of this room: its smallness meant there was always a piece of furniture or a wall within reach. Which proved extremely helpful as she dragged herself along as fast as her legs would take her, throwing open the door and bursting into the corridor.

She promptly connected with a hard body, and arms shot out to encircle her waist.

The corridor was dimly lit, but she could still make out the lines that appeared between Jonathan's eyes as he gazed at her, the cords that stood out against the sides of his throat. "What's happened? I heard a crash."

She didn't answer, simply wriggled her arm free to slam the door closed. Then, she pressed her weight into him, urging him back in the direction he'd come.

Fortunately, he took the hint, and they lurched backward, staggering into his room next door.

She pulled herself away as soon as her legs connected with the end of the bed, dropping onto the stiff mattress. The lone seat in this room made up of a bed, a nightstand, a hearth filled only with embers, and nothing more.

She set her hands on her knees, taking in shallow breaths as another door slammed, this time by his doing. Shutting them in together.

He was staring at her, his eyes wide and alarmed. Much the same expression he'd worn yesterday when he'd picked her up off the side of the road. A look containing an intensity that made her remember ... that nearly made her think he still felt ... *something* toward her ...

"I—" She paused, feeling her cheeks begin to heat. Perhaps he imagined her in some new crisis. Some life-or-death scenario. While the truth, it turned out, was decidedly inaner. "I saw a mouse run under my bed," she muttered, the warmth spreading up to the roots of her hair. If she thought to spend the rest of her days alone, she best start doing things to prove her independence and not flit about like a silly, squeamish girl.

"Oh." He pressed a fist over his mouth, and was it her imagination, or were his eyes crinkling at the corners like those of someone about to smile? Perhaps it was, for when he lowered his hand, his mouth was tight, and his brow remained furrowed. "Based on what I've seen of this inn, I can't say I'm surprised. I'm sorry. Had I known the state of things, I would have tried to press on with the carriage for a few more miles. We don't seem to be having much luck with accommodations, do we?"

No, they didn't. No luck with weather, either. Or with *anything*. However, those things didn't matter, she reminded herself again, as long as she remained on her way to Northamptonshire.

"We'll switch rooms," he said, retrieving his candle holder and shining the light around the perimeter of the room, where wall and floor intersected. "I can make no guarantees as to the state of this one, but I see no obvious holes in the wall, and I'll stuff my coat under the door when I go to provide an extra barrier."

"No." She shook her head, still feeling foolish. "No, that's not necessary."

"It *is*, Amelia." He set the candle back on the nightstand and reached for the valise he'd laid at the foot of the bed. "I want you to be as comfortable as possible. Besides, I've spent enough time belowdecks to have grown accustomed to the sight of rats. A mouse is practically a pleasure in comparison."

"No," she repeated, a whisper instead of a command. He was rushing, taking hold of his valise, turning away to reach for the door, ready to break out into the corridor. She couldn't let that happen.

She should be the one to go. To return to her room as if no upset had occurred and ignore the scurrying feet, the leaking window, the groaning walls, and whatever else came her way during the night. But drat it all, the mouse had startled her. Thrown her off balance. And suddenly, she didn't want to be alone.

More specifically, she didn't want to be without *him*. Because as much as the past should have taught her differently, she couldn't shake the sense, right down to her core, that he would keep her safe.

She cleared her throat, forcing more power into her voice. Willing it not to crack. "No, don't go. You should stay here. That is, we could both stay here."

He stilled in his position by the doorway, his fingers tightening around the handle of his valise. Her heart thrummed, each second becoming an eternity. Perhaps she'd shocked him with the suggestion. Heavens, she'd shocked herself. Ladies—spinsters—didn't make those sorts of propositions. Mouse or no, she had to remember herself, had to act on what was right and, more importantly, wise—

"All right." He lowered his valise to the floor, then turned, his expression unreadable. "I'll fetch the counterpane from your room so I can make a pallet for myself on the floor."

"That's not necessary." Her new phrase of choice. She shifted against the bed, drawing her feet up and settling on the far edge next to the wall. Scarcely able to believe what she was doing but unable to stop herself. "The bed is large enough for both of us."

He must have answered, for his throat moved, although the sound that came out was indistinguishable.

More seconds slipped by. More infinite moments to wait.

Until suddenly, he was loosening the buttons of his coat, sliding it from his shoulders. Undoing the waistcoat beneath.

Foolishly, her pulse quickened. Hadn't she seen him doff his coat that very morning, outdoors in broad daylight? Yet somehow, the shadows of this cramped space made the sight even more intimate. More revealing.

He bent down, bunching the garments into the gap between the door and floorboards, making the faint flicker of light from the corridor sconces vanish. Cutting them off from any animal visitors, hopefully.

Cutting them off from everything but each other.

His shadow approached the bed, the candlelight just bright enough to reveal the dark glimmer of his eyes. Still unreadable. She ran her tongue over the surface of lips turned dry, digging her fingers into the edge of the counterpane. She couldn't afford to let anything show on her face, either, for who knew what it might reveal? Her stomach reeled, and her thoughts rushed around in circles. She'd asked him for this. She *wanted* this. But at the same time, it felt, in part, far more frightening than the mouse.

"Shall I blow out the candle?" His voice hung in the air, filling the short distance between them.

"Yes." She threw back the counterpane, sliding down into sheets that felt rough, damp. The pillow was a lump beneath her head, the mattress so stiff that she would need to do a great deal of tossing and turning to find comfort. However, she didn't move from her position close to the wall, careful to leave the other side of the bed bare. "Yes, we should sleep. Perhaps we can then get an early start tomorrow and try to reach our destination."

With a puff of his breath, the room went black, taking what little she could see and turning it into shadows. Yet, from the lack of sight, her other senses became more alert.

The bed dipped, making a faint creak as he lowered himself to sit on the edge. Then, there came the rustle of hands against fabric, and a thud as his boots dropped to the floor.

Once again, her pulse skittered, and she remained frozen in place, not even daring to exhale. What would come next? The linen shirt gliding over his head? His fingers sweeping over the buttons of his fall? When she'd made the request that he stay with her, she hadn't considered his sleeping attire. Or lack thereof.

The bed creaked again, the mattress sinking inward as he stretched out along the length of it. Still clothed in his shirt and breeches, from what she could tell. Not even nestled in the sheets but atop the counterpane, where there was no chance their bodies could intersect without a barrier.

A relief. The twinge in her chest could signify nothing else, surely.

She stared at the black nothingness of the ceiling, sleep feeling like a faraway entity. Perhaps it would be easier if she turned to the wall and imagined the sprawling parkland of Foxhill, or a comfortable bed, or anything other than this too-small room at The Crooked Oak.

She *should* have done that. Only, her body turned the other way instead.

She lay on her side with her eyelids fluttering, her pupils adjusting to the dimness until she could just detect the outline of him. The broad shoulders that lay pressed against the mattress. The legs, even longer than hers, that stretched to the bottom of the bed.

That curious, spiced scent filled her nose again, for he was so close. Near enough that with a single motion, she could sweep her hand through his hair, over his jawline, along the taut surface of his chest.

She shouldn't be thinking these things. After all, between the hours in the carriage and the time he spent carrying her from one spot to another, they'd had their fair share of proximity over the past two days. It was enough that she should have become desensitized. However, there was something about lying down—on a bed—that heightened her awareness, making her skin prick.

With a single motion, she could be in his arms, imagining

herself as a girl of eighteen. A runaway debutante at an inn in Gretna Green. A wife.

With a single motion, her heart could fill with everything she'd spent the past decade longing for. Because he'd crushed it, and still, it yearned.

It damnably, perilously yearned.

She squeezed her eyes shut so even the shadowy outlines dissolved into blackness. This wasn't the time to remember the past, to pine for what could have been. If she was going to finish this journey no worse for wear, she had to remain in the present. For in the present, the Duke of Branscombe was accommodating and courteous, going along with her plan to travel north together despite her aloofness. The past two days hadn't been kind to them. And still, he'd persevered, trying to keep going because that's what she wanted.

That was all that mattered—that she could *allow* to matter. And at the very least, he deserved her acknowledgment for that.

"Thank you," she whispered, daring to peer out at the space once more. He was still there—of course, he was still there—lying on his back, the heat of his body radiating toward her.

Had he fallen asleep? He stayed very still, his chest barely moving. Which was perhaps for the best. It would be more appropriate for her to thank him when he dropped her off at Foxhill, when they were far away from this cloak of darkness and intimacy.

Except then, his body shifted, ruffling the counterpane as he turned onto his side. His face drew near enough that the warmth of his exhales fell upon her cheek, and whether the obscuring darkness was a blessing or a curse, she could no longer say.

She could just make out the glint of his eyes, watching her.

And then, a lone finger traced over a strand of her hair, the touch featherlight yet vibrating through her body like a lightning strike. Now, she was the one who stilled. She didn't so much as breathe while his head lifted from the pillow, coming closer, and his lips fell upon her forehead in the faintest, gentlest caress.

It was only an instant before his lips moved away, murmuring something close to her ear. "It's hardly worth speaking of." Her own words from the night before, repeated back to her.

She didn't know what to do, how to respond, for all she could think of was that finger traveling down her body, those lips meeting with her lips.

So, she did the only thing she could. Uttered the only response that wouldn't send her hurtling down a dangerous road from which she might never return. "Good night."

His head returned to the pillow. His hands, to his side. The counterpane remained between them as a mark of propriety—well, as much propriety as one could have when sharing a bed with a man who wasn't one's husband. Almost as if he'd never touched her after all.

The fabric of his shirt and breeches rustled against the counterpane as he settled himself. Still so close that she could never become unaware of his presence. She could hear the intake of breath as he opened his mouth, could detect the low sound in his throat, and for a moment, the world felt like an orb teetering on the edge of a cliff.

But only a single phrase emerged. A rejoinder to her own. "Good night, Amelia."

She forced her breaths to come, in and out. Now, she could attempt to sleep. Her heart pounded, making her chest feel like it might burst, but she would have to close her eyes and ignore it. She needed to rest, to prepare for a full day of travel tomorrow when, with any luck, they would reach

Foxhill. Then, they would go their separate ways once more. Because that's the way things needed to be.

She'd sworn she would remain in the present. Nonetheless, as she turned to the wall, curling her body beneath the counterpane, her imagination conjured up words that drifted into her ear. No more than a whisper but clear enough that she could nearly believe they were real.

Sleep well, my love.

9

A weight pressed into Jonathan's torso. A warm, soft weight, in counterpoint to the hard surface below him. It enveloped him like a dream, providing comfort he never wanted to leave, contentment that flowed through his limbs.

He cracked open an eye, blinking at the sunrays that streamed through the inn's grimy window, announcing the arrival of a new day.

The inn. Morning.

His other eye flew open, his brain rushing to catch up with the scene that unfurled before him. The bed was so firm and lumpy, he'd sworn he would spend the whole night lying awake, trying *not* to think improper thoughts about the woman next to him.

Except at some point, he *had* fallen asleep and rolled right into Amelia. His body cupped hers like she'd been created to fit there, for she was tall, but he was taller, able to surround her from head to toe. The well-worn counterpane lay bunched between them, but it did little to mask the heat of her.

And his arm ... his arm had stretched out, draping across her side, his hand coming to rest against the flat plane of her abdomen. She still wore her night rail and dressing gown, of course, but both garments were thin. Very thin.

Tentatively, he untucked his fingers from the flimsy silk and lifted his arm, and when she didn't stir, he flopped onto his back, stifling a groan. This seemed an inopportune time to realize that he'd awoken with a rampant cockstand.

He pushed himself up to sitting, trying to concentrate on musty inns with mildewed walls. Vermin. Rain that wouldn't relent. Mud.

It didn't matter. He could still smell apple blossoms. Had eyes for nothing but the hair fanned across her pillow, catching the sunlight, a sprawling curtain of gold and copper.

He bent over and grabbed his boots, shoving them awkwardly onto his feet. This had to stop. Immediately. She may have deemed his presence throughout the night more tolerable than that of a mouse, but that didn't mean she wished for him to become overfamiliar or to take liberties.

He nearly made it to the door before the voice stopped him.

"Your Grace?" Her words contained the huskiness of sleep, along with the same hint of confusion he'd just experienced as he opened his eyes in this strange situation and tried to piece the world back together again.

Jonathan. What he'd give to hear his true name cross her lips just like it used to, full of lightness and adoration. To hell with the honorific. He wanted none of that where she was concerned.

More inappropriate musings. He had to leave, to flee the confines of this room before he did something uncouth.

"I'm going to alert the coachman that it's time to ready the carriage." He placed his hand on the door, not daring to turn around. "I'll also ask for a small breakfast to be sent up, and then, we can get on our way."

He didn't wait for her response before snatching up his

discarded coat and waistcoat and bursting into the dusky corridor, which, thank God, remained devoid of people. Given her eagerness to arrive in Northamptonshire, she would hopefully appreciate his haste rather than find it peculiar.

He tugged on his crumpled garments. Adjusted his breeches. He intended to do just as he'd told her and arrange for their breakfast and departure.

First, though, he was going to need another minute.

To the coachman's credit, he'd stayed sober last night, making him efficient in bringing round the carriage at the appointed time and setting off down the Great North Road once more. And to the sun's credit, it remained high in the sky, not marred by so much as a single cloud. Not that Jonathan entirely trusted appearances after the events of yesterday. However, they were off to a promising start.

Amelia sat across from him as usual, her stockinged foot propped up on his bench. She'd told him, as he settled her in the carriage, that her ankle felt less swollen this morning. She'd also made a comment about a newborn lamb she spotted and a cluster of crocuses growing in a field.

Now, however, she stayed quiet, gazing out the window with a faraway expression. Perhaps she, too, had gotten little rest during their night in the ramshackle inn. Not that it had been entirely sleepless ...

Damn it, *no*, he was *not* going to think about the events of last night again. Or the way he'd woken up.

He needed to focus. If the carriage maintained its current pace, this could be their final day of travel, and he had yet to discern the reason behind her flight from London. He couldn't just drop her on the doorstep of Foxhill and be on his way without knowing for sure that she faced no sort of trouble.

For that matter, he was beginning to doubt his abilities to drop her off and be on his way, never looking back, under any circumstances.

Regardless, the past two days had taught him that straight-out asking her about it would get him nowhere. It was as if she could sense when he even *thought* about posing the question, and she then proceeded to grow distant, feigning sleep or changing the subject.

Perhaps the trick lay with approaching the matter less directly. Starting with trivial conversation, to which she appeared to have no objection.

"Do you travel to Northamptonshire often?" he asked, his voice cutting into the rhythmic bump and rattle of the carriage. That was an innocuous enough inquiry, wasn't it?

She must have heard him, for her forehead creased, but she didn't divert her gaze from the window. Maybe even that question had gone beyond the realm of what she was willing to discuss.

However, with her eyes still glued to the passing fields, she gave her head a small shake. "No. Very rarely. My brother, Nicholas—the Marquess of Rockliffe, if you recall—used to travel to Foxhill when he wished for seclusion. Which was often. In the early years of his marriage to Cecilia, when their daughter, Emily, was small, he invited me to accompany them there on an occasion or two. However, as time went on, he only wanted to go alone."

She blinked against the sunlight that streaked across her face, clasping her fingers into tight balls. "I suppose he wouldn't begrudge me staying there a while, though, now that he's gone."

Gone? While Jonathan had made inquiries about Amelia immediately after arriving in England, he hadn't thought to ask after the rest of her family. "What happened?" He spoke softly, knowing that one wrong word could close her off to him for the rest of the journey.

She swallowed, the muscles in her neck growing tight. "There was a terrible scandal. Cecilia took Emily and ran away with ... with another man. Intending to go all the way to India. Nicholas went after them. After that, I have very few details. As you're aware, letters travel slowly from that great a distance, and I don't believe Mother is very forthcoming with the news she does receive. All I know is that Cecilia contracted an illness and did not survive, and that Nicholas and Emily haven't returned. I don't know if they ever will, and—goodness, I'm sorry."

Her head darted forward, causing her gaze to connect with his at last. Her eyes had that sheen again, almost as if tears lurked close to the surface. "I shouldn't speak of such things. It's a highly improper topic, and there's already been so much gossip—"

"I want you to." He reached out a hand but then stilled it. Just because they'd shared a bed didn't mean she would suddenly welcome his touches. He desired nothing more than to place his hands over hers. Or better yet, to hurtle onto the bench next to her and gather her in his arms. To make her feel safe. However, as he might better accomplish that by keeping a degree of distance, he stayed where he was, peering at her, willing her to understand. To trust. "I want you to feel you can tell me anything and know I'll hold it in confidence."

Her fingers gave a couple quick swipes at the corners of her eyes before she lowered her hands back to her lap. "I miss them." She let her shoulders sag against the stiff seat back, her breath coming out as a shuddering exhale. "Just as I miss Samuel. For my second brother is gone, too, and he's not coming back. Did you know I received news of three deaths only months apart? Samuel. Cecilia. And then, Tobias Astley, the former Duke of Branscombe."

The Duke of Branscombe ... his uncle ... Not a man she'd known well, presumably, or at all. Yet he knew from speaking with one of the more loose-tongued grooms at Branscombe House that that's when rumors of his own death had run rampant. *We didn't know what was to become of us, Yer Grace, what with some folks saying the heir was coming from afar, while others said he'd been drowned at sea years ago.*

That Amelia had thought about him, amidst everything else ... That she'd endured so much ...

Damn restraint. He vaulted to the opposite bench, wrapping an arm around her shoulder and gathering her close. If she decided to shrug him off and tell him to go to the deepest recesses of hell, he would gladly oblige.

But she didn't. She let him hold her, allowed her head to sink against his chest.

Her eyes continued shimmering, but tears didn't fall. He could hear himself making hushing sounds nonetheless. Soft, calming words so she knew she wasn't alone. That he cared.

He wished he could draw away every scrap of pain she'd ever felt. On account of him. On account of circumstances with her family. On account of any way life had ever wronged her.

They stayed that way as the countryside continued to rush by, and Amelia's gaze returned to the window, the sun casting her in a golden glow.

"At least Samuel's sons remain," she said eventually, her expression distant, as if she'd traveled miles away. They'd just passed a group of children running through a field, their excited shrieks loud enough to drift into the rattling carriage, and her lips gave a momentary twitch upward. "If there could ever be a bright side to his loss, it's that I've gotten to know my nephews, who were estranged while he was living. They're darling boys. One even looks just like him. I shall miss them, too, now that I've left London."

Why did you leave? Could he ask that now? For she looked almost melancholy, as if the departure had gone against her wishes. Even though she'd so adamantly insisted on the hasty journey.

There had to be a reason for it. The truth must be close. Trust was a fragile thing, but after all she'd just shared, maybe it had strengthened enough between them that she would utter the words if he gently prompted—

"Your Grace." She stiffened in his arms, wriggling herself upward, and he bit down on his tongue to prevent himself from emitting a curse loud enough to rock the whole carriage. However, the alarm that filled her eyes wasn't directed at him but toward the window, where she pressed her face, tapping a finger against the glass. "Do you see that?"

He hurriedly leaned over, positioning his face near hers, and had to blink several times to comprehend the scene outside. A figure lay crumpled on the side of the road, covered by a tattered cloak and bonnet. So uncannily similar to the way he'd found Amelia two days prior that his stomach lurched from the memory.

Amelia was here beside him, safe and well. He allowed his shoulder to brush against hers for a split second of reassurance. That didn't change the fact that some other woman had met with misfortune and required urgent assistance, and there were no other passersby in sight.

The carriage began to slow and veer to the side, but he banged on the ceiling just in case, signaling the urgent need to stop. God willing, there was something he could do to help, that this wouldn't end in tragedy.

The bundle moved, sturdy hands peeking out from beneath the cloak and shuffling against the dirt. Alive. Yet the sensation that filled him wasn't a burst of relief. Not only did the woman stir, but so, too, did the leaves in the thicket of bushes that delineated the area between the grassy countryside and the dirt road. Suddenly, his chest went tight, the feeling more akin to deep-rooted dread.

The woman staggered to her feet, ripping off the bonnet, letting the cloak tumble back to the ground. Except it wasn't a woman but a short, stocky man, who had a face like a bulldog and a bald head that gleamed with beads of sweat beneath the sun.

The bushes rustled again, and the leaves parted, revealing another man so opposite the first that, under the right circumstances, it could have been comical. As tall and lanky as the other was squat and thick. Shaggy haired.

Yet they did have one thing in common. They both plodded toward the carriage with steadfast determination, their heavy boots scuffing against the dirt.

Jonathan pounded on the ceiling again as if the action could somehow reverse the past few moments. If the blasted coachman would just take up the reins, send the horses into a gallop—

There was an indistinguishable shout. A thump against the ground. The coachman's boots came into view, followed by the rest of him. He stumbled backward a step, looking like he might topple at any moment, his face even grayer than yesterday.

The sight was but fleeting, for in the next moment, he was bolting across the road, his legs flopping about wildly until he dove into the thicket, his body disappearing behind a tangle of branches and leaves.

Jonathan could only sit and watch it happen as if he'd become the audience to some outrageous play. Disbelief froze his limbs, his mind swirling in a dozen different directions, trying to determine the best course of action. His lips managed to move, though, letting a muttered curse escape. "I'll be goddamned."

What came next was pure reflex. He bolted upright, grabbing hold of Amelia's shoulders and sliding her down the bench. His head banged into the too-low ceiling in the process, but it didn't matter, for when he flopped back down, he and Amelia had changed places, so he now sat closest to the encroaching danger, his body able to provide at least something of a shield.

It was all he had time for before the carriage door flew open, revealing the bulldog-like man peering in at them with a humorless smirk.

Cocking a pistol, pointing it straight at Jonathan's chest. "Stand and deliver."

10

Amelia sat with her back wedged against the stiff carriage seat, her lungs ceasing to draw in air and her heart pounding at double speed. The carriage bounced and creaked, and then, heavy footsteps pounded on the roof above her. That black-toothed, lanky man must have climbed up to rifle through the imperial and see what he could pilfer.

A circumstance that was secondary to the fact that the other, stockier footpad stood outside the open door with a pistol aimed at Jonathan's heart.

Without looking away from the man, Jonathan leaned down slowly, retrieving the small valise he kept under the seat and handing it outward. "I suppose you want this."

It was remarkable. Why, he nearly sounded ... *bored*. As if this were some mundane transaction and his life didn't dangle on the line. The footpad snatched the valise away, and with gradual motions, Jonathan raised his body, dragging his hand toward his coat pocket, which was bunched up from the way he had to awkwardly bend his legs in the cramped space.

"Ah." Again, his voice was the picture of calm disinterest.

"If you'd allow me to step to the ground, I can better empty my pockets."

The footpad's craggy face twisted into a scowl, and Amelia had to bite back a silent scream. What could Jonathan mean by making such a suggestion? Perhaps it would serve him better if he freed himself from the confines of the carriage, if he could put more space between his body and the pistol. But at the same time, it wouldn't change how there were two ruthless—and armed—men looking to rob them, how anything could happen ... Blood pounded through her ears and rushed through her veins, feeling like it had turned to ice.

The footpad took a step backward with a grunt and a nod, and whether the action proved wise or not, Jonathan jumped down from the carriage, stuffing his hands into his pockets.

"Hey!" The footpad's gravelly voice cut through the air, as sharp as any bullet. The pistol wavered in his hand, and a burst of air suddenly shot into her lungs, ready to make her shriek, jump, surge forward.

Until she realized. The footpad's reaction wasn't in response to Jonathan. He was looking straight at *her*.

"She has n-nothing." Jonathan's words were rushed, overloud. The first crack in his composure. He wrenched his hand out of his pocket, dropping a fistful of coins into the footpad's free palm. "My wife has been injured and is unable to rise from her seat. However, you need only look at her to know. She has nothing."

She dug her nails into her thighs, her fingers curling around swaths of her blue muslin skirts. It was the dress she'd worn on the day she left home, which was now covered with mud. She had no adornments, nothing in her hair but a piece of limp ribbon that secured the end of her braid. The best she could do with no lady's maid to assist her.

She looked a fright, her face no doubt ashen and twisted

into an expression of horror. The carriage appeared not much better, its black paint peeling, the interior cramped and worn. Nothing to suggest it belonged to a duke.

Why the footpads had targeted them, then, she couldn't say. Yet if she and Jonathan could both keep calm and give the scoundrels enough coins to appease them, maybe they'd be free to go again. Lighter in the pockets but unharmed.

They *had* to get through this unharmed. Her fingernails sank deeper into her skin, trying to force her head to clear so she didn't get sucked into the black abyss of panic.

Jonathan dumped his pocket watch into the footpad's meaty hand, and the man shoved it into his tattered coat, temporarily satisfied. The pistol, however, remained in position, his finger against the trigger.

Amelia allowed herself a quick glance out the window toward the empty road. Why would another carriage not come along?

If only someone who was able to assist would appear. If only they'd brought a pistol of their own. If only the footpads would decide they'd had their fill and be on their way with their stolen coins.

If only, if only, if only …

She had no more time for fruitless speculation, for suddenly, her skin prickled, sensing the weight of a gaze upon her. The footpad continued accepting Jonathan's offerings, leaving the pistol aimed at his chest. His steely eyes, though, were on her. Glinting in a way that promised danger.

She made a small sound in the back of her throat, unable to hold it in.

From there, everything seemed to happen at once, faster than her mind could process. She only knew that one second, Jonathan was standing there with his back to the doorway, passing coins to the footpad. And the next, he'd pivoted to the side, his arms slicing through the air. One smashing into the footpad's wrist. The other grabbing the top of the pistol, wrenching it around.

The footpad gave an outraged bellow, his fist flying outward, connecting with Jonathan's gut. Jonathan staggered, just for an instant. But long enough for the footpad to grab his hand, trying to reclaim what he'd lost.

A deafening crack burst through her ears, and she screamed, the world suddenly reduced to nothing but the shot's forbidding echo and the smoky tang of gunpowder. She scrambled up from the bench, heedless of her ankle, heedless of how she seemed to be choking on sobs, heedless of anything but her need to get to Jonathan's side, even if she had to crawl there.

And then she realized. The pistol had flown through the air, coming to land at the edge of the bushes. There was no blood, no bodies crumpling to the ground. Both men still stood, the footpad's eyes stretched wide with disbelief, his face red with uncontained fury. He raised a hefty fist—the only weapon he had left—

And got no farther.

Jonathan's hand shot outward, his palm and fingers in a razor-straight line that slammed into the side of the footpad's jaw. He lunged forward, his other arm swiping past the footpad's throat until his elbow delivered a crushing blow.

Now, the fierce, stocky man was the one stumbling, his breaths coming out in strangled gulps.

But she saw no more. The carriage creaked above her, and a figure swooped down into her field of vision, filling the doorway. The other footpad—a man even taller and ganglier than she was—sprang down from the roof with all the agility of a cat, landing on his feet in just the right position.

His rotting teeth were bared, his dark-eyed glower boring

through her even more intensely than that of the other scoundrel. A shiver darted up her spine as his gaze traveled along her torso. And then, to the small bag that had previously been tucked behind her feet, and now, with her change in position, sat out in the open. A bag containing a decade's worth of savings, the product of dozens—no, hundreds—of magazine columns. The only thing she had to her name that was really and truly *hers*.

She had no time to think, not even about the tip of the silver blade that emerged from his palm. She raised her knee, heaving it forward with all the strength in her body, directly into the footpad's groin.

He reeled backward with a groan, beginning to double over.

All at once, Jonathan was there, his boot hitting the back of the footpad's knee, making him pitch forward. The knife fell, and once again, with a speed too rapid to track, Jonathan's elbows flew up, connecting with the footpad's shoulder blades and neck. The final blows that toppled their attacker.

Jonathan snatched up the knife before the man's face hit the dirt. As for the first footpad, he already lay facedown and motionless a short distance away, his arms sprawled out to the sides.

She remained by the open door of the carriage, unable to move, unable to do anything but gape. Her mind was still spinning nonsensically, her heart pounding, her chest too tight.

Until suddenly, a rustle in the bushes snapped her attention to the side of the road. The coachman popped up, his livery covered in twigs and leaves, his hat nowhere to be found. He looked like he'd seen a ghost. Rather, a whole village of them. Yet he crept forward a step toward the carnage as if testing to see if the ground would still hold his weight. All while grasping the used pistol within his shaking hands.

"Well, then?" Jonathan eyed the man, his brows rising on his dusty forehead. Not even sounding breathless. "Shall we be on our way?"

His words set the world in motion again. The coachman, with pink splotches spreading across his cheeks, hurried back toward the carriage, and Amelia slumped down onto the bench, tension draining from her seized limbs.

In the next instant, Jonathan appeared on the bench across from her, the carriage door slamming closed behind him.

Somehow, they were rolling into motion again, traveling down the road as if it were a morning like any other. The sun continued to streak through the windows and bathe the carriage interior in cheery yellow light.

Amelia didn't attempt speech. Her breaths were coming too fast for that, and she still couldn't be sure that everything she'd just witnessed was real. She kept her face turned to the floor, trying to let the sun's warmth calm her. Trying to make sense of the scene that played over and over in her head.

"Are you all right?" Jonathan's voice pulled her eyes upward onto his dirt-streaked face. Jonathan, who'd borne the brunt of the ordeal. He could have been *killed*. Yet his features were creased with concern for *her*.

She nodded, willing her breaths to slow. Because she *was* all right. As was he.

"What you did to that footpad ..." He paused. "How did you know ..."

"That?" She made a sound. A sob? Or maybe she was laughing. Her emotions ran in such a tangle that she could no longer distinguish them. "Growing up with older brothers can cause a lady to learn all sorts of unsuitable things."

An indeterminate noise came from his throat as well. Nearly a laugh, but not quite. "I'm glad for their teachings, then. For if anything had happened to you ..."

Silence fell over the carriage, but his brown-eyed gaze remained on her, intense enough to make her chest ache. She couldn't focus on the meaning of his words. Could only picture him standing there with the footpad's pistol pointed at his chest until suddenly, it wasn't.

"Perhaps the better question is, how did *you* know?" She could still envision his arms slicing through the air, his body darting about with almost surreal dexterity. "Those things you did. Those actions. What even *was* that? And are those rogues —um—*dead*?"

"Not dead. Merely incapacitated," he answered quickly, and whether the assurance brought her relief or not, she couldn't say. His fingers drifted down to his pocket, running mindlessly over the edge of the fabric, and a glint of gold appeared. The pocket watch. He'd gotten it back. "As for fending them off … much like older brothers, traveling also has the ability to teach a person new skills."

She made some nondescript comment in response. At least, she meant to. However, her ability to form words didn't seem to have fully returned. She was staring, her eyes suddenly refusing to leave him. Traveling to his rumpled shirt and cravat and the chest that rose and fell beneath. Back up to the strong jawline, the angled cheekbones, and skin that contained just a hint of a flush. The dark, disheveled hair, still coated with dust from the road.

So very male. And near. And *alive*.

Once again, she reacted without thought. One moment, she was sitting in her seat with her hands folded in her lap, unable to do anything but gape. And the next, she was launching herself across the carriage onto the bench beside Jonathan. Her body pressed itself against his, needing to feel its warmth, its strength, and her face tilted upward, locking eyes with him again, drawing close. So close that a wisp of air flitted across her cheek from the low sound he made.

His arm flew around her waist, his own face angling down, closing the final gap.

The moment their lips connected was like a reunion. A feeling of safety and familiarity. A decade may have passed, but the memory of his kiss hadn't faded. The pressure of his mouth was just as it used to be, gentle but passionate all at once. He took his time as if savoring every edge and contour of her lips. Making her feel cherished. Revered.

Sparks flared in her belly, igniting a fire she'd thought forever extinguished. And maybe it wasn't sensible or wise, but she let it burn.

She kept her mouth pressed to his while her fingertips relearned the feel of the soft hair skirting his nape. While she breathed in the scent of him—spices mixed with the outdoors. While his hand secured her body in place, tracing circles over her lower back. Not touching her because she required assistance but because he desired it.

She continued to give and receive the same tender kisses of their youth, although with each passing moment they stayed connected, the tentative fire within her grew closer and closer to a full-fledged blaze. She would gladly stay like this forever, her lips locked with his, where there was nothing but the confines of this carriage, and the past and future ceased to exist. Only ... a part of her yearned for more.

It was as if he sensed the burgeoning need within her, for his hands came to her hips, shifting her onto his lap. The feeling was delicious, of having his muscular thighs beneath her, of drawing herself inward so she swept against the solid surface of his chest. And with the change in position, he deepened the kiss, brushing his tongue along her lips to coax them open, sliding into her mouth.

Oh, Lord, it was too much.

No, it was not enough.

She braced her hands on his shoulders, allowing her

tongue to twine with his. To drink in the heat of him. The taste. How was it he knew just the way to caress her, so the world became reduced to nothing but feeling?

As a girl of eighteen, she'd kissed him in the garden more times than she could count. She knew what it was to want. Yet it had never felt quite like this. This moment consisted of fear, relief, shock, sorrow, desire ... So many things that heightened the sensations coursing through her body, scrambling them into something unnamable but powerful.

The carriage shuddered as it rolled over a bump, pitching her forward so their lips crashed together with even more force. So her breasts collided with his chest, sending a jolt through her sensitized nipples, and her thigh connected with hardness in his breeches, the heat of it shooting straight to her core.

She didn't know what was happening to her. Only knew that she wanted the carriage to hit that bump over and over again, for the sensations to keep setting her on fire, to build into something potent enough to raze cities to the ground.

Except they weren't careening over bumps any longer. Why, they were slowing down, the movement of the carriage nothing beyond a gentle sway. The wheels creaked and groaned beneath them, the carriage veering to the right in a movement that tipped her away from the center of his body.

"What's happening?" She pulled her face away from his, experiencing a sharp ache of protest. And a discomforting return to reality. Outside the window, a large half-timbered building was coming into view. A coaching inn with a wooden sign hanging above the door. *The Golden Lion*. "Why are we stopping?"

"Uh." Jonathan blinked, his eyes appearing out of focus. The sound came out strangled, and though her chest no longer pressed against his, she could still detect the rapid echo of his heartbeat. He turned to the window to survey the scene. Blinking again. "I—I suppose it must be time to rest the horses."

That made sense. In a way. Because they didn't live in a world that revolved around kisses alone, did they? Real life contained horses that required resting, footpads that jumped out of bushes, dingy, mouse-infested coaching inns, and so much rain.

He adjusted the loosened knots of his cravat. Ran a hand through his hair. "We should stop a while. See if I can speak to a local constable about what happened. It may still be possible to apprehend the footpads."

Yes. A good idea. Very sensible. Unlike everything that had just passed between them, which was the opposite of wise.

She made her body drop to the side, scrambling out of his lap and back onto the opposite bench. The place she should have stayed all along, except she'd let her emotions get the better of her.

Foolish. So very, very foolish.

"Would—would you like to see if they have a passable dining room?" He cleared his throat. Smoothed another fold in his cravat. "We could have a meal while we wait."

"Perhaps." She tried to smile agreeably and pretend the earth hadn't just shifted. In truth, she wouldn't manage to eat a bite. "I think I'd like some air first."

The carriage had rolled to a stop, giving a slight tilt as the coachman jumped to the ground. Bringing this leg of the journey officially to a close.

"Amelia ..."

Jonathan was looking at her. Speaking her name in that low voice. The one that contained a note of contemplation, seeming like it was a hairsbreadth away from opening a Pandora's box of questions.

That, she couldn't allow.

"Why don't you go ahead?" Her cheeks felt too hot, too brittle. Hopefully—if there was any mercy left in the world—it wouldn't show. Alongside the inn were several unpruned hawthorns, along with a large chestnut tree, just beginning to display its springtime green. That would be her refuge. "While you're inside making inquiries, I'll stroll over to those trees. My ankle is feeling well enough that I'm sure I can manage that short a distance."

He pursed his lips, and she could see the protest forming on his tongue. But whether something on her face stopped him or she simply had a scrap of luck on her side after all, he swallowed it back, letting out a barely decipherable sigh. "At least let me help you to the ground."

Denying him that small request would only draw attention to things she didn't want revealed. And so, once again, she found his arms upon her, gathering her weight against his chest. Setting fire to her skin, which remained far too sensitive.

Fortunately, the trip from her seat in the carriage to the ground was brief. Not short enough to leave her unaffected, but she should be able to walk it off. She hoped.

She tested out her ankle, letting it bear a small amount of weight as her other leg did most of the work in propelling her toward the trees. It wasn't a fast or elegant process, but she managed. In fact, she did very well, all things considered. Nonetheless, Jonathan stayed at her side. Not touching her but matching the pace of her bulky strides.

If she stumbled, he would be there to catch her. For some reason, that knowledge caused an ache to spread through her chest.

The trees neared, and up close, she could see that several large rocks had been pushed together beneath the chestnut's trunk, almost like a makeshift bench. How fitting. She'd happened upon the perfect retreat.

She shuffled the remaining distance and carefully lowered herself to the cool surface of the largest rock. Jonathan extended his arm to help her, but she didn't take it. She didn't dare.

"This is lovely." She glanced up at him, where he stood surrounded by sunlight so bright it made her eyes water. That made it easier, having something to obscure the view. "I'll be perfectly well staying here for a while. In fact, I'd welcome the opportunity to have a few moments alone. You go along. I can make my way inside unassisted should the need arise."

She may not be able to discern his expression, but once again, she could sense his hesitancy. Could feel his gaze boring down until she didn't know how she would stand it.

She needed him to go inside. To call for the constable, or seek out provisions, or do whatever else needed to be done so they could get on their way again as quickly as possible. The idea of reaching Foxhill before sundown was fast slipping away, which would mean another night at an inn if they didn't hurry. Another night when they were pushed together, and her heart pounded with longing for something she shouldn't want.

Her reckless, reckless heart, which seemed to have forgotten the way it had once been trampled.

His hesitation lasted another moment. More seconds in which he remained standing above her, and something inside her continued to swell. Willing him to go. To stay. She didn't know anymore.

In one fluid motion, he turned away toward the entrance of the inn. Before he took his leave, though, moving in long strides across the dirt and gravel, he said something. Barely identifiable words, for he muttered them under his breath, and his back was to her, giving her a view of nothing but his down-turned head and the broad shoulders beneath his dusty wool coat.

She heard them nonetheless, the low syllables causing her ears to prick. *This isn't over, Amelia.*

And though he was walking away, giving her the solitude she'd asked for, her heart pounded harder than ever before.

11

J onathan stepped through the door of The Golden Lion, back into the fresh springtime breeze. A stagecoach was just pulling up, its wheels creaking and the sound of its exterior passengers' chatter filling the air. However, he only had eyes for the tree-filled area to the side of the inn. Specifically, for the figure who sat alone on the large rock beneath the chestnut tree, not paying heed to the stagecoach, either, but facing away so all he could see was a red-gold braid glinting in the sunlight.

He took a few careful steps forward, even though the cacophony of the new arrival would mask any noise his boots made as they hit the dirt. He didn't want to disturb her just yet. Not until he had another moment to gather his thoughts.

This day had turned into a bloody disaster, where nothing went as it should. Not that that was anything new. Yet from the moment their carriage had rolled to a stop in front of the Golden Lion, it was as if a heaviness had settled in the air. Rather like a storm cloud, ready to burst open and release a deluge at any moment.

He'd sensed it as they sat down for luncheon—not in a

private dining room, unfortunately, but in a room so crowded that conversation became impossible. He'd sensed it as he awaited the constable—who, as it turned out, made no efforts to hurry to The Golden Lion and kept them waiting for the better part of the afternoon. He'd sensed it when the constable—a portly man by the name of Mr. Gibbs—finally did arrive and proved himself to be the utmost sort of prattler, leaving Jonathan with the task of extricating himself from the discussion while Amelia fled outdoors for another repose.

The day's obstacles were behind them now, and nothing remained but an open road and a clear sky. And still, he was on edge, waiting for that first crack of thunder. That first splash of rain.

The problem lay with how his memory kept diving back to the events of the morning. Not the pistol pointed at his chest, nor the ache in his ribs from the footpad's hefty fist. Those things he could sweep away. It was what came afterward that wouldn't leave him. Amelia scrambling across the carriage ... their lips connecting, their tongues entwining ... her weight on his lap, stoking his yearning ...

As if his reward for besting the footpads was to have his innermost desires come true.

Except then, the carriage had stopped, and he'd been pulled back to a reality he no longer wanted. A reality where criminals remained at large, and he had a duty to try to stop them. For that was the honorable thing to do, and if he let honor slip, he wouldn't be any better than his uncle, would he?

Only, looking back, he was beginning to wish he'd said to hell with honor and duty and remained in the carriage, lapping up Amelia's sweetness, relearning her every curve. Tasting her, touching her, letting pleasure build and consequences slip away.

Maybe then, he wouldn't feel ready to jump out of his damn skin.

He approached the rock, staring at how the gradually sinking sun immersed her in brilliant light. Not just her hair but the pale skin at her nape and the slender lines of her back, covered by clinging blue muslin. He'd been a fool to ever let her slip away from him and would do anything to get back what he'd once thought forever lost.

But were all mistakes—even the darkest, most egregious ones—repairable?

He cleared his throat, and her head darted around, her expression unreadable as she took him in. "Your Grace."

No. Not Your Grace *to you*. The title on her tongue—the formality of it—dug at him worse than ever. But before he could say a word, she pivoted her body so she faced him, giving the wrinkled material of her skirts a few quick tugs. "Is everything sorted with the constable? Are we able to go now?"

"Yes, it's been sorted, and Mr. Gibbs finally saw fit to take his leave." He took another couple of steps toward the rocks, eyeing the empty seat beside her but stopping short of taking it. "Word came while we were speaking that one of his men apprehended the footpads not far from where we left them. Apparently, they've been causing trouble in the area for several weeks."

"I'm glad." She gave a firm nod, although her face was too tightly drawn to display true relief. "We can be on our way, then."

"We can. But I was thinking ..." He ran a hand across a brow grown too warm. Reached down to smooth the edges of his coat. "There aren't many hours of daylight left, and it would prove impossible for us to reach Foxhill before nightfall. The accommodations here at the Golden Lion appear far superior to anything else we've encountered thus far. We may be better off staying here for the night, where we can be assured of some degree of comfort, and resuming the journey tomorrow."

"Staying?" Her eyes widened as if he'd said something shocking, and he didn't miss the small quiver in her chin. "But ... but we have a rare day without rain. Your coachman, to the best of my knowledge, remains sober. Should we not take advantage of that and continue traveling?"

He couldn't argue those points. However, whether or not they carried on for another brief stretch this evening, they would still have to face time on the road tomorrow. Would an hour or two one way or another really make much difference?

Besides ...

Selfishly, he wanted to keep her here. God help him, but he wanted his carriage's wheels to cease turning—the whole damn world to stop spinning—until they had a chance to *speak* to one another. Not meaningless niceties, but to get to the heart of all the unexpressed things that remained between them. Things that had been lurking ever since he'd first picked her up on the side of the road but had been sparked to life by their earlier encounter in the carriage. Things that now hung around too prominently—too *heavily*—to be ignored.

No, an hour or two farther north versus south wouldn't make much difference. But at the same time, every untraveled mile meant another stretch of minutes that remained until he had to let her go. He needed to make the most of every second they had before that looming moment swept down on them. In case there was something he could do to change it. Some way in which he didn't have to say goodbye.

"I really think we should keep going." Her voice wavered partway through, but she drew her spine up tall, crossing her arms over her chest. "We haven't encountered the best of luck when it comes to making progress with our journey, and the more miles we can put between ourselves and London—"

"Why?" The question burst out of him louder than he'd

intended, shooting up as an echo through the trees. Yet he'd skirted around it long enough, and suddenly, it refused to be contained. "Why the haste to leave London? Especially alone, *and* injured. Do you have any idea what could have happened had the wrong person discovered you on the side of the road? For that matter, did you think of the consequences were someone to recognize you at one of these inns? You could have been ruined. So *why*?"

His jaw began twitching, and a fire grew within his veins. It was as if the emotions of every event from the past week had come back to hit him all at once. The awe of seeing her again and the sharp pang of envy as he discerned the other man's hold upon her arm. The anger and humiliation of reliving childhood taunts, and his own desperation to flee. The all-consuming dread as he detected her motionless form in the mud. The frustration of being pushed away. The quiet, dreamlike bliss of waking up with her in his arms. The outraged shock of finding themselves threatened. The burning desire from having her lips, her body, on his.

And the regret. Always the regret ...

"I'm already ruined." Her voice was soft, a direct counterpoint to his near-shout. Yet it grabbed his attention instantly, making him freeze in place.

"Perhaps not in the way you think," she continued, taking in the horror plastered across his too-rigid face. She closed her eyes for a moment, pausing to take a long breath. "My ruination came from blackmail. For Felix Egerton—my companion at the Englewood ball, if you recall—discovered something about me he should not have, and he proceeded to use that information to offer me a bargain. His silence in return for my consenting to become his wife. For me, the price was too great. I could never agree to such a thing. Thus, my urgency to leave London. If I could do nothing else, I at least needed to be far away before he began dragging my name through the scandal sheets. I wouldn't be surprised if he already has."

Jonathan's skin became hot, his short-term relief at discovering that no man had taken unwelcome liberties with her quickly giving way to a wave of fury. *Blackmail ... Felix Egerton ...*

Any man who would do such a thing was the most detestable sort of swine. However, that particular name caused outrage to surge in his chest.

He may have never met the reprobate, may have only seen him that one time in passing. Yet Jonathan had attended Eton, spending years receiving insults and blows from the young Viscount Ward. Only to go to Brook's years later and be disparaged by the same man, now styled as the Earl of Stanfield. Otherwise known as Thomas Egerton.

No doubt some relation from a whole blasted family that was rotten to the core.

Amelia was all gentleness. That someone could use her in such a manner ... That such a thing was even possible, that unsavory information could even exist ...

"I see," he bit out between clenched teeth. "You are not obligated, of course, to tell me what this blackmail entails. However, if you're in some sort of danger ... if anyone has laid even a finger on you ..."

"Lady Lockheart." She stared down at the dirt-stained fabric of her skirts, her words a barely audible murmur.

Her fingers drummed against her sleeves, and maybe it wasn't wise, but he reached down, placing a lone finger beneath her chin. Coaxing her to look up until glimmering blue eyes met with his. He didn't have a clue what she meant but would give anything to find out. To have that trust ...

She didn't shrug him off or look away, but nor did she say anything.

That was fine. He would wait as long as she needed.

He waited as she bit her lip, worrying it between her teeth. As she took another deep breath, another long swallow.

And finally, she spoke.

"Mr. Egerton found out that I'm Lady Lockheart, the advice columnist from *The Ladies' Spectator*—a women's magazine that's grown in popularity beyond what I could have imagined. It's a secret I've held for years. One that, obviously, I never wanted revealed."

Jonathan felt his jaw slacken, and he pressed his lips together to keep from gaping. Out of all the things she could have divulged, he never would have predicted that admission in a thousand years. Amidst his intense urge to speed back to London on horseback, find Felix Egerton, and do things that would make his treatment of the footpads look mild, questions began to pop up, one after another. First and foremost ...

"Why?" He continued to watch her—the flush that spread over her cheeks, the slight tremble of her chin. "I understand your upset at having the secret stolen from you, and believe me, I have no shortage of things I could say about Felix Egerton, none of which are suitable for a lady's ears. Why, though, is the revelation terrible enough that you can no longer show your face in London? I know the ton has all sorts of unspoken rules, but to the best of my knowledge, there is nothing criminal about writing an advice column in a ladies' magazine. On the contrary, if your pseudonym has become renowned, why can you not own it with pride and tell Egerton to go hang?"

Her pale brows lifted in unison, and her chin jerked, moving away from his touch. "Do you honestly think my mother would approve of such a thing?"

He had to suppress a shudder as a pair of ice-blue eyes, set in a face of steel, sprang up in his mind. The Dowager Marchioness of Rockliffe. A visage whose coldness he would never forget. "Perhaps not, but—"

"That's not all." She let her stiff shoulders slump as if she'd suddenly grown weary. "Do you really not see? Lady Lockheart is popular because of the air of mystery she presents. No one wants to discover that the sagacious lady who is all-knowing in matters of the heart is actually a plain, meek little spinster. I'm sure to become a laughingstock, and the last thing I want is that sort of attention. My brothers may have had the wherewithal, and charm, to endure all manner of scandal. I, on the other hand, do not."

A pit opened in his stomach, his ribs feeling like they'd been dealt a blow all over again. How could she think so lowly of herself? A woman so kind and bright. The woman who had once taken his miserable existence and made it worth living. He'd never forgotten the way she'd worked herself into his heart. He never would.

"To hell with anyone who says a word against you." His fingers curled into fists, and he pressed them tight against his sides. Throughout his travels in the East, he'd spent countless hours working with masters to strengthen his body while simultaneously learning serenity and control. Nevertheless, there was nothing he'd like to do more at present than tear that blackguard Egerton limb from limb.

He hated the man. Hated anyone who'd ever made her feel less than adequate. Hated himself for any way his long-ago actions could have contributed to the sentiment. However, he couldn't let himself get caught up in unproductive loathing. His focus needed to stay on how to fix things.

"You're more than worthy of the ton's esteem, and anyone who thinks otherwise is beneath you." He dropped onto the rock beside her so their bodies were close, their gazes at the same level. "Don't let that idiot Egerton drive you into hiding while he remains in London, running his mouth however he pleases. Besides, what if it's not too late to stop him? I could *help* you, Amelia, in any way that's in my power. Regardless of what he already has or hasn't said."

The irony of the situation wasn't lost on him, for hadn't he, too, fled London because of a member of the Egerton family? He could assure himself all he liked of his responsibleness in tending to matters at his country seat, but at the end of the day, he'd run from the Season when things got uncomfortable. That was the truth of it.

Which suddenly seemed like an exceedingly poor decision. He was no longer an Eton schoolboy or a duke's misfit grandson hiding in a solicitor's office. He *was* the goddamn duke. Just as Amelia was a marquess's daughter and a bright, capable, talented woman. Why should they let anyone push them around?

It was all so much clearer now. Perhaps because previously, they'd each been left to face an exacting society alone. But that no longer had to be the case. What if they could re-enter London together? If they didn't part ways but posed as a united front. The Duke of Branscombe and Lady Amelia Prescott.

To the best of his knowledge, their relationship from a decade prior had remained secret. What if they could rekindle their union and make it known to the world? What if Amelia became a duchess ...

His duchess. Because if he had her by his side, he'd possess the strength to conquer anything and would do whatever it took to give her that strength in return. Mayhap they'd decide to escape the gossips of London once more in favor of a lengthy honeymoon. However, their departure would occur because they decided on it, together, and not from someone else driving them away.

"Returning is impossible, of course." Her clipped tone extinguished his musings as swiftly as a lone candle flame brought out into a deluge.

"It's not—"

"In any case, I think you're right." She dipped her chin, and for the briefest moment, hope existed that she'd changed her mind. In the next instant, though, she was clambering to her feet, shaking out her swollen ankle. Becoming the one who towered over him. "Upon closer reflection, I agree that we should stay here for the night and get some rest in proper beds. Then, we'll be ready to resume our journey early in the morning and can travel the final distance to Northamptonshire."

No. That may have been their goal when they set out, but it wasn't the way this could end any longer. Too much had changed. With everything that had passed between them and everything he'd learned, how was he supposed to leave her to disappear into the shadows?

How was he supposed to let her go?

"Shall we go inside to procure our rooms?" She looked down at him pointedly, leaving him no choice but to push himself upward, all while his mind scrambled to invent ways to turn this around, to make her see. All without scaring her away.

"Uh, yes." He held out his arm to her, and surprisingly, she took it, letting him lead her away from the trees and toward the entrance of the Golden Lion. Dozens of protests rose in his throat, yet his tongue kept them contained.

If nothing else, at least he'd paused time for one more night. This wasn't over.

"Come to think of it, after the day's events, a repose will be just the thing," she said as their boots brushed over dirt and gravel, catching the light of the weakening sunrays. "I can only imagine how weary you must feel. I'm sorry I didn't consider it sooner. Hopefully, a good night's rest will help us put it all out of mind and leave us better prepared to face tomorrow's travel. *North.*"

She enunciated that last word with unmistakable insistence, as if she recognized his thoughts before he voiced them.

He did as he knew she wanted and kept walking, not saying a word. They both realized this had little to do with his weariness and more to do with the pattern they'd fallen into of push and retreat. Damn, but the confrontation with the footpads was beginning to feel easy in comparison.

Be that as it may, this wasn't a final concession. He still had one more night.

One more night to change her mind. To make her recognize her strength, her worth.

One more night to see if broken trust could be rebuilt, strengthened. To see if she would let him in without pulling away, to allow him to stay by her side.

One more night to show her there was nowhere else on earth he'd rather be.

12

Ninety-eight, ninety-nine ...

Amelia ran her hairbrush from the top of her scalp down to her waist, marking an even hundred strokes. Her hair fanned out around her like a curtain, glinting beneath the light of the candelabrum she'd placed on the nightstand. Should she keep going, aiming for a full two hundred?

No. She tossed the brush onto the nightstand, giving her head a small shake. The distraction of the mundane task was proving far from sufficient.

Instead, she pushed herself up from her seat on the bed, stretching her sore ankle to rid it of some of the stiffness and letting it bear a little weight. Now that the swelling had grown less prominent, surely it was beneficial to have some periods of exercise so the ankle didn't become weak from disuse.

However, taking a turn about the room was proving no better a distraction than the meticulous brushing of her hair.

She gritted her teeth, forcing her legs to keep going, moving her from the bed to the washstand to the curtained window that overlooked The Golden Lion's courtyard. Just as she and Jonathan had predicted, the room was spacious and well-furnished, with a soft mattress and a window well-sealed from the elements.

Still, she felt just as on edge as last night at The Crooked Oak, when rain had trickled beneath the glass and tiny feet scurried across the floor.

She took one step after another, back and forth between each of the papered walls. All the while, her mind swirled, refusing to let go of the day's events. The footpads. The pistol. The kiss. The Lady Lockheart confession. And Jonathan's words: *I could* help *you, Amelia*.

She was weary and raw, her skin over-sensitive, her ears too alert. On one hand, a sort of lightness fluttered through her. The relief of having a burden lifted. The faint stirrings of hope. But at the same time, a weight pressed down, preventing the feeling from fully taking flight. Reminding her that life was never simple, and neglecting to keep her guard up could have dire consequences.

Like a coward, she'd run from it all, claiming she had no desire for dinner and sequestering herself in her room to rest. Which was unfair, she knew. After everything that had transpired today, Jonathan deserved more than having her shut him out so abruptly.

Under different circumstances, perhaps she would have done differently. However ... something was terribly wrong with her. Something beyond the aftereffects of facing a threat and revealing a long-kept secret.

The warring desires of her heart—the yearning to make free with her trust again and the opposing need to retreat— were bad enough. But now, adding to that was a series of knots and tangles in the center of her belly.

And lower.

The feeling tugged at her, making itself known each time she took a step and her silk night rail brushed against her thighs. Almost as if the garment had grown too tight. It heated her skin, made her breathing accelerate. All while her mind kept dropping her back into the carriage, atop Jonathan's lap, with her lips pressed to his. Reminding her of the solid warmth of his chest, the hardness in his breeches—

A door slammed in one of the nearby rooms, the resounding bang causing her to jump. A frisson of pain shot through her ankle at the sudden movement, and she stumbled, toppling toward the nightstand.

She threw out her arms, steadying herself before she ended up sprawled across the surface with her legs in the air. Except in the process, her hand swept into the brush she'd tossed there, sending it clattering to the floor and narrowly missing the candelabrum.

"Blast!" Her hand flew to her chest, hovering above her rapidly beating heart as she tried to catch her breath. Why did she have to be so clumsy? So skittish? It was a wonder her hairbrush hadn't cracked in half from the abuse she'd given it lately.

Something crashed against the floor next door, and again, her body tensed, her eyes darting to the shared wall. Not belonging to Jonathan this time, as he'd been placed in a room across the corridor, but to a stranger. One who sounded no more dexterous than her.

A shrill female voice pierced the air, launching into an unintelligible tirade. There was another crash—the unmistakable shatter of glass, and a booming male voice joined the cacophony, fighting with the female's for dominance.

And then, rapid footsteps, and a fist pounding upon a door. *Her* door.

"Amelia!" This time, the voice on the other side was familiar despite how it had become an anxious shout. "Amelia, open the door."

She spun around on her good ankle, her heart giving a fresh lurch as she hobbled across the floor with all the speed she could muster. Knowing who she would find when the door came open, and unable to stop the unbidden surge of anticipation.

Jonathan burst forward the moment she unlatched the door, coming to an abrupt halt at the threshold of her room. His eyes darted up and down her body, the sconces in the corridor revealing that his face had gone ashy and taut. "Are you all right? What in blazes is going on?"

"I'm well," she answered quickly, trying to slow the rise and fall of her chest so he wouldn't detect her breathlessness. The less he knew of her nearly falling on her face *and* starting a fire, the better. Besides, her momentary stumble and the resulting clatter of her hairbrush seemed insignificant compared to the rampage that continued next door. She glanced at the shared wall, behind which the woman's shrieking had gained the upper hand. "As for what's transpiring in the next room, I couldn't say, beyond that I don't believe those two like each other very much."

He followed her gaze just as a large object thumped against the wall, and a few of the woman's shouted words grew distinct enough to carry over. *You're a proper arse ...*

"Indeed." Jonathan turned back to her, his features tight. "I'm sure the proprietor won't delay in putting a stop to the disturbance. In the meantime, why don't you wait in my room? It's at least a little quieter."

"Oh, no." She could hardly spit the words out fast enough. Jonathan's room ... with Jonathan, who must have been relaxing before he dashed over to her, for he wore nothing but his gray breeches and a linen shirt that hung open at the neck. Lying next to him last night after the mouse incident had been challenging enough. But doing it now, with the way her head spun and her body whirred? Impossible.

She swallowed. "Thank you, Your Grace, but that isn't necessary."

"Don't call me that."

The unexpected sharpness of his tone made her blink. A change swept over his face, giving it a look of ... she didn't know what. She only knew that there was hardness and then softness, and he took a step forward, over the threshold, his voice a low hum near her ear. "Do you know what I would give to hear my name on your lips again? The way you always used to say it? I want no title from you. Only my name, just as I use yours. Amelia. *My* Amelia ..."

Her breath hitched, her lungs no longer remembering how to take in air. In fact, everything seemed to stop, even the shouts and crashes from next door giving way to a sudden silence.

There was only the flicker of flames and the echo of words spoken so reverently that something fluttered within her chest.

And Jonathan, standing so close that heat radiated from his body to hers, and she could feel the whisper of his exhale against her skin.

She didn't know how it happened. Only that one moment, there was a modicum of space between them, and the next, it was gone, for her chest was pressed to his, her lips against his lips.

The kiss wasn't gentle and tentative this time. Nor did she want it to be. His tongue slipped inside her mouth—teasing her, caressing her—as meanwhile, his hand reached up to grip her nape, his fingers twisting in her unbound hair.

Sensation consumed her until all she could think of was returning each stroke of his tongue, absorbing the slight flavor of brandy, inhaling the spiced, masculine scent of him. She hardly noticed that they were moving. It might not have registered with her at all, except suddenly, the hardness of a wall materialized against her back, and his weight pushed against the front of her, holding her in place.

Oh, this was even better. The closeness even more intense.

She let her fingers travel to the stubbled surface of his jaw. Down his neck and to his shoulder, the skin hot beneath his linen shirt. Her fingers took on a life of their own, wanting to explore every surface.

As for her body, it was abruptly overtaken by the urge to move. To drag itself up and down the length of him, to experience friction.

She'd never done such a thing, had never even imagined ... Yet if she dared, she knew it would be delicious.

So wonderfully, wickedly delicious.

A sharp, high-pitched cry tore through the air.

Not hers. Certainly not Jonathan's. It had to have come from the next room. The fighting couple.

Slowly, the reason Jonathan had ended up in her room came floating back, even as her lips remained locked with his, caring nothing for what existed beyond these four walls.

The woman's cry sounded again. However, it was no longer a shriek of fury. This noise sounded more animalistic, almost like she experienced pain, or—

The bedframe began creaking against the floorboards of the adjoining room, the cries intensifying, becoming recognizable words: *more ... harder ...*

Oh. Amelia jerked her head away, a fresh surge of heat spreading over her already too-hot skin. She may be an inexperienced spinster, but she'd overheard enough whispered words amongst married ladies not to remain ignorant altogether.

She unhooked her hand from Jonathan's shoulder and pressed it to her cheek, willing it to cool. Was there something in the air here at the Golden Lion? Something that made people go completely out of their heads until all they could think of was *that*?

Oh, Lord. She'd already thrown good sense to the wind, and only the tiniest shred of self-control remained in her possession. How was she to maintain what she had left with this sort of ... *background accompaniment* surrounding them?

"Um." The sound came out like a croak, and she cleared her throat to try again. "Perhaps I could wait in your room after all."

Even as she said it, her body raged at her, bemoaning anything that would remove this closeness—inopportune noises be hanged. However, in the next moment, she found herself not bereft but swept into his arms, being carted into the corridor with brisk, measured strides.

He threw open the door to his room and kicked it closed again behind them without missing a beat, bringing them into a candlelit space much like her own. At least, it appeared similar from a cursory glance. In truth, she only had eyes for the bed— the sturdy wooden frame, the plumped pillows, the patterned blue coverlet. All drawing nearer, for he was continuing to walk, just as she was continuing to stare, her stomach knotting with anticipation, a strange heat surging between her legs—

She stiffened in his arms, squeezing her eyes shut and then reopening them to look at the floor. *Only* at the floor. She'd suggested the change of rooms to get away from those sorts of thoughts. Not to have them intensify.

He must have sensed the change in her, for he stopped short of the bed, gently lowering her feet to the floor but keeping his arms around her waist as a means of support. Which, it seemed, was needed, for her legs had turned shaky.

She let him hold her there. Let their eyes lock. His had turned into large, dark orbs that glinted in the candlelight. Assessing her. Trying to read her. A challenging task, given that at present, she hardly understood herself.

The noises from the other room had lessened but not vanished. Even with a corridor separating them, wisps of words, intermingled with moans, drifted over. *Faster ... more ...*

And she felt it. Blast it all, but her pulse raced faster with each cry, her body making demands that she didn't know how to slake. Even when she didn't look at the bed, her mind still placed her atop it. And his weight atop her. Because somehow, that felt like the answer.

Her lips crashed into his again, hungry and searching, and he returned the pressure at once, his arms tightening to pull her closer.

Who was she fooling, thinking she could stand in his room, with him in his shirtsleeves and her in her night rail, and the sensations coursing through her would lessen? Thinking she still had a care for restraint?

She tried what she hadn't dared back in her own room, pushing herself up on her tiptoes, letting her body slide along his. Just like yesterday in the carriage, a hardness in his breeches brushed against the aching spot between her thighs, the sensation so potent she let out a whimper.

Yes. This was what she wanted. At least, the motion provided her with a hint of relief, yet it also left her desiring more. She moved again, traveling back down, and if his groan was any indication, he took pleasure from it, too.

Encouraged, she rose to her tiptoes once more, her fingers sinking into his shoulders, seeking an anchor to keep her from floating away.

He made another low sound, his hands gripping tight to her waist, his heartbeat a rapid thump she could detect against her own chest. But then, his body became still, his muscles tensing around her.

"Amelia." His lips broke away, his breath a shudder as he rested his forehead against hers. "We will do only as much as you want to do, I swear it. Only, the longer you make those motions, the more difficult it becomes for me to think straight."

Her eyes flew open, falling upon his parted lips. On the muscle that twitched in his jaw.

"I want ... I need ..." She didn't have the right words to describe the longing pouring through her veins, or to explain the ache. Her gaze shifted to the bed behind them. To the bare patch of skin where his shirt hung open, revealing a glimpse of the sculpted chest beneath. To the bed again. "Please, I ..."

"It's all right." He shifted his head, the rough surface of his cheek grazing her overheated skin until his mouth hovered just above the shell of her ear. "I can help you, if you'll let me."

She didn't need to think on her answer before letting it glide off her tongue as a whisper. "Yes."

She became enveloped in his embrace and found herself being led backward and lowered to the bed. Her head hit the pillow, the ceiling above blurring through her haze of desire. His hands were on her legs, lifting them onto the coverlet, and the thin silk of her dressing gown proved an inadequate barrier in preventing another shower of sparks from igniting in her core.

He lowered himself, too, his body stretching along the bed, running parallel to hers.

"Would you like me to touch you, Amelia?" The mattress shifted as he rolled onto his side, and he leaned in, his mouth returning to her ear. "The way you touch yourself when you're alone in the dark?"

A wicked thrill coursed through her. Having his hands upon her—*everywhere*—sounded like heaven. Except—"I've ... I've never ..."

The coverlet rustled as he pushed himself up onto his forearm, and she could feel his gaze boring down on her, although she couldn't meet it.

Had she shocked him with her inexperience? She'd never been more aware of all the things she *didn't* know. Yearning had never flared in her this way. She'd never allowed it to.

Which was beginning to feel like a mistake. Had she taken better care to … *educate* herself, perhaps her insides wouldn't be tied up in knots, making her desperate for something unknown and just out of reach.

"We can change that." His voice was low, raspy, and when she dared to look up, his lips were quirked in a semblance of a smile. Not scornful but full of promise.

"Yes." Again, the word escaped her without preamble. She would take whatever he thought to give her, for he must know the answers to things she did not.

He turned to the nightstand, blowing out a quick breath, and the light from the candelabrum vanished, leaving them with nothing but the glow of flames flickering in the grate. Then, his head returned to the pillow beside her, and she lay in perfect stillness, waiting as he leaned in and reached for her —hand.

That wasn't what she'd expected.

But in the next moment, he was guiding it down, using his other hand to grasp the hem of her night rail and slip it up her legs. The silk slid upward until it connected with her hand, and he coaxed her fingers to curl around it and raise it the rest of the way. Baring her most intimate flesh to him.

"Good," he murmured into the dimness. "Beautiful."

Making any passing instinct she had to cover herself dissolve. She'd never been in a position of such vulnerability. However, in the low light, with Jonathan's palm to guide her, she also felt safe. Eager. Free.

He led her hand over her thigh, and she realized, with a flash of heat to her cheeks, that the skin near her apex was wet. Yet if he noticed, he seemed unbothered by it, and suddenly, she couldn't bring herself to care, either, for her hand was at her entrance, circling over the sensitive flesh. More wetness coated her fingers, and he guided her upward again, through slippery, hot folds, and then—

Her finger hit a place that was pure sensation, and her hips jerked against the bed from the shock of pleasure.

"There." He pressed his index finger atop hers, making it trace slow circles over the bundle of nerves. "Is this the place that aches to be touched?"

She tried to agree, although the sound came out more like a moan.

Yes, that was exactly the spot, and now that they'd started, she never wanted it to end. With his finger leading her, she sped up the pace, gasping as she experienced jolt after jolt of bliss.

Something was building inside her, leading her to a precipice where she had merely a vague notion of what existed on the other side. Whatever it was, her body felt like a wound coil about to spring free, a dam about to burst, and she wasn't sure how much more she could bear.

"Please," she sobbed, her hips rocking upward, chasing the pressure of their joined hands. "I don't know ..."

"You do, my love." Without breaking the rhythm of his finger, he drew closer, his tongue trailing over the edge of her earlobe. Down to the pulse point in her neck. "Just let it come."

And then, his mouth was on her breast, enclosing the section of silk that covered her hardened nipple. He drew her in, laving her through the fabric, and all at once, the tension within her broke.

She cried out, her intimate muscles pulsing as she was inundated by wave after wave of pleasure. His hand—his mouth—stayed with her, carrying her through each swell until, eventually, the feeling receded, leaving her with limbs that felt warm and pliant.

Now, she understood why she'd heard other ladies whispering about a *crisis*.

Jonathan sank back onto the pillow, his hand leaving hers to stroke her hair. "How do you feel?"

Sporadic aftershocks continued to pulse through her, and though it was dark, her skin felt as though it were bathed in sunlight. "Better. Wonderful."

She stretched her back like a cat, savoring his featherlight caresses. Yet beneath the satiated glow, something tugged at her. He'd seen to her pleasure. But what about his?

She turned her head, trying to clear her thoughts enough to fully take him in. His eyes were still large, reflecting the subtle glow of firelight. His body still radiating heat.

"And you?" she managed to say, her voice coming out unsteady. "What do *you* need, Jonathan?"

Her mind flashed back to the rigidness in his breeches. Could she touch him there, the way he'd done to her? Or how would it feel to have that hardness between her legs? She'd thought herself replete, but another twinge rose in her core.

His lips twitched upward as she spoke his name, and he moved them to her hair, brushing a kiss atop her head. "Right now, I have everything. We don't need to rush. There will be plenty of time for more later. Whenever you're ready."

The words made her breath catch, and suddenly, it was as if the sun streaking through her had been replaced by ice. Because they didn't actually have plenty of time, did they?

She shut her eyes, tensing against the shiver that bolted up her spine. They had tonight. Nothing more. For tomorrow, she'd be in her bed at Foxhill. Alone.

Her stomach sank as the cold bite of the truth set in, and her heart pounded in protest. But that's the way it needed to be. Better she come to terms with that now than allow what existed between them to go even farther.

Already, she knew the feel of his mouth, his touch, would stay forever engrained in her memory. Were she to open her body to him even more—to join as if they were one in an act that would undeniably bring the greatest bliss—her heart would never recover. For it would yearn, and it would love.

Leaving itself out in the open, where it could be trampled again.

There came another rustle of fabric, and she realized he was tugging at the coverlet, trying to pull it out from under them so they could rest beneath it.

He didn't want her to be cold. For some reason, the tiny gesture put a lump in her throat.

She shifted her weight obligingly, pushing up onto her side and then sinking into soft sheets as the coverlet floated back down to envelop her. More rustling, and Jonathan nestled beneath it, too, his body coming against hers, his chest to her back. He surrounded her like a fortress, one arm draped across her waist, the other returning to her hair.

Her eyelids fluttered closed again. Beneath them, an unpleasant sting emerged, and she twined her fingers with his, trying to make it go away. She let herself press against the solid heat of him, attempting to think of nothing but this moment. For morning would come to snuff it out soon enough.

Tomorrow, she would go to Foxhill to shut herself away from the world. To be safe.

But tonight—just this one final time—she would allow herself the fleeting comfort of falling asleep in his arms.

13

The morning deluge came as no surprise. Amelia drifted awake to the sound of it beating against The Golden Lion's roof while glimpses of a gray, foggy dawn appeared between the gap in the curtains.

A fitting finale: the journey that had started with rain would end with it, too, putting the hints of sunlight they'd experienced along the way soundly out of mind.

She rose from bed with both stealth and speed, not even giving herself a final moment to relish the warmth of Jonathan's embrace or a lingering glance at the peacefulness of his face in sleep. By prolonging the inevitable, she would only make things harder on herself.

Back in her own room, she dressed quickly, throwing on the same mud-stained blue dress and cloak and tying her hair in a haphazard braid. Then, with her scant belongings stuffed in her bag, she limped down the stairs, seeking out the innkeeper to request a few provisions for the road and sending a message to the coachman to say that Mr. Maxwell would like the carriage readied straightaway. The latter involved a small lie. However, as her forwardness in issuing such an order would speed up the process of getting them underway, surely Jonathan wouldn't find fault. After all, they'd already experienced enough delays to last a lifetime, and he, too, had a destination to reach.

She was standing near the front window, nibbling on an oatcake she didn't want and watching the rickety black carriage pull up near the inn's entrance when his voice came up behind her.

"Amelia?"

The bewilderment in his tone caused a painful knot to form in her stomach. Nonetheless, she couldn't change course.

"Good morning, Your—um, Jon—um, *husband*," she settled on due to the other patrons that wandered about the inn's common area, although as soon as she said it, it seemed like the worst option of all. She turned to face him, feeling the knot tighten as she took in his creased brow and parted lips. The hair that hung chaotically over his forehead, the coat that had one of its buttons unfastened, and the cravat that wasn't done up quite right. He'd obviously dashed out of bed with even more speed than she had.

She tried to smile, although her face felt pinched. With any luck, her voice would at least come out sunny. "I took the liberty of calling for the carriage. I thought it best we get on our way before the weather has an opportunity to worsen."

He stood with his chest heaving up and down, gazing out at his carriage and the rain. Gazing back at her. "You ... you're ready?" His shoulders looked too stiff, and his fingers—oh, she shouldn't think about his fingers—were clamped to his sides. "You've already packed your things? You've eaten?"

She nodded, the few crumbs of oatcake she'd consumed suddenly sticking in her throat. "Yes. I arranged to have a basket packed as well, should we grow hungry along the way."

He pressed his lips together, the line across the bridge of

his nose deepening. The silence between them seemed to stretch, overtaking the chatter that hummed all around them. Until finally, some quiet words. "I ... I-I need to retrieve the things I left in my room."

"Of course. I'll wait in the carriage."

And before he could say anything else, she staggered away, through the inn's entrance and out into the driving rain. If there was anything she could give thanks for today, it was that her ankle felt much better.

Either that or the ache in the rest of her had taken precedence.

She allowed the coachman to help her into the carriage and flopped down on the under-stuffed seat cushion. Peered out at the familiar sight of raindrops, trying to count them as they hit the glass. Anything to distract herself from the look of bafflement she'd just put on Jonathan's face, the roiling in her stomach, and the memories that wouldn't fade of his hands, his mouth ...

Just a little longer. She pressed her hands into her lap, the carriage feeling smaller than ever before. They would be underway soon, with Foxhill not thirty miles ahead.

The, for better or worse, this would all be over.

The carriage door flew open, and Jonathan tossed his valise inside before jumping up and positioning himself on the seat directly across from her. Staring straight into her eyes, leaning forward so their knees nearly touched. "Could we talk about this first?"

Oh, no. No, no, no, she didn't have the strength for that this morning.

"What's there to speak of?" She tried to sound light, though her body felt like it was laden down with boulders. "We're continuing with our journey north, as we've been attempting to do all week. With any luck, the rain won't linger, and we can make good time."

"Did you at least think about what I said? About turning around?" His voice became a little deeper, a little more strained, and tightness formed in her own throat. "I meant to explain myself better last night. There were so many things I wished to say, but then we ... well, then I didn't, and I'm sorry, for I shouldn't have left it until morning. I'm not always good with words, but I want to try. I want you to know that—"

The carriage gave an abrupt lurch as it set into motion, jostling them both so their knees crashed together and they careened to the side. She gripped the door handle to steady herself, using the pause to suck in a breath. The lump she'd just swallowed rose right back up.

"It isn't too late," he continued, pulling himself upright, his hands curling around the edge of the seat. "When we get to the end of the lane, all I need do is tap the ceiling, call out instructions, and we can go south, not north. You don't need to hide or let some worthless bastard have control over you. You can return home, and I swear, I will support you through whatever is to come. In fact, there's nothing in the world I want more than to remain by your side. For always. Perhaps I don't deserve another chance, but if you're willing to grant one, I'll spend the rest of my life proving my love and devotion to you. However ..."

As it picked up speed, the carriage began a steady sway, free from bumps, but he halted as if he'd been shaken again, the corners of his mouth growing tight. "If your hesitation lies with not—not wanting our association to continue, then say the word. I'll make myself scarce in London if that's the way you'd prefer it. No one need ever know about this journey."

Not ... not *wanting*? Her eyes burned at the corners, tears rising dangerously close to the surface. Didn't he see that the opposite was true? She wanted him *too* much.

She wanted him at her side in London. In Northamptonshire. Anywhere in the world life happened to take them, be it the shores of England or some foreign land across the sea.

She wanted his help in confronting all the things she was afraid of. To no longer do it alone.

She wanted him to fill her nights with unthinkable pleasure and to wake up each morning in the safety of his arms.

She wanted it all.

Except then, she'd have to live with the possibility that it could be snatched out from under her, just like before. How was she to tolerate that risk after she'd sworn, all those years ago, that she would forever safeguard her heart? For the cost of losing was so great, so terrifying, so earth-shatteringly painful—

A deafening crack split the air at the same time the carriage shuddered and jolted, pitching her out of her seat. It all happened so fast that she didn't even have time to make a sound. Around her, there were shouts and whinnies, and she began falling until strong arms shot out to grab her—

And then, she was crumpled on the floor. Not alone but sheltered by the solid surface of Jonathan's body, which had broken the worst of the fall.

He clasped her tightly, his breaths coming in rapid pants beside her ear. "Are you hurt?"

She waited a moment for the stars in her vision to clear before giving her head a tentative shake. No, nothing smarted too badly, beyond a bruise or two she may have acquired from the incident. However, they were no longer on a level surface but listing toward the ground.

Whatever had happened, the carriage was very much not all right.

Tentatively, he raised his hand to the door handle, and the door dropped open, nearly low enough to hit the ground. He eased himself out first, releasing his hold on her so he could slide down, planting his feet in a muddy rut. She didn't miss his look of wide-eyed disbelief before he snapped his face in the other direction, out of her sight.

He recovered himself quickly, turning back to extend a hand, words beginning to form on his lips. But by that point, she'd already scooted to the doorway, heaving her body out and letting her feet drop to the ground.

Discomfort shot through her ankle from the abrupt, clumsy movement. A gust of wind and a smattering of raindrops pelted her in the face. She hardly noticed any of it. Her face seemed to have frozen, likely into an expression of shock akin to Jonathan's. All she could do was stare.

The carriage's back left wheel was lying alone in the mud. As a result, the carriage sat stagnant at the side of the road, sloping to one side like some injured, overlarge animal.

Words floated around her, fragments of a heated exchange between Jonathan and the coachman. *Rut. Rain. Broken. Disrepair.*

They had no meaning. It was as if she'd gone into a trance where nothing was quite real. Her legs moved, one rigid step after another, to the back end of the carriage. A rusted axle hung loose, and a few scraps of metal littered the ground.

Suddenly, she was on the ground, too. Her knees sank into cold mud, but instead of shrinking from it, she crawled forward until she rested amidst the carnage. Wood, metal, and glass, as well, for a window must have shattered.

She peered down at the ruins beside her palms. Peered up at the leaning carriage that loomed above her, bringing her face next to the damaged underside, her eyes traveling over pieces of muddy, rusty iron.

She thought she heard her name, but she wasn't certain. Her brain was slow to process the scene, each object before her appearing foreign, like something she'd never seen. Until all at once, the truth of the matter snapped into place.

The carriage was gone. Perhaps, after extensive repairs, it

would become serviceable again, but not today. She'd spent the week running, desperate for any means to get north, to get away. No longer just from society's censure but from her feelings, too, and the ever-growing danger to her heart.

But no more. The carriage was gone.

Some far-flung, foggy place in her mind tried offering up suggestions about stagecoaches or rented post chaises, but it was too late. Her knees began wobbling, and abruptly, she sat, landing in a shallow puddle. Water splashed up around her, soaking her to the skin. However, she couldn't bring herself to move. Her limbs were too numb, too shaky, her chest too tight.

She squeezed her eyes shut, trying to draw in a breath.

It wouldn't come. Her lungs had ceased working, and her throat had closed over.

No. This couldn't be happening.

Her eyelids flew open, bringing her back to the rutted road and the vast gray sky that released a deluge. Except it was no longer vast but shrinking, the thick clouds drifting down and closing in on her, the rain streaking across her face to choke her.

No, no, not now. Not after all these years, not after everything she'd managed to endure this week …

"Amelia!"

She detected her name again and a figure dropping next to her on the ground. She couldn't turn her head to look, for her muscles had seized, unable to do anything but quiver uncontrollably.

"Amelia, what's wrong?"

There was a frantic edge to the voice, but it quickly got swallowed up by the blood pounding through her ears. She grasped her knees tight to her chest, digging her fingernails into her skirts in an attempt to hold on, to save herself from drowning. But it was no use. Her heart was beating too fast, her chest constricting, her stomach flopping about like she was going to be ill—

"Amelia, I need you to look at me."

Fingers pressed against her chin, nudging it upward, and through the miasma that threatened to consume her, a hazy version of Jonathan appeared, kneeling on the ground directly in front of her.

She tried to tell him that the rain blurred her vision, that it was suffocating her, that she was about to be crushed. But when she opened her mouth, nothing came out but a strangled gasp.

He continued to cup her chin, sinking down so his eyes became level with hers. "I need you to take a breath. Can you do that for me?"

She tried, going through the motion of inhaling, which was supposed to come without thought. A small burst of air entered her lungs, but it wasn't enough. She blew it out, attempting to suck in more. Yet all she could get were tiny puffs, in and out, in and out, as rapid as her racing pulse.

"That's good. That's so good." One hand dropped from her chin, going to her shoulder to give it a gentle squeeze. "Keep looking at me. Do you think you can try it a little slower this time? We'll do it together."

There was so much rain, so many clouds, so little air. Yet behind it all, there was a familiar set of brown eyes, unwavering in the way they peered into hers. She made herself focus on them, at the calming glimmer amidst everything else around her that had turned dark and stifling.

She felt her hand being eased away from her knee and brought to rest below the collar of his coat. The wool had become sodden and cold. But beneath it, his heartbeat resounded through her palm, and his chest rose in a slow, deliberate movement.

Her body shook, ready to collapse, ready to drop into the

mud and not get up. Yet Jonathan wouldn't let go of her chin or hand, and from somewhere within her, the strength came to take in a large mouthful of air.

It was a weak imitation of his measured breathing, and another choked sound escaped her from the effort. Nonetheless, he pressed her palm tighter to his coat, giving an encouraging nod. "Good. Let's do it again."

His chest lifted once more, pausing and then sinking back down as he let out a long exhale. Her breath shuddered as she followed him in releasing it, her body greedy and protesting, demanding to keep drawing in quick gulps of air. However, she forced herself to copy his rhythm, not inhaling again until he did.

Breathe in. Pause. Breathe out. Again and again, as steady as she could, counting the seconds to try to keep herself on tempo.

One, two, three ... This feeling would pass; it always did ...

"You're doing so well, my love." His voice drifted into her head like a lulling wave. So calm. So reassuring. He leaned closer, his gaze upon her never faltering. "You're going to be all right now, I promise. I'll keep you safe."

The rain hadn't stopped, nor had the clouds retreated. But still, she believed him. He was near and steady and encouraging, his masculine scent filling her nose even amidst the smells of drenched earth and horses, his words filling her thoughts despite her pounding heart. He hadn't wavered, hadn't left her, hadn't stared at her like she was stark raving mad.

And she believed him.

His arms were there the instant her overwrought body tilted forward, gathering her into his lap, hugging her tight to his chest. "You're going to be all right," he repeated, brushing his fingertips along her cheek, and whether the wetness he wiped away came from raindrops or her tears, she couldn't say. "Let's go back to the inn now, where it's dry."

Back.

Not pressing forward, as she'd been so desperate to do, but heading back. Stopping.

She'd fought him—and fought her own heart—so many times along the way. She should be protesting now. Instead, she dropped her head to his chest, letting it rest there as he rose to his feet. She nestled in, finding the perfect place against his heart so the beat thumped next to her ear. Giving her back that comforting rhythm as she waited for the remaining tremors to flow from her body.

They began moving, his footsteps sturdy despite the wind and the never-ending mud below his boots. Perhaps because they only had a short route to travel, and he already knew it well. Not because they'd traversed it on foot before, but his horses had.

She didn't take a last glance at the broken carriage and bemoan what they'd lost. Instead, she looked to the half-timbered facade of The Golden Lion, and the candles burning in the window to stave off the day's dreariness, and the painted front door, ready to welcome them back.

She was tired of running.

14

The next stretch of time passed in a blur. Amelia was weary. So weary, and her head remained wrapped in a haze.

She knew that the front door of the Golden Lion creaked open, and suddenly, the air was no longer dank and oppressive but warm and calming, filled with the steady hum of chatter. She detected several voices drawing nearer and Jonathan uttering words in return. Whatever he said, it led to them rushing up the stairs, back to the same room where they'd just spent the night together.

She felt her cloak being unfastened and pulled away, and her body being lowered onto the familiar bed. For a moment, her muscles tensed, protesting the loss of contact with his chest. However, as her head hit the pillow and her boots and wet stockings were eased from her feet, she realized that her breaths had fallen into a normal rhythm, even without his consistent heartbeat to keep her on track. Likewise, her chest no longer contained the weight of the world, and her stomach had settled to a gentle flutter.

She was going to be all right, just as he'd assured her.

With that realization, she was able to close her eyes. Resting but not fully asleep, for certain things still reached her awareness. A knock, and careful footsteps, and the diminishing fire flaring back to life in the grate. Their luggage being deposited beside the door. A mug of beef tea pressed into her palm, which she heartily drank, savoring the rich warmth as it traveled through her. More footsteps pattering across the floor, and a scrape and a shuffle, and water sloshing.

And then, Jonathan's hand upon her shoulder and his voice close to her ear. "Come. There's a bath waiting for you."

She rubbed her eyes, focusing on the spot across the room where steam rose invitingly from behind a screen. Exactly what she needed to cure the chill that had seeped into her bones.

She pushed herself upright, clutching his outstretched hand for support. No doubt he would carry her to the tub if she showed even the slightest indication that's what she wanted. She opted to try her legs instead, though, still a little wobbly as they moved across the floor but able to manage because she had him to lean on. They shuffled together until they reached the other side of the screen, where the tub of steaming water awaited, along with a folded sheet of toweling and a bar of soap that rested atop a chair.

Without letting go of her arm, he pivoted his body so he stood in front of her, giving her another glimpse into those eyes of warm, calming brown. In fact, all of him had become warm, for he was no longer clad in wet wool but in a dry shirt and breeches, and his face was no longer streaked with mud and raindrops.

He was very close, his breath a hot trickle against her skin as he uttered a single phrase. "Will you let me help you?"

She nodded. The proper thing would be to fend for herself or to ask for a maid. However, she didn't care about proper anymore.

He carefully spun her around, his hands going to the tapes of her dress, her stays, the ribbon that secured her shift. One by one, damp garments fell to the floor, and surely, she should have at least a vague sense of reticence. Yet as the final scrap of fabric came away, all she could think of was his hand in hers, supporting her, and the delicious warmth that enveloped her as she sank into the tub.

The water had a floral tang—lavender—and it poured over her, a soothing balm to her shaky limbs. She tilted her head back, letting it saturate her hair and then dunking her head below the surface, washing away a little more of the day.

When she came back up, Jonathan was sitting in the chair beside the tub, leaning in with a soft scrap of cloth to dab at her face. Her neck. Her shoulders. Every touch reverberated through her, traveling deep, to her very essence. Not in the same way as last night, when she'd been rendered frantic and desperate. These strokes left her with a sense of calm. Of contentment. Of feeling like nothing could hurt her again.

He tugged loose the ribbon of her braid, setting it aside and retrieving the soap. His fingers began a thorough massage of her scalp, a sensation so lovely she nearly hummed from the pleasure of it. Eventually, he reached into the water to gather the rest of her hair, working it into a soapy lather as he rubbed his hands through the strands again and again.

And again, his motions growing more vigorous before abruptly, he stopped.

"Um." He sat back in the chair, setting the diminished bar of soap aside. "I may need to run downstairs for a moment. To ask for some, uh, flour, or—"

"What?" She whipped her head in his direction, the motion causing her mass of hair to flop over her shoulder and fan out into the water before her. In a split second, confusion became clarity. Which became horror. The red-gold tresses were coated in thick streaks of black.

She made a small sound as she gathered the mass into her palm and lifted it out of the water, inspecting it like something foreign and unknown, much like she'd done with the damaged carriage.

Another flash of clarity. She'd been down on her hands and knees underneath the carriage as she tried to make sense of what had happened. In the process, she must have brushed against the broken axle, transferring the thick black grease from the iron to her hair. She scrubbed her fingers against the oily strands, just as he'd spent countless minutes doing, but nothing happened other than that she now had black fingers, too.

"It's all right." Gently, he slid the clump of hair from her palm, letting it fall back into the water. "We can fix this. I already got the worst of it out near your head, and as for the rest, I heard somewhere that flour can help to remove this sort of thing, or maybe we could send to the village for a different type of soap ..."

She closed her eyes against the sudden rush of queasiness in her stomach. For a moment, she was no longer at The Golden Lion but a girl of eighteen with her head in a basin back at Rockliffe House in London. When she opened them again, though, the tub returned, along with the chair and the screen, and Jonathan.

"That isn't necessary." She knew he didn't like when she said that. Furthermore, he was obviously worried about her sinking back into a state of panic.

Her chest did hurt a little from the familiar knots suggestive of fear. However, she wasn't being crushed, and the walls didn't close in. She could still breathe perfectly well. As for her head, it felt clearer than it had all day.

"I don't need flour or more soap." She said it not to put distance between them but because it was the truth. Because she'd already decided what needed to happen instead. "But while I finish up here, would you mind fetching some scissors?"

Amelia's reflection stared back at her in the small mirror above the washstand. Flushed skin from the heat of the bath. A thin face with faint shadows beneath her eyes. Long fingers that trembled slightly as they clutched a pair of scissors, bringing them ever closer to the braid she'd refastened and slung over her shoulder.

Her hair. Her one point of beauty. Marred with stubborn black streaks that the mirror wouldn't let her forget.

"Are you certain you want to do this?" Jonathan's face came up alongside hers in the mirror. Dark hair. Steady brown eyes. "Because if you've changed your mind, we could—"

"Yes." She couldn't think on it any longer. She'd already made up her mind, so there was no sense allowing doubts the chance to creep in. She spared his reflection one more glance before turning back to her own. Her fingers pried open the scissors, enclosing her braid between the blades. There came a distinctive snip and a featherlight thump against the floor.

She started backward, the scissors tumbling out of her hand, flying into the washbasin with a clink. Had ... had she really just gone through with it?

She staggered again, her mind in a whirl. But as they'd been all week, a pair of arms was there to catch her, to wrap around her waist and guide her to the wing chair that sat near the fire.

She lowered herself with his gentle prodding, purposefully not looking back toward the mirror or the floor below it. Instead, she skimmed her hand up her body—over the patch of her dressing gown that had grown damp from the wet braid that no longer remained—and above her shoulder, stopping when she connected with loose hair near the level of her chin. The wet ends felt strange, so short and jagged, and—

"Beautiful." Jonathan crouched down beside her, his hand going up to run through one of the strands.

A protest began to form on her tongue because no, of course she wasn't beautiful, especially not now. Yet it died away before it crossed her lips. The way he said the word, she could almost think it true.

He stroked her hair again, sweeping the limp pieces away from her face. "I can straighten it up for you a little if you like. I cannot claim to be an expert, but after all the years I spent at sea without a valet, I do have a bit of experience cutting hair."

She squeezed her fingers one more time around the rough edges of her hair, then dropped them to her lap. In performing the shaky cut, she'd made up her mind that her appearance couldn't matter. However, as she peered down at him where he lingered by her feet, she found that, once again, she believed him. He could make it better.

With a single nod from her, he was on his feet, going to retrieve the discarded scissors. She still didn't glance in that direction, not ready to see her braid lying across the floor. However, as long as she looked straight ahead, toward the fire, a sense of calm filled her. The upper floor of the inn was quiet at the moment, for the guests in the surrounding rooms must have already vacated. All that remained was the patter of rain against the roof. The crackling of flames, which shrouded her in warmth. And then, a quiet snip as Jonathan positioned himself behind her chair and made the first cut.

For a while, the rain, fire, and scissors were the only sounds to fill the space as Jonathan worked, the combination gentle, like a lullaby. Part of her felt like she could sit there indefinitely, not thinking, just losing herself to the quiet rhythm. Yet, at the same time, a memory she couldn't fully erase lingered below the surface. Pushing a little harder, a little harder, until eventually, her voice crept up, breaking into the lull. "Did I ever tell you about how I was sent away before my first Season?"

The scissors paused where he'd brought them around to do the left side of her hair, and from the corner of her eye, she could see him shake his head. No, she hadn't told him, had she? She'd never spoken of this to anyone. But suddenly, she wanted to.

"I was seventeen," she continued, peering into the dancing flames, "and with the scandals that had cropped up surrounding both my brothers, Mother thought it best I go elsewhere, to put some distance between myself and the family before I had to come out in society."

Her eyelids fluttered closed, and for a moment, she became a girl bouncing along a rutted road in the Rockliffe traveling coach, her stomach twisted with apprehension. "She arranged for her friends the Earl and Countess of Rowley to have me at their country estate in Essex. Their daughter, Miranda, was to make her debut at the same time as me. The problem was, I didn't wish to go. I don't mean to sound ungrateful, but I'd never been away from home before, and I was so anxious. Likewise, Miranda was none too pleased with the companion who'd been forced upon her." *The worst companion, who tripped over her own gangly legs and spent too much time at her escritoire.*

"I began having ... episodes." She swallowed, placing a hand atop her beating heart. Willing it to stay steady. "Like I did earlier. Where all of a sudden, I would find it hard to breathe, like I was going to be crushed. Lady Rowley was beside herself. As for Miranda, whatever distaste she had for me to begin with became so much worse. She used to call me ... well, I'd rather not repeat the names. Suffice to say, no one understood. No one ever did anything but ridicule. Not until you."

It suddenly occurred to her that the snip of scissors had vanished from the array of background noises, and she glanced up to find Jonathan peering into the flames with a faraway expression, as if they contained images of his past.

"I would never ridicule. *Ever*. Many years ago, my father used to have incidents sometimes where ..." He broke off, a muscle in his jaw twitching. "N-not that it's the same situation at all. My point is that during his times of struggle, I tried to treat him with understanding, not disdain, for I never wanted him to think himself lacking for things beyond his control. Just as no one should have made you feel that way. Compassion takes little effort, yet some people seem to have great difficulty exhibiting it."

"Indeed." She captured her bottom lip with her teeth, watching the firelight flicker across his face, illuminating each shadow and twitch. The room's quiet seemed to be evoking his own memories of a past of which she knew only bits and pieces. But before she could think on it any longer, he shifted his position to stand in front of her, taking hold of one of the strands that framed her face.

He leaned down so they were at the same eye level, his brow furrowed in concentration as he made another cut. "Does it happen often?"

A tiny wisp of hair floated to her cheek, and she brushed it away, letting it fall to the floor with the others. "No. Not anymore. In fact, the episodes all but stopped when I was finally allowed to go back to Rockliffe House just before my first Season began. I cannot explain it, for I possessed plenty of apprehension surrounding my debut. In any case, there was only one more incident after that."

She sensed the small increase in her pulse and dug her fingers into the silk of her sleeves, trying to remain steady. This was the main reason the story had come to mind in the first place. She braced herself with a long inhale. "The day before my court presentation, Mother invited Lady Rowley and Miranda for tea. Outwardly, all very civil. I was sitting at the escritoire when they arrived, and Miranda approached to ask if I'd like to take a turn about the room. Looking back on it now, it's almost funny to think of how many times she drew attention to my clumsiness during my stay in Essex. For that afternoon, it was *her* elbow that went flying into the inkwell and caused the contents to splatter all over my dress and hair."

A lump formed in her throat, but she pushed through it, willing herself to keep going. "A ruined gown meant little to me. But my hair ... and only a day away from being presented to the queen ... I don't know what came over me. I couldn't breathe, couldn't think straight. All I could do was retreat to my bedchamber and scrub my hair as if my life depended on it."

Again, a pause with the scissors, and Jonathan's mouth grew taut. "I'm so sorry—"

"Ultimately, it was far from the end of the world, though it may have felt like it at the time." She gave her arms another quick squeeze, a reminder that she was here, in the present, and far removed from that long-ago afternoon. "Mary, my lady's maid at the time, helped me get out the worst of the ink, and a few strategically placed feathers were able to cover what we couldn't remove. I got through my presentation without incident, and while Miranda may have whispered all manner of things to the other ladies behind my back, her malice was short-lived, for she quickly became distracted by the attentions of a Scottish earl."

Just as Amelia had become distracted by a duke's mysterious grandson sitting alone in a garden.

She pulled herself up a little straighter against the chairback, squaring her shoulders. "Miranda—or Lady Murray, I should say—rarely returned to London after her marriage. Rumor had it that the earl was near bankrupt, and they didn't have the funds for travel, and I can't pretend to be sorry for it. Her absence made it far easier for me to take part in the Season year after year." *And to deal with the other trials that came her way.* "However, as silly as it now seems, I've never fully forgotten the incident. As for the matter of my hair … I suppose I didn't want to risk feeling today the same way I did all those years ago. I just want to let it all go."

"Not silly." His voice came out low but insistent, and he gave his head a small shake. He gently took hold of a strand beside her face, making one final cut before letting it slip through his fingers and turning to place the scissors on the mantle. "I'm finished. Would you like to see?"

For the first time, she allowed her gaze to travel to the floor, to the reddish-blond tufts that glinted in the firelight. And in that moment, she knew she was ready.

"Yes." She rose to her feet, accepting his proffered arm as they started toward the washstand. Keeping her eyes on the floor until they stopped, and then, she didn't delay any longer. She lifted her face to the mirror, where a stranger peered back.

No, not a stranger exactly, for she still had the same blue eyes, pale lashes, and freckled nose. But instead of a long braid trailing to her waist, her hair fell in loose, even waves that ended just below her chin.

She looked so … *different.* But not in a bad way. She was lighter now, somehow, and—

"Beautiful." That word again, and Jonathan's face beside hers in the mirror, gauging her reaction. "You know that, right?"

She ran a hand through her hair, watching as her mirror image copied the movement. How much time had she spent *not* knowing that? Trying to hide her true self, thinking of all the ways she was lacking. But the way he said it—again, it felt like the truth.

"Beautiful," he repeated, circling his arms around her

waist, turning her gently so she no longer faced the mirror but him. Dropping the softest kiss upon her forehead. "Resilient." Another kiss, just below her left eyebrow. "Brave." A kiss to the right. "Strong."

Each brush of his lips sank far below the surface of her skin, traveling straight to her heart with a power so great that tears welled beneath her closed eyelids. She'd run from London not feeling like she possessed any of those qualities. However, it wasn't too late to change that. He believed in her. In turn, it was time she started believing in herself.

His lips traveled farther down to each of her flushed cheeks. To the sensitive skin at the edge of her ear. Worshiping her, filling her. Making her feel ... *new*.

A new Amelia who had short hair and possessed the confidence not to run away. Who could have a second chance.

A new Amelia who knew what she wanted to make the transformation complete.

And so, she reached out, letting her hand cup the side of his face, and asked for it. "Make love to me."

15

Jonathan's breath caught as Amelia's fingertips connected with his jawline. As he discovered her blue eyes fixed on him like two glimmering pools. As her whispered words floated into his awareness. *Make love to me.*

He pressed his forehead to hers, taking a silent moment where there was nothing but the steady thrum of raindrops against the inn and the quiet pop of flames. Creating a space so warm and intimate that it felt almost dreamlike, which begged the question: had he possibly imagined what she'd said?

But no, her cerulean gaze continued to fall on him, intent. Anticipating.

"Amelia, I—"

He what? Was honor-bound by a decade-old vow that they wouldn't consummate their relationship until after marriage? Wanted to be sure she wasn't driven purely by the emotion of everything she'd gone through that day, that she didn't ask for something she would later come to regret?

"I want you." Her voice was a little louder this time, and the edges of her nails pricked his heated skin. "I want to go back to London with you, just like you said. To have you beside me. Not to hide anymore. But first, I want ..." Her fingers left his jaw, sliding down to rest against the bare patch of skin where his shirt gaped open. "I want ..."

His mouth connected with hers, pressing hungrily into her soft lips. Because, oh, how he wanted, too. With her words, she'd just granted him everything he'd been hoping for, even if he scarcely dared to dream it.

He broke the kiss only long enough to scoop her into his arms. An action that had become commonplace over the past few days but suddenly held more significance—more intimacy —than ever before. He carried her to the bed, depositing her atop the plush coverlet. Again, an action he'd completed the night before when she'd grown frantic with a desire she didn't know how to manage, and he'd been consumed with the need to give her pleasure.

That yearning had returned, spreading fire through his veins. However, it wasn't frantic this time. On the contrary, it had become something he wished to savor, to draw out, to let bring them together until he no longer knew where he ended and she began.

He lay alongside her, giving her one more kiss before pulling away so he could watch her face as he unbelted her dressing gown and nudged the silk folds open. As he revealed the only garment she wore underneath—a flimsy shift—and reached for the ribbon at her neckline that held it in place.

Last night, when she'd come to his bed, he'd extinguished the candles and plunged them into darkness, not willing to take a chance that shyness could interfere with her burgeoning need. But today was different. She'd already shown him so much vulnerability and, dare he say, *trust*. She'd proceeded to voice her desires with newfound confidence. In turn, he wanted the mixture of muted gray daylight and golden candle-light to illuminate every inch of her body as he explored it.

He went slowly with loosening the ribbon to make certain she was willing, drawing the delicate shift open bit by bit. The translucent white silk already gave a glimpse of the body beneath it—the small slope of her breasts, two pearly pink nipples. She didn't shy away from his gaze. On the contrary, she watched him, emitting a quiet sigh as his fingers traced over her skin.

He let the ribbon come undone and pushed the shift from her shoulders, exposing her to him fully. She was perfect, just as he'd known she would be, with creamy white skin adorned by a sprinkling of freckles across her chest. Skin he wanted desperately to taste.

He lowered his mouth to the freckles above her right breast, giving each tiny fleck its own caress and then tracing a trail downward until he met with the hardened point in the center. He circled his tongue over it and captured it between his lips, relishing the feel of her without the barrier of fabric. She was so sweet, like blossoms and honey and spring.

He lavished her breast with strokes and flicks, feeling her nipple harden further before turning his attention to the other side. Soft mewls escaped her throat as he laved her, and he added the attentions of his hand, drawing it from her throat to her abdomen, where her shift hung slackly just below her breasts.

With a light tug, he eased it down, raising himself so he could pull it the rest of the way over her hips and legs and cast it aside. Which left her lying before him completely bare, with her long, slim body accentuated by the soft glow of candles.

He took her in, emitting a throaty sound of his own. Amelia's beauty didn't lie in lush curves but in perfect, straight lines. Almost like she'd been carved from alabaster, dotted by tiny flecks of the sun. He would never get enough of her.

He took hold of her slender hips, coaxing them apart so he

could kneel in between them. So he could stretch out and lower himself along the bed once more, bringing his lips to the flat surface of her belly. To her navel. Lower still, to the edge of her nest of curls—

"Wh-what are you doing?" Her head popped off the pillow, her hand shooting out to clutch his hair.

"Kissing you," he murmured, raising his mouth just a shade so his breath still floated across her skin. He skimmed his fingers along her inner thigh, bringing them upward until they brushed along her intimate folds. Her skin was damp and smooth, and the scent of her arousal permeated his nostrils, making his own desire flare.

"I want to kiss you everywhere. Including here." For the briefest moment, his finger connected with the bud at the apex of her sex before he drew it away, back onto her thigh. "May I?"

She hissed out a breath, her mouth gaping as she glanced at his lips. His fingers. Her own unclothed body. Back at his lips. And suddenly, understanding flashed through her eyes.

She dropped back to the pillow, uttering a single husky word. "Yes."

Yes. He nearly repeated it back as a shout of yearning.

He hooked his hands beneath her knees, encouraging them to bend and splay, leaving her center fully open to him. With that, he took his first taste, swiping his tongue along the wetness that had trickled to the seam of her thigh. More sweetness, and headiness, and he was beginning to feel like a man in his cups.

She shuddered beneath his mouth, the word crossing her lips again. "Yes. Please."

He continued, his tongue traveling into her folds. Up to the peak he'd teased with his finger. Back down again. Discovering every intimate part of her while she continued to grasp his hair, holding him close.

She'd begun making breathy noises again, and he used them to adapt his movements, lingering when a sound grew especially fervent or her body bucked in unison. Last night in this bed, she'd seemed overwhelmed by her own desire, uncertain what to do with it. Now, she embraced it, rocking her hips toward his mouth, chasing what she wanted.

With his tongue still circling over her swollen bud, he brought a hand to her sex, sliding a fingertip into her entrance. Right away, her muscles drew him into the tightness, and he gave a few careful strokes, watching her face as she absorbed the unfamiliar sensation.

Her head was thrown back, her breath coming in a relentless series of shallow pants. Her hips hadn't stopped swaying, leaning into the caresses of both his mouth and hand. Judging by the way her body began tensing, she had to be close to her peak.

He slipped another fingertip alongside the first, gently stretching her, as his mouth kept up its ministrations, circling, caressing—

She shattered, her muscles pulsing around his fingers as she let out a sharp whimper. Her fingernails sank into his scalp, and he continued lapping at her sensitive flesh, wanting to draw out each wave of pleasure for as long as possible.

He stayed there until her shuddering body stilled, all the tautness draining away, and her arms flopped to her sides. And to think, only hours ago, she'd been unaware of the fulfilment of desire.

She was a fast learner.

She was exquisite.

He pushed himself up to his knees, taking hold of his shirt and casting it over his head. Hardness strained against his breeches, for everything about her enthralled him. The smell. The taste. The sight of her splayed out before him, her body awash with the glow of pleasure. He'd risen only seconds ago, and already, he yearned to sink back down and have her heated skin beneath him once more.

However, he stilled himself, not moving from his knees despite his body's implorations for *more* and *faster* and *Amelia, Amelia, Amelia*. He wanted her, more than he could remember wanting anything in his life. That he could have her seemed almost too good to be true. Did she really still desire this? For if there was even a chance she could come to regret what passed between them—

"Please." Her fingers came up to his chest, sweeping over it with the lightest caress. "I've waited so long. I've *wanted* so long."

His blood pounded, and his chest grew very tight. Tight and tingling and full, bursting with a combination of sensations so powerful that his eyes stung in a way they hadn't in many, many years.

He'd sailed the world thinking his mistakes would define the rest of his life. That there was never any going back. That regret was an indissoluble burden.

Yet here he was, back in England, with things he'd imagined impossible lying before him to reach out and take.

Redemption.

Forgiveness.

"Me, too, my love," he rasped, his voice beginning to break. He reached for his fall, his fingers unsteady as he unfastened the buttons. More unsteady still as it came loose and he rose to push the breeches from his hips, all while Amelia peered at him in wide-eyed wonder.

He stretched himself out once more, lowering his body to align with hers. Bare skin against bare skin, setting his nerve endings aflame. His arousal hovered near her entrance, where she remained so hot and slick. He'd tried his best to make her ready, hating the thought of causing her even a second's pain.

He inched forward, using every scrap of restraint he had to

move into her with painstaking slowness, halting the second she let out a gasp. "I'm so sorry." He dipped his head, dropping a kiss to each of her flushed cheeks. To her parted lips. "The last thing I want is to hurt you. Is it too much?"

"No." She gave her head a tiny shake, planting her hands securely against his hips. "Please, I wish for you to keep going."

"The discomfort will just last a moment; it will get better, I promise—"

He broke off, capturing her mouth with his before pushing himself the rest of the way home. For that's what it felt like to be nestled deep inside her: warm, and embracing, and so utterly blissful that he let out a groan. At the same time, a soft noise escaped her throat, and he deepened the kiss, allowing it to swallow up their sounds.

His body was on fire, insisting he move. However, he held himself still, giving her time to adjust. He ran a hand through the shortened, silky hair that spilled across her pillow. Ran his tongue along hers with a featherlight stroke. And then, he lifted his mouth, rising just enough so he could study her face. "Are you all right?"

Her forehead contained a slight crease, and she captured the lip he'd just been caressing between her teeth. "I feel ... full." She made a tiny movement with her hips, sending a jolt of desire to his already throbbing cock. Yet, despite how it overtook his senses, he didn't miss the moment her face relaxed nor the subtle upward twitch of her mouth. "I think I like it."

With her words, he allowed his body to relax, pulling himself up and lowering back down with a careful thrust. Her mouth fell open, her hips making a more forceful motion, popping up from the bed. "Yes," she breathed, her fingernails searing his skin with sharp points of pleasure, "I *do* like it. I don't want it to stop."

He repeated the movement, getting another euphoric shock from the friction. *Like* was too insignificant a word to describe the feelings coursing through him. This was heaven. A place that kept driving him higher and higher because she was here with him, coming to meet each of his thrusts.

Already, he could feel a climax bearing down on him, easily attainable with just a few quick motions. And still, he went slowly, with gentle glides in and out. For the first time in his life, this act became about so much more than chasing fleeting physical pleasure. More important was prolonging the intimacy of every moment, of savoring the way each stroke drew them closer together, erasing a little more of the lost decade between them. Erasing the guardedness, and the remorse, and the gut-wrenching ache, until all that remained was her body joined with his, and the same blue eyes that had once gazed at him in a frosty garden and left a lasting imprint on his heart.

He kissed her once more, upon her lips, her ears, her throat. Her breaths were growing rapid again, her movements becoming more insistent. Was she close to reaching another peak? The thought caused him to plunge down with several quicker, unsteady motions. Because yes, he wanted this closeness to go on forever. But at the same time, what would feel better than having her reach her crisis around him? And finally, allowing himself to let go, too.

She released a soft moan with the change in tempo, and he slid a hand up to her breast, taking the taut nipple between his thumb and forefinger. Another cry escaped her, and his simmering yearning burst into an inferno, his strokes coming fast, with abandon. After holding it in check, his need flew at him, screaming to be fulfilled. Yet he wouldn't give in to it until he'd seen to hers first.

With his fingers still tweaking her nipple, he drew her earlobe between his teeth, then brought his mouth up to the shell of her ear. "You could touch yourself," he managed to say amidst his own hurried breaths. "The way I showed you last night."

Her exhale came out as a shuddered sigh against his neck, and he pulled his face back up so he could peer into her eyes. Her golden lashes fluttered, and her pupils had gone large, shining from both candlelight and desire.

He couldn't tear his gaze away, couldn't think of anything but Amelia and each bliss-filled second. Yet he became cognizant of her hand slipping between their bodies, of her muscles growing rigid—

And of her eyes screwing shut as release overtook her again, leaving her throbbing around him, crying out something that nearly sounded like his name. *Jonathan.* That was all it took for him to hurtle over the edge as well. Pleasure consumed him, pounding through his blood, washing over him in torrents as he spilled his seed inside her tight heat.

How much longer did they stay that way? Seconds? Hours? He'd lost all concept of time. He only knew that it felt so right, hovering above her as the waves diminished, leaving his body slack and sated.

When the moment came that he at last rolled to his side, she followed him, turning so they lay chest to chest, legs still entwined. He hugged her close, pressing a kiss to her forehead. "Beautiful." It warranted saying again until he was certain she had it engrained in her just how exquisite she was, inside and out. For that matter, he planned to say it every day for the rest of their lives.

They could stay together, forever ... The concept was still too surreal to grasp. Yet here she was, back in his arms. In his bed. The love for her that had never stopped smoldering in his heart, regardless of how much time or distance passed, no longer had to be fruitless. The dreams they'd once shared could have another chance to come true.

"Jonathan?" She pressed a hand to his temple, pulling him out of his reverie and back to focus on her eyes of perfect, peerless blue. "I haven't changed my mind about us returning to London. I still want to. Truly. Only, before we leave this bed ... do you think we might take advantage of it again?"

He laughed, a sound of genuine joy that had often eluded him. "That sounds like a clever plan, my love. In fact, perhaps we should do so two or three times. To ensure we get our money's worth out of this room we've procured, of course."

She giggled, too, a bell-like timbre that had his heart near to bursting. Her upturned lips had become a vivid rosy color, slightly swollen from the effects of his own lips and teeth. Just as her skin contained a dewy flush, and a few locks of red-gold hair hung haphazardly atop the pillow. Overall, she appeared thoroughly mussed.

Which made her suggestion fortunate indeed. It would have proved a great struggle to pull away from such a sight so quickly.

He reclaimed her lips, becoming absorbed in the plush softness once more. Beyond these walls, the future awaited them, full of trials to conquer and fears to face.

But as for the remainder of today ...

After so many lost years, today could be just for them.

16

Once again, Amelia found herself sitting atop one of the shaded rocks outside The Golden Lion, watching as an early stagecoach swayed down the road, growing smaller and smaller as it faded into the distance. Heading to London, most likely. Soon, she and Jonathan would follow.

She took a long breath of the brisk morning air, made heavy with low-lying gray clouds that promised rain, although nothing fell just yet. With any luck, the weather wouldn't drive her indoors before she had a few more moments to sit amidst the trees and clear her head, nor would it interfere with the plan she and Jonathan had made to hire a chaise to take them south.

She shifted against the rock at the memory of their murmured conversations—and other activities—in bed last night, the subtle ache between her legs reminding her it had all been real. Then again, she'd recognized that shortly after opening her eyes this morning, when she'd glanced down to find herself covered by Jonathan's outstretched arm, a twisted bedsheet, and nothing else.

Her body had hummed with contentment, as well as the

faint stirrings of desire. How could she help it when his warm, solid weight pressed into her, providing both protection and pleasure, even when he remained asleep?

Except then, a different sort of anticipation had set in. The type that made her stomach quiver, enough that she could no longer lie there, enwrapped in a pleasure-filled haze. Instead, she'd slipped out from Jonathan's embrace and silently dressed, sparing him a final glance before tiptoeing out to the corridor and making her way to her rocky perch for a brief period of solitude.

She would just take a few more minutes to wait for the unsettled feeling to go away and then return to the room as quietly as she'd left it. Perhaps Jonathan wouldn't even realize she'd been gone. After years of spending nights aboard ships, he must have learned to block out his surroundings as he slept, for he hadn't so much as stirred as she'd crept about the room, his features remaining relaxed and untroubled.

She smiled to herself at that despite the tightness in her throat. *They were together. They could have another chance. All would be well.*

A door banged, and boots came pounding across the dirt, the sound rapidly approaching her shaded retreat. She whipped her head toward the inn's entrance, the smile vanishing from her lips. Jonathan was running toward her with both her small traveling bag and his valise upon his arm, his jaw tense and his forehead furrowed with concern.

Because he thought she'd run away again, just as she'd done yesterday. His fears were written all over his face. He thought she'd changed her mind.

"I'm sorry." She uttered the words the moment he came to a stop in front of her, dropping the bags to the ground as he tried to catch his breath. "I thought I'd be back in the room before you'd awoken. I just wanted some fresh air before we begin our journey back to London. Join me?"

She patted the rock beside her, and he sank down, wrapping his arms around her waist and pulling her in for a quick kiss. "I thought—"

"I know." She kissed him again, then let her head rest atop his shoulder. "Nothing has changed since last night. It was truly just a desire for some time outdoors."

She meant the words. She *did*. However, a knot pulled in her belly, making her voice waver at the end.

He ran his fingers through the loose waves that hung around her face. "Are you certain there's nothing troubling you?"

She nestled herself more tightly against the warm wool of his coat. "I'm a little anxious about what will await me in London." That was the obvious answer, and it did hold a sprinkling of truth. Yet, if she were being honest with herself, it wasn't what had driven her outside to gather her thoughts.

"You won't be alone. You know we're in this together—"

"Yes." She nodded, peering out into the distance at the endless stretch of road. A well-traveled path that led travelers back home to the loved ones who awaited them. Or that carried them far away, to remote corners of England and Scotland, or maybe even to the docks, where they would board a ship and never return. "But what if it all goes away again?"

Finally, the question that lay heavy on her heart was out in the open. She lifted her head so she could meet his eyes. *Perhaps I don't deserve another chance,* he'd said, *but if you're willing to grant one, I'll spend the rest of my life proving my love and devotion to you.*

She'd made the decision to allow that chance. To let herself trust. To let herself *love*. And still, the past refused to be silenced.

She hated the thought of hurting him with her doubt. Yet now that she'd started down this road, she couldn't seem to stop. "What if—what if something happens? What if you change your mind? What if you disappear just as swiftly as last time and I never see you again? How would I bear that?"

Tears were falling again in silent rivers down her cheeks. She wanted so much to accept without question the future he'd offered her. To honor all the words and promises they'd spoken to one another when they were little more than youths, as if the decade in between had never happened. Except it *did* happen, and her wounded heart didn't know how to let go of fear.

"Amelia." His voice came out strained, his features reduced to a watery blur through her tears. "I wish there was something I could say to make everything better. There isn't. What I did was inexcusable, and there's no cure for that. All I can ask is for the chance to prove my constancy in the future. No more secrets. No running. Perhaps it's fruitless voicing it now, but my biggest struggle on … on that night was finding the will not to rush to your bedchamber window and beg for you to see me. If only so I could look upon your face one last time, even if it was filled with disdain. I couldn't abide the thought of not having a farewell, of knowing we'd already had our final encounter without even realizing it. Yet, in the end, I decided to respect your wishes and stay away, leaving behind nothing but a letter that you could read or not as you pleased. I could at least give you that much, for my own desires had become meaningless. Please tell me you knew it was never a matter of me not caring deeply enough and certainly not of changing my mind."

"My wishes?" Her body was raw, overtaken by waves of old, concealed hurt that kept rolling up and crashing into her. Yet his last words parted the sea, allowing an uncomfortable spark to take hold deep in her belly. "What do you mean by my wishes?"

She gave her eyes a few impatient swipes, forcing the moisture away so that Jonathan came back into focus. His face appeared pale against his dark hair, and his body was stone still. "The ones you expressed in your note."

Her note ... her note? Her head pounded, trying to put all the pieces of what she was hearing into place, but nothing made sense. Her mind flew back to that fateful night when the stableboy approached her window with the missive, and her dreams shattered with a few hastily scrawled lines.

That was Jonathan's note. But *hers*?

She knew before opening her mouth that the words would come out thick. "What note?"

Jonathan remained sitting beside her, his body a statue, his face a mask. Nothing in the world made a sound outside of her pounding heart. Until suddenly, he snatched up his valise, wrenching the clasp open and tearing at the contents.

Starched white cravats flew to the ground. A waistcoat. A notebook. He discarded it all into the dirt like a man possessed until his hand came up holding a lone sheet of creased paper.

"I kept it." He thrust it toward her, his movements jerky. "Perhaps that makes me pitiable. But I thought it better to retain some part of you than be left with nothing at all."

She accepted the paper into her trembling fingers, somehow finding the dexterity to unfold it. Words flashed before her on the page, and she gave her eyes another dab, making the letters crystal clear.

Jonathan,

Let me be brief. I know you've been keeping secrets from me. As a marriage should be based on honesty, I find this breach of trust unforgivable. I assume you understand why we cannot carry on with our arrangement. Please do not attempt further correspondence or meetings. Anything that existed between us has been shattered.

Amelia

The neat whirls and loops were unmistakably in her hand. The letters of the signature spelled her name. But ... but ...

"I didn't write this," she choked out, her body turning to ice. "You were the one who wrote to me."

She became vaguely aware of his widened eyes and slackened mouth, although her vision had clouded again, and her head spun.

"Of course, I wrote to you." He enunciated each word carefully, almost like a question. "I at least had to explain, to let you know how sorry I was, on the off chance you would consent to read it—"

"No." She shook her head repeatedly, too dazed to stop. Nothing made sense anymore. She may have burned his letter moments after receiving it, but its contents remained imprinted on her heart like a brand. "You wrote to tell me our betrothal was a mistake. That you'd come to realize how foolish you'd been and that we could never see each other again."

"I didn't!" His body shuddered as if he'd been punched. "Jesus, Amelia, you were the only bright spot in my miserable existence. I may not have deserved it, but I *wanted* to elope to Gretna Green and make you my wife more than anything else."

"But then ... but how ..."

Additional speech failed her, for the world was turning far too fast, taking every bit of knowledge she possessed and flinging it away. The letter remained in her shaking hands. The scrap of paper that contained her words, but at the same time, not her words. As for the long-ago letter that had come to her window, crushing her heart and altering her future, those hadn't been his words, either.

Those hadn't been his words.

She stared into his face as if assessing a stranger. Or rather, someone she hadn't seen in a very long time: the man of nineteen who'd made her promises of love and loyalty before they'd been torn apart.

Because someone must have found out about their secret union.

Someone must have interfered.

The realization hit her at the same time a carriage thundered down the lane toward The Golden Lion, appearing as a streak of black in her periphery. Horses whinnied as they ground to a halt near the inn's entrance, the sharp noise causing an inexplicable shiver to dart up her spine.

Still, she didn't look away from him, didn't even blink. For with the jolt of clarity—both cathartic and horrifying at the same—came another tangle of questions that made her stomach churn.

Why did the paper within her hands accuse him of keeping secrets?

Why had he attempted to write her a letter of apology?

Why did he say he'd done something inexcusable?

A carriage door creaked open, followed by a distinctive thump against the ground. One that sounded again, and again, a quiet but ominous beat that began to draw nearer.

Another burst of clarity shot through her, sucking the air from her lungs.

She staggered to her feet. Turned toward the inn. The streak of black was now stagnant, revealing the sleek lines of an elegant traveling coach with a telltale crest emblazoned upon the door. A phoenix, surrounded by flames. The Rockliffe crest.

In front of which stood her mother, tapping her cane against the ground as she strode forward. She squinted, pressing her hand against her lined forehead as if she didn't comprehend what she was looking at. Nor did Amelia, for that matter, for her surroundings had taken on a nightmarish quality. Dread-inducing, but not fully tangible.

But in the next instant, their eyes locked, and suddenly, the truth of the situation hit her like a blow to the chest.

It was too late to do anything but stand there and accept her mother's wrath, or whatever else fate had in store. Not that proceeding otherwise was ever a possibility. Her body was frozen, ready to smash into thousands of icy shards from the faintest knock.

The recognition that flared in her mother's pale eyes didn't make her walk any faster. On the contrary, she continued with the same measured steps—*thump ... thump ... thump*—that turned each passing second into an eternity. An eternity in which Amelia had the sinking feeling that her world was about to detonate once more, yet she was powerless to run for cover.

Her mother's countenance gave nothing away. Not until she came to a stop in front of them, and the cluster of trees and rocks became a sanctuary no more. Only then did her silver brows rise and her head tilt, betraying her incredulity as she took in Amelia's cropped head of hair. The mud coating her hem. And most of all, the man who'd just risen from the rock beside her.

Her mother was far too fierce for fainting couches and vinaigrettes. Nonetheless, her slender body gave a small twitch, and she clamped down on her cane, her fingers tightening until her knuckles turned white.

She parted her curled lips, and Amelia braced herself. Her mother had never been the sort for shrieking and hysterics, and today proved no exception. Only, the steely-toned rasp that came out instead was so much more terrifying. "*What* in God's name have you done?"

A strong hand pressed into Amelia's back, holding her steady. Jonathan had promised he would support her every step of the way, and he was starting right now. However, the resolve she'd summoned yesterday seemed to have fractured along with so many other parts of her. "I ..." Oh, she was dizzy, and her pulse wouldn't stop throbbing erratically.

She pressed her spine against Jonathan's palm, taking whatever shred of comfort she could find. "How did you discover me?" she muttered, the only words that would come. Not that the answer held much significance at this point.

A vein pulsed in her mother's neck, and a dangerous glint flashed in her eyes. "Don't think I didn't find your sudden departure for a holiday to Brighton with Theodora and the boys exceptionally peculiar," she hissed. "Not nearly as peculiar, though, as when I was driving through Hyde Park the next day, and whom should I spot running about but Benedict, Alexander, and that dog. It took naught but a few discreet inquiries afterward to surmise the true direction of your travel."

"Oh." Amelia sounded so dull, so nonsensical. Something hot and painful simmered deep within her, chipping away at the ice, but her mind struggled to catch up. Or perhaps it simply didn't want to see ...

"Well, never mind that now. We're well south of Gretna Green, so I trust you haven't done anything irrevocable." Her mother gave a pointed glance toward the Rockliffe carriage, where the coachman remained atop his box, and a footman waited by the door. "Get in the carriage, Amelia. You and I have a thing or two to discuss *in private*."

"No." Amelia's body bristled. Her mother's commanding speech made it impossible to ignore what was right in front of her any longer. Someone had written false letters to tear her and Jonathan apart.

That someone now looked her in the eye.

"You knew," she gasped, squaring her shoulders, trying to make her limbs stop trembling. "You've always known. *You* tore us apart. You tricked us! Why would you do such a thing?"

"For heaven's sake." Her mother gave her cane an impatient tap against the ground. "I thought you would have long since learned your lesson where *His Grace* is concerned. As it seems you haven't, even as a woman approaching thirty, let me explain very clearly. I did it to protect you. To save you from a life of entanglement with Branscombe rot. Because that family had every intention of using you. Of deceiving you and then crushing you. Just as they do with everything. That isn't speculation on my part. It's fact."

Beside her, Jonathan stiffened, his hand going tense against her back. The words cut her as well, sharper than any knife. But instead of making her cower, they caused the deep-rooted fire within her to flare to the surface, turning her voice every bit as acerbic as her mother's. "What right have you to make such accusations? You don't know the current duke! He's nothing like his predecessor."

Her mother's eyes had grown wide while her mouth hung agape. Amelia had never shouted like that at anyone before. Certainly not at her parents. But while the outburst caused her mother an uncharacteristic moment of bafflement, she vanquished it quickly, her eyes narrowing and her lips becoming taut once more. "Is that so? Why, then, was he willing to forgo the betrothal and disappear when the promise of funds became involved?"

"It wasn't like that!" Jonathan's hands flew to her shoulders, turning both of their bodies so they no longer faced the Dowager Marchioness of Rockliffe's notorious glower but each other. "It wasn't—"

"Wasn't it?" Even though her mother was out of sight, her voice permeated the air between them, dripping with disdain. "Did I say something false, Your Grace?"

"Yes. No. Y-yes. You don't ... d-don't understand." He shook his head violently, just as she'd done when she wanted to negate the terrible truth. "I didn't ... I had to ... it w-wasn't ..."

Her heart ached for him, even as it was splintering on her own account. She knew how he sometimes struggled with words when he became flustered and how deeply it shamed him. She wanted to sink into his arms and make that burden disappear for him. To tell him elocution didn't matter. Because it didn't.

This wasn't about words. It was about deeds. And that, she had to get to the bottom of without delay.

"You do not need to explain anything." She set a careful hand atop the front of his coat, over his thundering heart. "Only answer this question with a single word. Did you leave England in exchange for payment from my mother?"

The muscles in his throat strained, and his fingers sank deeper into her shoulders until the pressure nearly hurt. His dark eyes flared, becoming frenzied, desperate, pleading ...

Guilty.

And then, he uttered the word that smashed the final pieces of her heart. "Yes."

"Just as I said. He took the bribe. Money was the greatest motivator of all." Her mother's words hit the edge of Amelia's awareness, delivering a final agonizing knock. The ache consumed her, no longer hindered by uncertainty but crashing down like a breaking wave.

She'd thought he was different. That was the whole reason she'd fallen in love with him in the first place. He didn't flatter her with false words or put on a show for the large dowry he served to gain. Instead, he accepted her for who she really was, just as she did him. Money played no part in it.

Except it had all been a lie.

She snatched her hand from his coat as if it had turned to flames and shrugged herself out from under his grip. "I thank you for your honesty, Your Grace."

She spun away, ignoring the shot of pain in her ankle. The Rockliffe carriage awaited, if only she could reach it.

Her footsteps were stiff, her knees on the verge of collapse, and the closer she got to the polished black coach, the more it appeared like a nefarious cavern.

Her mother had come for her. Her mother had betrayed her. Because the Dowager Marchioness of Rockliffe was hard and calculating, willing to do whatever it took to turn things the way she wanted them. But she was also no fool.

I did it to protect you.

Her mother must know things she did not. She'd seen through to Jonathan's true motivations all those years ago while Amelia had yearned for him blindly. And was it any wonder? For who was she but plain and silly Lady Amelia Prescott, ignorant of the way the world worked?

Little had changed. The fact she'd spent the past decade giving advice to others was almost laughable. And in this moment, she knew less than ever before.

From behind her came a clash of voices. Jonathan's. Her mother's. She barely heard them. Couldn't *allow* herself to hear them. She couldn't manage any further blows to her heart.

She kept going, accepting the footman's proffered hand to help her into the carriage, where she dropped upon one of the plush velvet benches. Rain had started again. That, or her eyes had once more clouded with tears. Whatever the case, the glass in the window blurred, and her mother's outline as she climbed into the carriage appeared misty.

Rain or not, the carriage glided into motion, so smooth and sturdy compared to the rickety vehicle that had tossed her about for the past week. She didn't know which direction they were going. Didn't care.

It all felt so wrong.

But the right thing didn't seem to exist anymore.

17

Amelia stared out the rain-streaked window as familiar scenery rushed by. The same fields and budding trees. The same fences and toll gate. She was on her way back to London, just as she'd planned, and her mother had ordered the coachman to travel as quickly as possible. No doubt hoping that in another day or two, they could pretend this fruitless detour had never happened.

If only that were possible. If only five days on the road hadn't ravaged her heart in a way she would never forget.

She peered at heavy gray clouds and relentless raindrops, waiting for them—wanting them—to swoop down and crush her.

But they didn't. Her world had been torn apart, dealt a blow even more devastating than the one from a decade prior, and still, she remained upright in the carriage. Not in the throes of panic but numb.

She waited for admonitions, questions, *something* from her mother. However, the dowager stayed surprisingly quiet, sitting across from her with a posture like an iron rod. Did that mean she was thinking, calculating? Or was she letting her ire wordlessly build until it exploded into something of epic proportions?

Whatever the case, her gaze pricked at Amelia's skin, and the silence became deafening to the point she could no longer bear it.

"I wasn't eloping," she muttered to the window, unable to meet her mother's eye. Even the word and what it suggested —*eloping*—was painful. Yet, if nothing else, she could at least make it clear that she hadn't purposely made the same foolish mistake twice. "My meeting with Jon—the duke happened by chance. I intended, upon leaving London, to travel to Foxhill. Alone."

Her mother's cane shifted against the carpeted floor. "May I ask *why*?"

Amelia's head did dart around, then, so she could assess her mother's face. Her narrow brows were arched again, her lips pursed. If anything, it was a look of bewilderment, not anger.

She didn't know.

She may have always been aware of Amelia's secret dealings with Jonathan Astley, but as for the Lady Lockheart debacle, she didn't know. She couldn't, for surely, she would give some indication had her daughter's name been cast into scandal all over London.

Felix Egerton must not have revealed anything yet. Which meant there was still time to get back, to stop him.

However, the realization brought but cold comfort. She could hardly make herself care about Lady Lockheart any longer. About scandal. What difference did it make if that aspect of her life fell apart with all the others?

She slumped against the seat back, too weary to maintain proper posture. "I suppose I wished for a break from society for a while. Just as Nicholas used to."

Silence fell over the carriage once more, save for the abrupt breath her mother drew in at the mention of the marquess's name. While she would never consent to speak on the subject, it was clear that her oldest son's disappearance troubled her greatly.

As for the matter at hand, there was no way Amelia's vague answer could have satisfied her. Amelia, too, had disappeared. She'd lied. She'd rebelled. All things for which her mother must want an explanation.

But instead of demanding it, she settled back against her seat, sparing a glance at the passing countryside. "I made it well known that you fell ill the night of the Englewood ball and haven't been able to leave your bed since. We can keep up the facade for another day or two after our return, should you still feel the need for a break."

Amelia tilted her head, feeling her lips part. The words were far less harsh than she could have expected. Despite her mother's continued stony expression, they rang almost kind.

She didn't know what to do with that. In a way, perhaps it would be easier to have fury shower down on her so, for once in her life, she could rage back. Her anger, while muted by shock, hadn't fully disappeared. On one hand, she despised the woman sitting across from her, who'd learned all her secrets and not said a word. Who'd gone behind her back and destroyed her youthful hopes and dreams. But on the other ...

I did it to protect you ... The phrase wouldn't stop turning through her mind.

"Why did you trick me?" Despite how dull and lifeless she felt, the question slipped out before she could stop it. At once, her mother turned from the window, and their eyes locked, filling her with a fresh wave of misery. "If you had concerns about Jon—*His Grace's* intentions, why couldn't you have simply addressed them with me?"

"Because." With that single word, any hint of warmth in her mother's tone rushed away, and all that remained was the typical woman of steel. "I had to ensure you understood the gravity of the situation. You surprised me, Amelia. I would have expected that sort of rebellion from your brothers but from you? Never. As I could no longer be certain I knew you, I therefore couldn't trust that you would heed my warnings. And it was imperative, given my knowledge of that swine Branscombe and the rest of his family, that you did."

"What knowledge, exactly?" Amelia's body was cold as if her veins had filled with water from the depths of the ocean.

"I'm sure I don't need to tell you about the former Duke of Branscombe's unsavoriness. The ton certainly spoke of it often enough, for he only became worse as the years went by. I always made a point to steer clear of the man and his relations, as any person of good sense should do. Therefore, it never even crossed my mind to be wary of him as I guided you through your first Season. Imagine my shock, then, when it reached my ears that the duke and his equally detestable offspring had been overheard bragging that they would soon be in possession of the Prescott dowry."

The chill set in deeper, sending a shiver up Amelia's spine.

"I wasn't familiar with the duke's nephew at the time I discovered what was transpiring behind my back. No one was, with the way he'd been kept shut away in a solicitor's office prior to that point. Regardless, he was one of *them*." Her mother's lips curled in distaste like her mouth had been flooded with something bitter. "I began reading your correspondence, Amelia; I won't pretend that I didn't. And when it became apparent that you were on the verge of making a life-altering mistake, I sought out Jonathan Astley immediately. I made it *very* clear that I was onto his family's schemes, and you weren't to be trifled with, and surprisingly, the sum it took to make him cease the whole endeavor wasn't even that high. However, just in case he thought to come crawling back for another attempt, I arranged for him to receive a note making it plain that you no longer welcomed his presence."

Amelia pressed a hand to her chest, choking down a cry. Her heart had already shattered once today, and now, it did so all over again. Everything she'd learned in that fateful confrontation outside The Golden Lion seemed so horrific, so far beyond belief, that she could almost think she'd misunderstood.

But no. Her mother's words dealt a blow that solidified the truth. Jonathan hadn't loved her. He'd used her for money, and when procuring her dowry hadn't gone as planned, he'd taken what he could get and fled.

"I'm tired." Abruptly, she turned her face to the window, shuffling her body until she was pressed into the corner of the carriage. She closed her eyes, shutting out her surroundings. Wishing she could shut off her thoughts. "Perhaps anything else that requires discussion could wait for another time."

Her mother uttered some surprisingly placid words of assent, but Amelia hardly heard them. She tugged her cloak tighter around her body, trying to let the sway of the carriage lull her.

Trying, but nowhere close to relaxation or sleep. Her chest was far too heavy. Her head too addled. Once again, she'd become a hapless bystander, getting tossed about in a world too powerful for her to control.

She squeezed her eyes more firmly closed, but if anything, that only made the pounding of hooves, whirring of wheels, and beating of raindrops against glass even louder. Sounds that had become a near constant over the past week. So much so that she could almost think herself back in that ramshackle carriage with a large, strong body crammed into the seat across from her and dark eyes assessing her with such intensity ...

The memories hurt. But even as the ache weighed her down, something else, vague but insistent, wriggled its way into her awareness. A question. A faint, half-formed protest. Jonathan was more than just the successor to a bankrupt dukedom. Thanks to Maxwell and Son, he'd found success and wealth in his own right. Surely, he had little need for her dowry at this point. And if that was the case, then why … why had he spent the past days making renewed promises of their future together?

She shivered, grabbing at her cloak's hood and pulling it around her head. It didn't erase the noises surrounding her, but at least it muted them.

Best not to travel down that road. Best not to think at all. For if she couldn't sleep, she also couldn't let herself hope.

Hope only led to disappointment.

18

Jonathan cast the account book he'd been holding onto the cluttered desktop, leaning back in his uncle's chair—no, *his* chair—with an exasperated sigh. He was good at figures, usually, but after spending the better part of the day going through page after page of shoddy account keeping, where the overarching theme was that the Edgecote estate required a vast amount of funds to make it serviceable again, his head was beginning to swim.

The lone chambermaid who remained at Edgecote Hall had gotten a fire going before he entered the study in the morning and had been surprisingly diligent about keeping it stoked throughout the day. Still, a damp chill hung over the room that penetrated to his marrow. It would no doubt take time to undo the lengthy period of neglect in the house. Likewise, ghosts from the past couldn't be vanquished with only a few flames.

As he reclined, his gaze fell upon the wall in front of him, and he could feel his lips turn down in a scowl. As his first order of business, he'd ordered the oversized portrait of Tobias

Astley, the Fifth Duke of Branscombe, to be removed from the study and shut away in the attic. Perhaps his uncle had enjoyed having his likeness peer down on him during those rare moments when he conceded to sit at his desk and attend to duty. Jonathan, on the other hand, would rather peruse ledgers in the ninth circle of hell than look upon that haughty face. However, the portrait had left its mark, creating a large, perfect rectangle that stood out amidst the faded wallpaper around it. Refusing to let him forget its existence.

For that matter, every surface of the study held the taint of the former duke. The quills he'd once held in his fingers. The threadbare carpet he'd once trod on. The whole damn house was haunted. There was no denying it and no way to fix it, either.

Just days ago, he'd allowed himself to imagine differently. To dream of soft footsteps, the gentlest voice, and red-gold hair illuminating the gloominess within these walls. In time, maybe there would even be the patter of tiny feet and a host of delighted laughter. Until, eventually, the darkness would be replaced by something pure and good.

But that dream was gone now.

He lunged forward, grabbing the crystal brandy decanter he'd placed upon the corner of his desk. And stilled, a muttered curse crossing his lips. The old duke would have dealt with his troubles by becoming foxed enough to forget them. The new duke was supposed to do better.

He slumped his elbows against the desktop, pressing his fingertips into the bridge of his nose. He'd stepped back onto English soil *trying* to do better. Instead, the past had caught up with him, and everything had fallen apart.

As he sat in silence, attempting to push away the tension in his forehead, even the dulled mahogany beneath his elbows began to feel tainted. For his uncle's shirtsleeves had once rested here, too, as the distasteful man sat barking out orders. Concocting schemes. Just as he'd done all those years ago in his study in London on that fateful day when Jonathan had been summoned.

Witless, nineteen-year-old Jonathan, whose head had been so filled with memories of secret meetings in gardens and the softest, most kissable lips that he didn't think to feel trepidation or dread regarding what ton event he might be summoned to next. In fact, he'd walked into the study with lightness in his step. All until his uncle had fixed him with a knowing sneer. A look that was equal parts gleeful and malicious, that tore into him and seemed to expose him down to his soul. *So. It seems you're not as dimwitted as we believed.*

"Your Grace?" A crackly voice cut into his thoughts, and his gaze traveled across the room, where Davis, the ancient butler, stood in the doorway, his arms laden with a paper-wrapped bundle. "Your secretary sent along the"—he paused to clear his throat—"*documents* you requested."

Jonathan hurriedly straightened against the chairback, sweeping the pile of account books to the side to leave a bare space on the desk. "Please, set them down here."

Davis hobbled in, holding the bundle tight in his knobby arms. When he arrived beside the desk, he deposited it carefully before lifting his hunched shoulders. "There you are, Your Grace. Will there be anything else?"

Jonathan glanced up at the butler's craggy face. Why the man had stayed on with such a detestable—and then absent—employer for all this time, Jonathan couldn't say. Force of habit, mayhap? Whatever the case, Davis had always seemed a decent enough sort. Far more attentive than the staff of the London house. Not apt to look at Jonathan with derision, even all those years ago when he'd been a stammering schoolboy and not a duke.

"Nothing." Jonathan shook his head, making a note to himself that Davis required a raise. And an increase in his pension, whenever he chose to take it. "Only, Davis? Close the door on your way out, and see that I'm not disturbed."

The butler offered him a stiff bow, and Jonathan watched him retreat, drumming his fingers atop the brown paper as he waited for the door to close behind him. Only then did he tear the paper apart, revealing the contents of the bundle. Letting the dozens of issues of *The Ladies' Spectator* spill across his desk.

He spread them out, these years' worth of Amelia's secret writing. The key to a hidden part of her.

All he had left.

Dates were printed at the top of each cover. *February 1806 ... December 1805 ...* He thumbed through them, working his way back through time. Certain months were missing here and there, but for the most part, the issues kept going. *January 1802 ... May 1799 ...*

He set them all to the side, the haphazard pile growing and growing until, at last, a lone magazine remained untouched, and the dates went back no farther.

July 1795. He may as well start at the beginning.

He flipped through pages one by one. Fashion plates. Poetry. Needlework patterns. Nothing of particular interest to him, yet his pulse thrummed with anticipation. He kept going, past a short story and a gossip column. Until finally, just a few pages from the back, there it was. *My Dear Lady Lockheart.*

His fingers tightened around the magazine's edge, and although he could make out the words perfectly well while it rested on the desktop, he lifted it, bringing it closer to his face. And read.

My Dear Lady Lockheart,

I accepted a gentleman's marriage proposal, thinking for sure he reciprocated the great love I developed for him. But as it turned out, everything he told me was a lie.

He did not desire a life with me after all, nor did he hold any true feelings of love. For—it pains me to write this—he jilted me right before our wedding. Not even to my face, but through a hastily scrawled note claiming he had made a mistake and would never see me again.

How could I have been so terribly misguided? Our courtship was obviously naught but a game to him. For me, however, it was real. How can I recover from this devastating heartache? And most importantly, how can I ensure this never happens again?

Sincerely,

Miss Lovelorn

Amidst the stillness in the room, Jonathan realized his hands had begun shaking. *Everything he told me was a lie ... He did not desire a life with me ... Nor did he hold any true feelings of love ...*

She'd written this about herself. About what he'd done to her. He drew in a ragged breath, feeling like he'd been punched in the stomach.

She didn't understand. That wasn't the way of things at all.

He clenched his fingers to make the page stop wavering, and his eyes traveled over the remaining words.

My Dear Miss Lovelorn,

Gentlemen can be fickle creatures, I'm afraid, which it seems you've learned the hard way. Alas, this false gentleman of yours has come and gone, and there's naught left to do but forget him.

I understand full well the eagerness of young ladies to make a suitable match. However, I would advise that in future, should another happen along who catches your fancy, you take the time to truly learn every aspect of him. Trust is too vital a thing to forge in an instant. It may take weeks. Months. Whatever the timeframe, I cannot emphasize enough the importance of waiting to ensure it's there and that the two of you will suit. If you'll permit me the boldness, I would even go so far as to say that if you cannot swear, with every fiber of your being, that this trust exists and you're certain of his sentiments and intentions, you should forgo the union altogether. While this is surely an unpopular opinion, I would argue that remaining unwed is preferable to a marriage filled with heartache and misery. The heart, after all, is a delicate thing, worthy of safeguarding at all costs.

With my sincerest wishes for your future prosperity and happiness,

Lady Lockheart

"No." Jonathan's strangled voice crackled through the silent study. This was all wrong. So bloody wrong.

She'd spent the past decade building walls around her heart. Thinking she'd been trifled with by a fickle, faithless cad. Not that she was mistaken in disdaining him. He had plenty of sins to atone for. He hadn't been honest with her. Yet amidst the tangle of half-truths and regrets, one thing had remained a constant. He loved Amelia Prescott to the ends of the earth and to the stars in the sky.

And she didn't know.

She didn't know because she'd never received his final letter. A forgery had reached her instead.

He lowered the magazine back to the desk, letting the pages slip from his rigid fingers. Once again, his eyes fell upon the unfaded patch of wallpaper that had formerly displayed a portrait. That damnable relic of the past containing the likeness of a man so depraved he made the Dowager Marchioness of Rockliffe's scheming seem downright pleasant.

Suddenly, a realization hit him, its force more powerful than the waves on the night he'd jumped into the South China Sea.

He'd accepted Lady Rockliffe's money, but to the best of his knowledge, she hadn't been aware of his intended use for it. She'd referenced his family's duplicity, but did she really know the whole truth of the situation? For his uncle, despite his typical carelessness, had ensured it remained a well-guarded secret. And if the dowager didn't know, then Amelia didn't, either. She had no explanation for his departure but greed and a changeable heart.

He slumped his body back toward the desk, letting his head rest in his hands again. What was he doing, shut away at Edgecote like this? Especially after his grand speeches about facing adversity head-on.

He'd retreated because Amelia would no longer welcome his presence alongside her. Because without her, what else did he have in London? Another tainted house. A club whose members ridiculed him. The House of Lords, where he was more apt to become a laughingstock than to deliver successful speeches on the subject closest to his heart.

It didn't matter. The Rockliffe coach had headed south—presumably to London—so that's where he needed to travel, too. Amelia may very well refuse to speak with him, but he at least had to try. To tell her the things he'd kept hidden so she could make up her mind based on the truth. Having her listen, of course, wouldn't guarantee anything. She may still consider him irredeemable, and he wouldn't blame her for that. However, if there was even the smallest possibility she could see her way to forgiveness ...

It was a chance he had to take, daunting though it may be. The past was a heavy, dangerous thing. But once all the long-kept secrets came out in the open, then maybe ...

Maybe there was also hope for the future.

19

A commotion was afoot in the Rockliffe House entrance hall. What had started as a knock upon the front door led to an exchange between muffled male voices, accompanied by occasional quips from a female voice, which eventually caused Flynt, the house's stoic-faced butler, to begin shouting. As the volume rose, fragments of his irate exclamations floated into the drawing room. *Impossible ... Not receiving visitors ...*

Amelia shifted on the sofa and glanced up from the novel she'd been trying, unsuccessfully, to read. It wasn't every day that Flynt lost his temper. In fact, it had never happened in her lifetime, from what she could recall.

Even so, her spark of curiosity lasted only a moment before her eyes fell back to the page of words she didn't care about. For five days now, she'd been back in London, and still, her weariness wouldn't abate. Her heart wouldn't stop aching.

And so, she'd taken advantage of the rumors circulating that she'd fallen ill and used them as an excuse to live as an invalid. Not leaving the house. Not seeing anyone. Even her mother had respected her wishes for solitude and left her be, allowing her to take trays in her room and not pushing her to get back into society.

This in-between existence couldn't last forever, of course. The outside world couldn't always be held at bay. However, for the time being, that's exactly where it remained, and she wasn't ready for that to change. Which was exactly why she didn't let herself get caught up in the events transpiring in the entrance hall. They'd originated beyond these walls, and therefore, they didn't concern her.

All until her flush-faced lady's maid, Gwen, burst into the drawing room, her movements so rapid that she stumbled over her curtsey and her words came out breathless. "My lady, there's a gentleman here to see you."

Amelia's heart was foolish enough to skip a beat.

"A Mr. Felix Egerton," Gwen continued, and all at once, the flutter in Amelia's chest became a cold, heavy weight. "He's been here every day for the past week. Your mother advised Flynt that you were not accepting callers, but Mr. Egerton has been growing more insistent, and with Lady Rockliffe on Bond Street for the morning, I wondered if perhaps ... well, I thought I would ask if you might feel differently today."

Gwen regarded her with a knowing glint in her eye. As the person who'd secretly assisted with the Lady Lockheart venture for all these years, she was also willing, it seemed, to go against the dowager's instructions and facilitate a meeting between Amelia and her gentleman caller if that's what she desired.

If only Gwen knew the truth about the gentleman in question.

Amelia brought a hand to her nape, finding it dotted with small beads of perspiration. Why couldn't Flynt, in addition to yelling, toss Egerton into the street? The male voices continued echoing through the entrance hall, the rejoinder to

Flynt's becoming loud enough that she could recognize it as belonging to the man from the Englewood ball.

Until suddenly, another voice burst into her awareness. Not real but a crystal clear memory. *You don't need to hide or let some worthless bastard have control over you.*

Her heart skittered again. Life as she knew it had been pulled out from under her since Jonathan had spoken those words, and she *did* want to hide. To disappear and wallow in her misery until she found the strength to regain her footing.

Except then, another memory flashed to the forefront. Felix Egerton's rakish face looking up at her on the Englewood House terrace, smug with the knowledge that he had the upper hand.

He could very well be wearing that look right now, growing haughtier each time he visited only to be turned away. For he alone realized the circumstances preceding her sudden illness and disappearance from society. He knew he'd been the one responsible, could no doubt picture her cowering within the walls of her town house, growing more desperate by the hour as she faced an impossible choice: submit to his will or have her secret blasted into the open.

"My lady?" Gwen peered at her quizzically, and she realized that her teeth were clenched, and her hands had balled into fists around the airy muslin of her skirts.

You don't have to let some worthless bastard have control over you.

No, she didn't, did she? Much may have changed in the past week, but those words still rang true. She had a choice. It was time she made the right one.

"Send him in, please, Gwen."

She nearly clamped her hand over her mouth the moment the words escaped. The voice that came out, so smooth and cold, sounded less like her own and more like the Dowager Marchioness of Rockliffe's. The woman with whom she'd always thought she had nothing in common beyond shared blood.

But if ever there was a time for her to adopt her mother's steely resolve, this was it.

She didn't miss the way Gwen's eyebrows shifted upward from the uncharacteristic tone. In the end, though, her maid simply nodded and left the room, going off to manage the commotion in the entrance hall.

Only then did Amelia scramble, shoving her book beneath a cushion and pulling her ankle down from the mound of pillows atop the footstool in front of her. Felix Egerton needn't know about her ankle injury. He needn't see any signs of weakness at all.

She was in the midst of straightening her bodice when Gwen's footsteps returned to the corridor, followed by the steady thump of boots. She pressed her hands into her lap, squeezing them together, willing them not to tremble.

There was no more time. Gwen and Flynt appeared in the doorway, and the top of a sandy-colored head emerged behind the butler's shoulder.

"Mr. Felix Egerton, my lady." Flynt stepped forward, his nose wrinkling as if he smelled something unpleasant.

"Thank you, Flynt." She kept her eyes on the perturbed butler and her perplexed lady's maid, not paying heed to the man who approached from behind them. "You may go, but please, keep the door open on your way out. Gwen, if you could kindly wait in the corridor, I would be much obliged. Mr. Egerton and I shan't be long."

They both had doubts about obeying her; she could see it in their faces—perhaps because Lady Amelia wasn't the type to give orders, especially if they involved something on the edge of impropriety. However, because obeying was what longtime servants at Rockliffe House were well trained to do, they both departed without another word, Flynt heading back down the corridor, Gwen taking up her post outside the door.

Leaving Felix Egerton free to swoop in, his steps downright jaunty as he approached the sofa.

"How good to see you, my dear Lady L—" He paused, his grin widening to display a gleaming set of teeth. "Amelia."

He would never tire of that jest, would he? She frowned, not inviting him to sit, although he did anyway, lowering himself into the wingback chair to her right. In the light of day, everything about him seemed sharper. The carefully styled curls atop his forehead. The angles of his boyish face. The gold threads in his paisley waistcoat.

There was no denying that his revolting interior was veiled by youthful good looks. There was even less denying that she despised him.

Yet she squeezed her fingers again, refusing to let him see anything but indifference. "Mr. Egerton." She gave him the barest of nods.

"I confess, I was beginning to grow worried." He was staring at her in a manner that wasn't altogether polite, his gaze resting on the loose locks of hair that ended above her shoulder. "Lady Amelia Prescott, taken ill at the Englewood ball and not seen since. What, I wonder, could have caused such a terrible thing? It's peculiar, though. You look well enough to me."

She tilted her chin upward, forcing herself to keep meeting his eye. "It was nothing serious, and any reports you heard to the contrary were exaggerated. I'm quite well now."

"Oh, but I'm glad to hear it." He smiled again, the humor in his expression tinged with malice. "Might that be because, after a period of reflection, you've determined that the solution to your troubles is really quite simple?"

She snapped her lips together, not willing to dignify that

with an answer. There was nothing simple about this! Her mind traveled back to the day of the attempted robbery on the Great North Road, when her knee had sprung up, almost of its own accord, to connect with the footpad's groin and send him reeling. If only she could perform a similar action on Mr. Egerton.

He gave an irritated huff that broke the silence. "I trust you've given more thought to my proposal," he prodded. "I'm most eager to hear your response."

Her knees began trembling beneath her skirts, and she clamped them together, forcing them to be still. Stiffening her shoulders, making her spine remain tall.

Beautiful. Resilient. Brave. Strong. The words Jonathan had spoken to her between kisses, the qualities he'd recognized in her even when she didn't see them in herself. Since that day, so much she'd believed about their relationship had been revealed to be a lie. However, that didn't mean those words were no longer true.

She'd felt strong within his arms, like she could conquer London or anything else that came her way. She would do herself a disservice by not believing she could conquer it without him, too.

This was her pivotal moment. And suddenly, she knew exactly what she needed to do.

"I have," she said. And she smiled. That sweet, welcoming Lady Amelia smile she'd spent years practicing, displaying to the ton even amidst scandal, loss, and secret heartbreak. The look caused Felix Egerton's eyes to light up, for him to lean toward her in his chair. She leaned forward, too, so there could be no mistaking what she was about to say. So he could recognize the exact moment when the smile fell from her lips and her face returned to a mask of ice. "I wouldn't marry you if you were the last man on earth."

Mr. Egerton recoiled instantly, his pale eyes turning flinty.

"Was I not clear enough on the consequences should you refuse?"

"Perfectly clear," she spat, her hand going toward the end table, to the little bell that would call for Flynt to show him out. "Will there be anything else?"

He scowled, then turned toward the window, his forehead creased in thought. His boots tapped against the rug, a quiet thump that proved grating nonetheless. Until all at once, his feet stilled, and he turned back to her, his face eerily placid.

"Nothing else for the moment. I'll take my leave." He grinned again, sly and dangerous. "I won't call again without your invitation. However, I certainly hope your health will permit you to attend Lady Symonds's ball this Friday."

Her stomach roiled, filled with a blossoming sense of unease. Her mother had mentioned the event to her in passing as Amelia half-listened, unable to summon anything but disinterest. Yet, with Egerton's seemingly innocuous question, the ball took on a note of foreboding.

Still, she remained statuesque, managing speech despite a throat grown too tight. "I wouldn't miss it."

"Good. I have a feeling it will be the talk of the Season." He rose from his chair and straightened his coat, the unmistakable promise in his words making her stifle a gasp. "Well, good day, Lady Lockheart. I'll see myself out. And remember, if you have any second thoughts before Friday, you need only send word. I am, after all, a reasonable man."

With that, he swept from the room, the tails of his fine green coat flapping behind him with each of his arrogant strides. She held her breath, watching him go, staring at the doorway with a razor-sharp gaze.

Only when his footsteps faded back into the entrance hall and Flynt bid him some indistinct but brusque words of farewell did she slump against the sofa back and blow the air from her lungs, pressing a hand to her pounding heart.

"My lady!" In the next instant, Gwen appeared, rushing over to the sofa and kneeling at her side. "Forgive me. I thought you might want to see the gentleman, but that meeting didn't sound altogether amicable. Has something happened?"

Amelia peered at the carpet, struggling to catch her breath. "He knows," she choked out, feeling her face go bloodless and cold. "About Lady Lockheart. He knows, and he plans to tell everyone."

Gwen let out an audible gasp. "Oh, no, my lady, surely—"

"I could have stopped him." Amelia shifted her eyes upward to a face as stricken and pale as her own must be. "For a price. But I didn't."

While Felix Egerton had remained in the room, she'd almost felt like she stepped outside herself, as if someone else controlled her speech and movements. However, now that the confrontation was over, and she spoke the words aloud, the magnitude of what she'd just done hit her with full force.

"I didn't," she repeated, shaking her head, while visions of the future dashed through her thoughts. The ball in two days' time, an annual event that was always well attended by the most prominent members of the ton. So many eyes upon her, so many whispers involving her name. A decade-long secret hers to keep no more.

Gwen remained beside her, silent and contemplative. Waiting for any instructions her mistress might have or requests she could fulfill that would ease Amelia's distress.

But what else was there to say or ask for? Nothing would make this go away.

Amelia had two days. Two days before she became Lady Lockheart to all of London, two days during which she could still change her mind.

She wouldn't, though. In a world where she could trust very little anymore, there was one point of which she was absolutely certain. *Nothing* would make her go crawling to Felix Egerton with her tail between her legs. If last week's disastrous road trip had taught her anything, it was that she was better than that.

She wouldn't waver. Whatever that decision meant for her future—be it a barrage of the ton's gossip, or another Prescott scandal, or she and her column both becoming a mockery—she *wouldn't*.

Whether that made her incredibly brave or incredibly foolish remained to be seen.

20

The back garden of Rockliffe House hadn't changed much over the past decade. The hedges were perhaps more prominent. There was a two-tiered stone fountain, carved with birds around the basin, that hadn't been there before. The trees, showing their first signs of springtime buds, had grown taller.

Those things aside, though, Jonathan could notice little in the moonlit garden to differentiate it from the space he'd traversed frequently as a young man of nineteen. Notably, the stately oak still stood near the house, one of its sprawling branches leading directly to Amelia's bedchamber window, where candlelight flickered behind the thick panes of glass.

He approached the tree trunk, moving cautiously so his boots wouldn't crunch against the gravel path. An action in which he'd once been well-practiced. The difference was that back then, he'd always known Amelia awaited him, ready to give him a welcome comprised of kisses. Tonight, on the other hand ...

A pit formed in his stomach as he bent to pick up a small stone next to his foot. Tonight, he'd received no invitation.

Warranted no welcome. She might very well regard him with contempt, if she deigned to look at him at all. All because of circumstances he'd brought about with his own detrimental mistakes. Still, he had to try.

He positioned himself beneath the oak's wide, most significant branch, casting the stone upward so it hit the window above with a quiet knock.

The stone fell back to the ground, followed by silence. Stillness. Not even a breath of wind to shake up the cool midnight air. He waited, feeling like both a green boy anticipating an encounter with his first sweetheart and an old, enervated traveler with the weight of the world on his shoulders. His heart pounded, fast but heavy. Until suddenly, a shadow moved behind the glass, and all at once, a face appeared. A slender, beloved, beautiful face that peered out into the night, scanning the garden with eyes that seemed far away, as if they belonged to another time.

She looked out at the branches and the starry sky beyond. And then, she looked to the ground. To him. She was far above him, the intricacies of her features unclear behind the glass. Yet he could still detect the moment her lips parted and her eyes grew large, the way her body jerked and then froze.

For a long moment, they peered at each other through the window, separated by a trivial distance that simultaneously felt wider than the oceans, and all he could do was stand there, willing her not to turn away.

She didn't. Instead, her hands went to the sash, and in one swift, noiseless motion, the window came open, and she stuck her head out into the darkness. "What are you doing here?" Her face had become blank and her voice monotonous, giving away nothing about how she felt toward the uninvited visitor in her garden.

He chanced a step closer to the house. He was here to explain. To atone. To lay all his shameful misdeeds at her feet.

So that at least if she deemed his actions unforgivable, she would be making the judgment based on facts and not with secrets left between them.

A familiar lump rose in his throat, the one that made his words catch and tangle. "I need to speak with you." He would need to focus, to maintain his composure, or speech would become altogether impossible. "P-please."

Another pause, and another of Amelia's assessing looks. If she rejected him, he wouldn't have the words to convince her to change her mind—

"All right."

All right. His body nearly sagged from relief. That was the first step successfully completed, in any case. Even if what followed would prove more challenging still.

She reached out, her fingers skirting the oak branch where she used to plant her feet before hopping to the ground and into his waiting arms. "I'm afraid tree-climbing is beyond my abilities at present. That being the case, I suppose you'll have to come up."

An invitation to Amelia's bedchamber. The idea seemed almost surreal. However, he didn't have time to ponder it. In the next instant, he was hefting himself up the oak tree, grasping at rough limbs until he reached the branch that allowed him to slide through the open window.

At once, he was enveloped in a warm, intimate room, illuminated by the glow of a vigorous fire and scented faintly by her sweet apple blossom perfume. He couldn't help but glance around, to take in this private space and the small details that spoke of her presence. The bed, with its plush floral counterpane, where she dreamed her dreams and cried her sorrows. The dainty gilded escritoire where she must write the words of advice so beloved by the ladies of London. The vanity, atop which rested the same silver hairbrush she'd brought along during their travels.

But most important of all, there was Amelia herself, clad in a white dressing gown of billowy cotton that draped around her and dusted the floor.

"Well?" She pulled the window back down, shutting out the springtime chill. Shutting them in together. When she turned to him, her eyes caught the firelight, making the blue glitter like lakes beneath the sun. "What did you wish to speak of? My mother and my lady's maid are already abed, but still, I think it best we not take any chances by dawdling."

I don't deserve your love, but I love you anyway, and I'm sorry, I'm sorry, I'm sorry ...

He swallowed. One step at a time. He needed to explain everything—every painful detail—in a way that would obliterate any misunderstandings. "You didn't receive the letter I tried to send you all those years ago. Before I left England." He enunciated each word carefully, willing himself not to stumble. "I would like to explain what happened."

Her arms came up to cross her chest, her fingernails sinking into the white cotton at her arms. "I'm not certain we need to discuss the past any longer. What's done is done."

He hated the flash of pain that marred her features before she schooled them back to neutral, hated even more that he'd put it there. But he had to keep going. Whether that made him brave and persistent or a selfish bastard, he no longer could say, but he had to keep going. "Please."

Her chest rose and fell with her silent inhales and exhales, and the column of her throat, golden beneath the flickering flames, appeared tight. Until finally, a barely perceptible sigh of resignation and more words, the same ones as before, the best ones he could hope for. "All right." Without another second's hesitation, she strode away, her footsteps pattering across the carpet until she reached her bed and lowered herself to sit on the edge.

Taking even greater care than he had on the gravel outside

to ensure his boots didn't make a sound, he followed her to the bedside. Where he stilled. The counterpane beneath her appeared soft and inviting, and if he could only sit down beside her, he would feel the warmth of her body, the gentle motions of her breath. His mind flew back to a stiff, uncomfortable bed that had become the best place in the world because he'd awoken there with her in his arms.

He didn't merit that privilege now.

She was looking up at him with her arms still crossed. Waiting. He would talk to her as he was, then, standing close enough that he wouldn't have to raise his voice above a murmur to be heard. Not so close as to cross a prohibited boundary.

"I'm not sure how my uncle discovered our association." He spoke deliberately again, knowing the words were only going to get harder. Not wanting to relive that period of his life but needing to. "Regardless, when he summoned me to Branscombe House, a fortnight after the Englewood ball, he was more complimentary toward me than ever I'd seen him. Being the heartless sot he was, he could see it only as a scheme I'd concocted to obtain a dowry, and in turn, he considered how the funds could serve him. His gross mismanagement of money had left him with copious financial woes, even back then."

He held back a grimace, the mere mention of his uncle's depravity leaving an acerbic taste in his mouth. "I tried not to think of him. You made me feel happy and hopeful for the first time in so long, and I wanted what we had together to be my sole focus. However, as the days progressed, his summons grew more frequent and his comments more insistent. That's when I began thinking we should elope. To go far from society and especially from him. My uncle seemed to have a talent for taking all things good and destroying them, and I couldn't abide the thought of him doing that to you. To us."

He took a breath, the long-held dull ache within him augmenting to a sharp stab of pain. "Perhaps we would have escaped to Gretna Green and then lived our quiet existence in a cottage somewhere had I kept my mouth shut. But I didn't. After all the years I spent choking and stammering in my uncle's presence, I finally found the voice to shout at him. I told him he would never see me again, that he would never get a penny of any funds I happened to accrue. And that's when he said ..."

He broke off, his throat feeling raw. His chest tight. This was the part where all his shame, regret, and sorrow would come to the forefront, and it would hurt. But he had to keep going. Or rather, to go back and fill in the missing pieces. "Uncle Tobias became my guardian when I was ten years old. My mother had died of a fever two years prior, and as for my father ..." He paused again, finding the words he'd been long ago forbidden to reveal. "Her death exacerbated some long-time struggles he dealt with, and he was eventually declared *non compos mentis*. Insane."

Amelia sucked in a quick gulp of air, her shoulders stiffening. In that moment, what he'd grown to suspect became blatantly apparent: she hadn't known.

"He was sent to a private madhouse in Greenwich, and on rare occasions as I grew older, I was allowed to visit him. My uncle, however, never wished to speak of his younger brother Robert, to be reminded of the taint of madness in the blood. As my father had chosen to spend his adult life in the country, away from society, Tobias found it easiest to put out that he'd died. He said that if I ever dared to publicly contradict him, I'd be apt to end up in a madhouse myself, given how I, too, had an affliction bordering on idiocy."

Jonathan curled his hands into fists, trying to quash the intertwining sensations of outrage and despair that had so often kept him awake at night when he was a youth. "That's the way it stayed until that day in the Branscombe House study when I shouted my intentions to disappear. That's when, after close to a decade of refusing to speak with me on the subject, my uncle said ..."

He released his fingers, digging them into the sides of his breeches to keep himself steady. He was back to where he'd started, and he had to get the words out. He *had* to. "He said my father's board was growing too expensive and that if I didn't see fit to procure a dowry and give him his due, my father would have to be moved elsewhere."

Again, Amelia let out a quiet gasp, and strained lines appeared around the corners of her eyes.

"It was never about the dowry for me," he rushed to say. "Please, if nothing else, believe that. All I ever wanted was you and the quiet cottage. But the situation with my father ... I knew then that I had to tell you everything."

Because while he'd never told her a deliberate untruth, nor had he cleared up the common misconception regarding his father. They'd simply never spoken on the subject at all, preferring to keep their conversations light, as if the turmoil of the real world didn't exist. Until it had all blown up in his face.

"I went to Rockliffe House that night." His stomach roiled, the same way it had back then as he'd hurried over the familiar roads while clinging to the faint hope that he could salvage everything despite his mistakes. "However, when I arrived in the back garden, it wasn't empty for a change. Footmen appeared out of nowhere, and then ... then, your mother."

Amelia's face still looked tense, although she didn't gasp or startle at that revelation. Perhaps the Dowager Lady Rockliffe had already told her this part of the story. Regardless, as long as he had her sitting rapt on the bed before him, he needed her to hear his side of the story, too.

"The dowager marchioness didn't mince words. She

informed me that she knew of my deception and my family's scheming, and that you'd been made aware of it as well." His jaw stiffened at the memory. Knowing what he did now about the forged letters led to a question: how much of what the dowager had told him that night was truth and how much had been due to trickery of her own? "I insisted that I needed to see you to explain, while she insisted just as adamantly that you wouldn't consent to it, and she wouldn't allow it. And then, she made me an offer."

He swallowed down bile, reliving the desperation that had clawed through him as he stood in the garden and his life fell apart. "One thousand pounds if I never showed my face again. If I swore I would leave you be. I thought you despised me, that I had ruined everything by withholding my secret from you. And so, I accepted."

Amelia's eyes were beginning to glimmer with moisture, and a sting crept up in the corners of his own. "I accepted," he repeated, "and by the next morning, I had two things in my possession. A sealed letter from you and the funds. I couldn't allow myself to think. I simply took the money to Goodman House in Greenwich. If I could do nothing else, I had to ensure my father's living arrangements didn't get disrupted. He may have been far removed from his former self and the world around him by that point, but there was a garden where he liked to sit, and he had his own bedchamber, clean and comfortable. Far superior to some of the asylums, about which I'd heard horrific tales."

Jonathan had done so well with his words, getting them out, one after another. However, that last part made his voice waver, and he could feel himself spiraling downward, his limbs beginning to shake. "I was t-too late. My uncle, the goddamn liar, had seen him moved three weeks prior. It wouldn't have mattered if I'd procured all the riches in England, for the duke had already decided his brother wasn't worth the expense."

Amelia's face creased with horror, and his own mouth grew tight, not wanting to keep moving, although he couldn't stop. Not yet. "At least, with the right amount of coin, I was able to convince one of the orderlies to tell me where," he said, his voice a low, strained hum. "An establishment in Hoxton. I rode there as quickly as I could. But ... but I was too late."

Again, that terrible truth, the one that would never cease plaguing him, even were he to live until the end of time. "I found him in the stable. Chained to the wall, crammed in with the other pauper lunatics." It was a scene that came to him just as vividly as the day it had happened. The dark, the damp, the filth. The smell that had caused him to retch. The plaintive, nonsensical shouts. "The conditions in that stable weren't fit for a rat. Yet it had become my father's home. He lay on the floor, ravaged by fever. B-because I was too late."

He wasn't sure exactly what happened next. Only that one moment, a soft hand reached out, the slender fingers becoming entwined with his, and the next, he was atop the bed, sitting next to her. No longer needing to support his weight, able to sink his elbows into his lap and rest his head in his hands. "I was too late to save him. On time only to sit on the floor beside him as he ... as he t-took his last breaths."

A strangled sound tore from his throat, and suddenly, her arms were around him, her chin pressing into his shoulder. "I'm so sorry," she whispered, her words choked by a sob. "I didn't realize. I'm sorry."

She continued to hold him tight, as all he could do was stare into his lap, inundated by the weight of the secret he'd carried around the world but had never spoken of aloud. It tore him apart, the memory of the day he'd lost everything that meant anything to him. And yes, he could curse the old Duke of Branscombe for his treachery and the Dowager Marchioness of Rockliffe for her interference, but at the end of the day, the burden of blame lay on Jonathan's shoulders, too. He'd failed the only people he loved.

"Why did I hide the truth?" Finally, he managed to look up into eyes of pure, perfect blue. She was so gentle, so trusting. He didn't deserve her. "When I was young, my father used to practice words with me on his good days. He would have me read passages from books. Recite poetry. *Take your time*, he would say. *Keep trying, and you'll get it*." His voice broke again, his entire body frigid and excruciatingly aching as if he were being torn apart limb by limb. "He was never ashamed of me. Why did I not give him the same courtesy in return? W-why was I not there when he needed me?"

"Your father's death wasn't your fault." Soothing hands stroked his hair. Clasped his arms. "You had not yet reached the age of majority, and your uncle played guardian to you both. There was nothing you could have done to stop him."

He shuddered despite her warming touch. *Maybe* ... Yet the questions would always remain: What would have happened had he been more attentive to his uncle's dealings? And what would have happened had he been honest with Amelia right from the start?

He cleared his throat, pushing back bitterness, tightness, and a guttural moan of anguish that lingered right below the surface. There was one final piece of the story to tell. "I went to the docks that night—the night we were supposed to depart for Gretna Green. There was nothing left for me in England any longer. I stopped only to post my newfound funds to Goodman House in the hopes that the money would allow them to take on some charity cases and spare them the misery of a madhouse like in Hoxton. Then, I stopped at Rockliffe House one final time to deliver one final letter. I handed it to a scullery maid. But I suppose it shouldn't surprise me that it never reached you."

"I wish it had. I wish I'd known." She peered at him, long

and deep, the flickering candlelight illuminating her sorrow. "I wish I'd always known."

The muscles in his chest clenched. How he wished, too.

For a moment, they simply sat together, silence enwrapping him in a web of regret and grief. Some things could never be undone, and some aches could never heal. Yet, if nothing else, he'd at least managed to give her the honesty she deserved. Without the burden of deceit on his shoulders, he could go forward a tiny bit lighter, knowing that whatever was to happen between them would be based on truth.

"You don't have to say anything else about it right now." He clasped the delicate hand that still rested atop his arm, giving himself a final moment to savor the touch he would always long for. "I know none of this is to be taken lightly, and I want you to have time to think ... to consider ..."

With great difficulty, he pulled his hand away, reaching into his pocket to retrieve the sealed sheet of paper and depositing it into her lap. "After what happened with our previous correspondence, I wanted to deliver this letter to you myself."

They gazed at one another again, and in the span of seconds, he attempted to memorize every intricate detail he could. The pattern of freckles across her nose. The slight curl to her golden lashes. The tiny indentation in her chin.

If he never had the privilege of sitting this close to her again, these details would have to sustain him for a lifetime.

"You are under no obligation to read it." His fingers went to a stray strand of hair that fell across her cheek and, just one more time, tucked it behind her ear. "Just as you are under no obligation to grant me forgiveness. However, when the time comes that you feel ready—*if* that time comes—I want you to have no doubt as to how I feel about you."

She glanced down at her lap as her hand curled around the page, and when she looked up again, her eyes were a wide, shimmering blue, seeming to contain depths they hadn't before. Yet, at the same time, they were still recognizable as belonging to the girl who'd claimed his heart in a frosty garden all those years ago. And to the woman with whom he'd spent a disastrous week on the road, falling in love all over again.

And because he wasn't as strong as he should be, he leaned in until his lips brushed against hers in a light, reverent caress. The farewell they hadn't gotten a decade prior.

Only then did he tear away, pushing back up to his feet before he could find himself lacking the strength to do that, too.

"I'll be at Branscombe House," he said when he reached the window, his voice turning into a low rasp. "If ... if you ever wish to send word. Or if you need anything."

He lifted the sash noiselessly, the resulting blast of cold air providing a stark reminder of the outside world. He possessed little more than the shell of his body, for the rest of him remained beside her on the bed. Wanting her. Loving her. However, it was time for him to go.

He allowed himself one final look at the figure sitting atop the counterpane. She hadn't said a word, hadn't moved, although her fingers still clutched the letter tight. Hers to open —or not—as she pleased, depending on what she did with the weight of everything he'd told her.

There was nothing left but to wait. To give her time.

And so, with one deft motion, he grabbed hold of the awaiting tree branch and slipped back into the night.

21

Amelia spent the night tossing and turning, waiting for the first light of dawn to streak through her bedchamber window. Her mind raced, returning to the late-night tap against the windowpane and the resulting scene that would have felt like a dream had the revelations it contained not been so shockingly devastating.

And if there was ever any doubt, she had proof of the encounter. A letter, folded and stamped with a ducal seal, which she kept beside her on the pillow while the endless stretch of hours ticked by. However, she couldn't open it yet. She already had too much to sort, too many thoughts tangling in her head. She had to take this one step at a time, and before she could allow herself to consider anything else, there was another pressing matter about which she needed to learn the truth.

When, at last, servants' footsteps began shuffling through the corridor as they attended to their morning duties, and a hint of weak sunshine appeared behind the filmy curtains, she jumped from bed, pulling her dressing gown tight around her body to guard against the early chill and slipping from the room. While her mother didn't believe in idling in bed all morning, nor was she likely to be up and about at this time of day. Nonetheless, Amelia didn't have it in her to wait any longer.

She scurried down a flight of stairs and a corridor she rarely had cause to traverse until she came to the intricately carved oak door that guarded the marchioness's rooms—her mother's once more, now that Cecilia was gone and Nicholas showed no sign of returning, either.

As a child, Amelia had always found approaching this part of the house intimidating. At the moment, though, she knocked on the wood with abandon, and when there was no response, she did it again. Her fist pounded against the door over and over until a voice croaked from within. "Stop that infernal racket and enter."

She burst inside, where her mother sat in the center of the vast tester bed as coolly as ever, propped up by an array of pillows. Had her cap not gone askew, letting a single disheveled curl spring free, there would have been no signs she'd even faced a disturbance. However, the instant her eyes fixed on Amelia in the dimness, her mouth slackened, and her hand went to her chest. "Amelia! Has something happen—"

"What do you know of Robert Astley?" She charged forward, an unstoppable force rushing toward the bed. Her mother often chose to forgo pleasantries in favor of getting straight to the point, and at present, Amelia planned to do exactly the same. She wanted no more delays. Only answers.

Her mother blinked several times as if she hadn't quite shaken off the vestiges of sleep after all. "I beg your pardon?"

"Robert Astley. The former Duke of Branscombe's brother. Jonathan's father." Remarkably, Amelia managed to get the names out without trembling, although her insides were tangled in knots, filled with a sickened sort of anticipation. "What do you know of him?"

Her mother's uncharacteristic, dazed silence lasted a moment longer before she pursed her lips. "What an absurd question. How would I know anything when I made every effort to avoid that family? Besides, he was never out in society, and he died so many years ago."

Amelia took another step closer, peering down at her mother's creased face through the low light of dawn, seeking any flutter or twitch that could signal duplicity. Her days of blindly trusting were gone, and something didn't add up. "You said you began reading my correspondence at the time of my planned elopement. Did you not intercept a final letter from Jonathan, one that came even after you'd warned him away and paid for his disappearance?"

"I did not."

"Tell me the truth." Amelia's slipper-clad foot stamped against the floor. "I won't stand for more schemes and deception."

"Don't be impudent! That is the truth. Although ..." The haughtiness in her mother's tone faded into something that nearly resembled resignation. Strongly peppered with annoyance, of course, for there were few things the dowager disliked more than not having total control. "If you're going to be so demanding, you may as well know. There *was* an incident at the time, wherein I came upon that delinquent lady's maid of yours in the kitchen with a sealed page clasped in her fist. I'd already made it clear to Mary that she was to have nothing more to do with delivering letters if she wished to retain her employment, and the moment she saw me, she startled and threw the paper in the grate. But I hardly see why that's significant, beyond it putting Mary out of work, and what difference does that make now?"

The scene of the dim bedchamber began whirling in front of her, and Amelia had to catch herself before she staggered. If everything her mother said was true, that meant ... that meant Jonathan's final letter had gone into the fire, still sealed ...

Her mother shook her head with an irritated huff. "Are you going to tell me why my knowledge of Robert Astley and some bygone letter caused you to burst in here at whatever ungodly hour it is?" Her brows drew together, her frown speaking of a sentiment that crossed her face only on the rarest occasions: perplexity.

Suddenly, Amelia's legs went weak, and she dropped to the edge of the bed. Her mother, who so often seemed omniscient, hadn't known the truth. She released a shaky exhale, letting the revelation sink in. All through the night, she'd twisted with the fear that the Dowager Marchioness of Rockliffe *had* been privy to the Astley family secrets and that she'd used Jonathan's father's illness against him. That, Amelia would have considered an unforgivable crime. However, it would appear instead that, for once, her mother had been mistaken.

"You were wrong," she croaked, words she could scarcely believe she had cause to say but that hit her more forcefully with each passing second. "About Jonathan being no different from his family. About his intentions all those years ago. Do not ask me how I know that, for it's not something I'm at liberty to disclose. Please, for once, just trust that I am a grown and capable woman, and I *know*. You were wrong."

The dowager took the accusation with far more grace than could be expected. Indeed, for a moment, she said nothing at all, simply turned to the bed curtains above her with a face deep in thought. When she returned her gaze to Amelia's, she let out another short sigh. However, it was no longer a sound of annoyance but of resignation. "I can see we're going to need to discuss things that I hoped could remain in the past."

Amelia tensed. "What things?"

Her mother crossed her hands atop the brocade counterpane, making a perfect stack of slim, crepey fingers. "This may be hard to believe, but I was a girl once, caught up in the excitement of my first Season. A girl foolish enough, I'm ashamed to admit, to find herself taken with one of the ton's most notorious rakes. The heir to the Duke of Branscombe, Tobias Astley."

Amelia gasped. The name rang through her ears, and still, the fact her mother had uttered it hardly seemed real.

"I should have known better than to listen to a cad's fanciful words," her mother continued levelly, "just as I should have considered how my generous dowry would mean far more to a reprobate and perpetual gambler than something like true regard. But I didn't. I thought only of how clever I was to capture the attentions of the heir to a dukedom."

Amelia could feel her mouth gaping, but she was powerless to close it. She was powerless to do anything but sit there and absorb revelations that went far beyond anything she could have imagined from the mother she'd always viewed as indomitable.

"In any case, my father possessed wisdom that I did not. The moment he discovered my ambitions of wedding Astley, he had me betrothed and then married by special license to the Marquess of Rockliffe." Her mother's voice wavered, just enough to be perceptible, as meanwhile, Amelia blinked rapidly from yet another shock. "I was furious. I barely knew Rockliffe, and I was so convinced I'd made a better match—a match I actually *wanted*—all on my own. In the end, though, my father deserved thanks for his interference. While Astley pretended great sorrow at our separation, I discovered later that he'd been making romantic declarations to two other wealthy debutantes at the same time, and he married one shortly thereafter. A woman who likely considered her death in childbirth a mercy, if rumors of the state of their marriage are to be believed."

Her mother shifted against the pillows, and although she didn't sink or slouch, her face creased in a way that made it seem as though she shouldered the weight of a burden. "I consider myself fortunate for escaping such a miserable fate. My affection for Rockliffe grew in time, and I was far better off building a life that contained no trace of Astley. He went his way and I went mine, and I thought that was the end of it. However, when I found out what was transpiring between you and Jonathan Astley—in secret—all those years later, it was as if the past were determined to repeat itself. That jackass Tobias Astley—or rather, the degenerate Duke of Branscombe by then—bragging about the dowry, thinking that, through his nephew, he could accomplish with you what he couldn't with me. I refused to let that happen, Amelia."

Amelia's head spun as she took in the face she'd known her whole life yet simultaneously belonged to a stranger. The revelations she'd just discovered would take far longer than the span of a few moments to process. Yet above everything else, it occurred to her for the first time just how small the dowager appeared in the vast marchioness's bed. As if maybe, despite her demeanor of steel, she possessed weaknesses, just like everyone else.

Amelia reached across the counterpane, pressing her hand carefully atop her mother's—for the dowager was afflicted by bouts of rheumatism despite her reluctance to admit it. Fortunately, she didn't flinch from the gesture but let Amelia remain there in a rare moment of closeness.

The Dowager Marchioness of Rockliffe was a force to be reckoned with. The one who *caused* the hurting while remaining far too impenetrable to experience her own hurt. Except now, that assumption had been turned on its head. Not only could Amelia see an aging woman in her nightclothes, who, if one didn't know better, could almost be described as *frail*. She could also envision traces of a girl not so different from herself, who'd dreamed dreams and ached with heartbreak.

To speak to her mother of that sort of vulnerability would be akin to sacrilege. Therefore, Amelia said nothing as she held her hand. The dowager, after all, was a shrewd woman. With any luck, she could sense her daughter's gratitude for the honesty that couldn't have been easy for her to share. For with that honesty, the anger and hurt that had kept Amelia awake through the night dimmed enough to show a path to forgiveness.

At the same time, though, she was more certain of her own beliefs on the subject than ever before.

"Jonathan is not his uncle." Her awareness trickled to the folded piece of paper she'd tucked into her bodice, refusing to let it leave her person until she felt ready to survey its contents. "If you couldn't believe that all those years ago, please, believe it now. He's grown wealthy enough in his own right to have no use for a dowry, and still ..."

The memory of his strong arms enveloped her, of them picking her up whenever she stumbled. Of hands that washed away mud, that protected her from footpads, that cut her hair, that caressed her as if she were a creature to be worshiped. "Still, over our week on the road, he proved his devotion to me. He made me feel loved. And in return, I love him deeply. I always have. There was never anyone for me but him."

Amelia held herself tall, bracing for words of protest. But instead, her mother sank back into the pillows, finally letting herself recline with a long exhale. "Well. I suppose that's all there is to it, then. Far be it from me to stand in your way. You've become a veritable force to be reckoned with this morning."

Amelia's lips twitched into a smile that she couldn't hold back. That had to be the most un-dowagerlike phrase she'd ever heard. Then again, this confrontation had already solidified itself as one where nothing went as expected, so perhaps she shouldn't be surprised. Her mother had given as much of a blessing as she could ever hope to receive. She wouldn't interfere.

Now, if only matters could be as simple as running into Jonathan's arms and living happily ever after.

Amelia let her body drop as well, leaning forward to rest her head in her hands. There was another obstacle to deal with before she could plan for the future. After all the confidences she and her mother had exchanged this morning, it was just as well she reveal this one, too, and get it off her chest.

"Our family is going to be involved in another scandal. This time, of my making." She dared to look up, back to the matriarch on her throne of blankets and cushions. She half-expected her mother's face to have returned to steel, to see ire flash in her eyes. However, she merely continued to sit there, not so much as blinking.

"Felix Egerton—the Earl of Stanfield's younger brother—is using blackmail in an attempt to force me into marriage." Amelia let the words pour out before she had a chance to clam up and second-guess them. "He discovered something I didn't wish to be revealed. Namely, that I am Lady Lockheart."

"Lady ... Lady Lockheart?" In what had to be a record, her mother's silver brows rose in bewilderment for the second time that day.

"Yes, from *The Ladies' Spectator.*" Amelia nodded, for what sense was there in shying away from the title now? While her mother had always dismissed the publication as drivel, Amelia knew full well that she was as aware of the notable columnist as most other ladies of the ton. "It's me. It's always been me. Samuel helped me get started with it, and when I no longer had his assistance, I managed to carry it on by myself. For close to eleven years, I wrote the column without incident, with no one any the wiser. That, unfortunately, has changed, and so, I face a choice. Marry Egerton, or have my secret announced tomorrow night at the Symonds's ball."

Her mother's lips formed the beginning of a single silent word. *How?* But before it could come out, her mouth snapped closed, and her posture became rigid once more, her fingers drumming against the counterpane.

"Perhaps an appropriate sum of money would entice him to back away," Amelia said carefully, studying the unsettling calm that had spread across her mother's features. "However, I hate the thought of him receiving even a farthing of Rockliffe money, and the last thing I want is for him to get the impression that I'm his to command."

She blew out a breath, reliving the impossible problem that had been on her mind ever since the fateful night of the Englewood ball, and the solution she'd decided upon, which, though terrifying, felt more right than ever. "Marrying Felix Egerton is out of the question, obviously, which really just leaves one option. I need to let the secret come out. No, it's not how I wanted things to transpire, and I'm sorry for the gossip it will bring upon us. Yet I've come to the decision that enduring the ton's talk and embracing who I am is far better than cowering in a corner and letting others walk all over me."

Her mother's jaw tightened, and again, Amelia steeled herself for a deluge of irate words. She'd been disobedient, after all, and secretive. Dishonest. All qualities that incensed the dowager to no end.

Yet her mother's cheeks didn't color in anger, nor did her voice become icy. Instead, she still appeared rather ... stunned.

For a moment, she simply locked eyes with Amelia as if she, too, had discovered a stranger in the room that day. Periods of silent stillness from the dowager tended to be ominous, like the calm before a storm. When at last she did move, though, it was to give a firm dip of her chin. "Quite right. Prescotts do not *cower*."

A sound rose in Amelia's throat, part gasp of surprise and part laugh. No, they didn't, did they? She'd spent so many years thinking herself lacking, *less*, but didn't she have the same blood running through her veins as the rest of her family? She was just as strong. Just as capable.

"Thank you," she whispered, her throat going tight as she reached for her mother's hand once more. The simple words felt inadequate when there was so much else to say. However, as her mother wasn't the type to welcome flowery speeches, Amelia merely sat on the edge of the bed with her a moment longer, hoping she understood the depth of her appreciation.

No doubt they both still had a great deal to process about everything they'd discussed throughout the course of their conversation, for between the two of them, it was difficult to say which one had shocked the other more. But above all else, one message rang clear to Amelia. Her mother accepted her. She supported her decisions.

The force that had torn her and Jonathan apart would no longer stand in their way. Just as the fear that her writing was frivolous and shame-inducing no longer had to be a factor.

What happened next was all in Amelia's hands. If she could go forward with even a fraction of the fierce resolve her mother possessed, things were bound to turn out the way they should.

22

The yellow brick facade of Brooks's loomed before Jonathan like a behemoth gleaming in the sunlight, making his palms sweat and his cravat feel as though it had been knotted too tightly about his neck. Still, he went forward, leaving behind the safety of the pavement outside and stepping into the entrance.

He hadn't been back to the gentlemen's club since that first disastrous night after his foray into the House of Lords when his words had failed him, he'd been made a mockery by his former schoolmates, and he'd sworn he had no cause to return. Yet here he was again, exchanging greetings with a steward, shrugging out of his greatcoat, and heading toward one of the drawing rooms as if he belonged.

Because maybe it was time—no, not maybe; it *was* time to start believing he did.

He continued walking through the club, even though his heart pounded and his tongue felt far too heavy for speech. Turning back wasn't an option. Not after he'd spent close to a week on the Great North Road encouraging Amelia to return to London and confront her fears. Yes, Amelia was gone now, silent ever since he'd deposited the letter in her lap and climbed back out her window. That didn't mean he no longer had a duty to follow his own advice.

He wanted Amelia, plain and simple. Without her, he didn't feel whole. However, if he couldn't have her—a thought he never dwelled on too long for the ache it caused—he could still see to his other responsibilities as the Duke of Branscombe. Namely, he could return to Parliament. Give the speeches that lay upon his desk, already partially written, about the need for more stringent regulations around madhouses and making these establishments accessible to noblemen and paupers alike. If he was going to propose bills, though, he would need to garner support to ensure they passed. Have allies. And potential allies could be found here at Brooks's.

"The blasted fool just can't stay away."

The voice from the drawing room cut through him as soon as he reached the threshold, before he even had a chance to observe the scene within. He froze, squeezing his eyes shut and taking a moment to steady himself. Despite how hard he'd tried convincing himself that this visit would be nothing like the last, the very man whose words plagued him had popped back into his imaginings.

Only, they weren't just imaginings, for when he opened his eyes, there sat the Earl of Stanfield at the same table, in the same drawing room, as before. His posse was diminished this evening, comprised of only two other men who surrounded him at the table, glasses of brandy in hand. Nonetheless, he was very much the same Stanfield with the devil-may-care look in his eye. The earl, who had once been a boy at Eton, skilled with both fists and vitriolic taunts.

"You'd think he would have learned his lesson after Naughton nearly discovered them sneaking off at Vauxhall the other night, but no." Stanfield took a long swallow of brandy, and when his glass came away, his mouth curved into a grin. "Just yesterday, he and Sophie sought to have a little fun at Naughton house, and when the viscount came home early, she apparently had to stuff Felix in the clothespress. Good thing he's short!"

Stanfield and his companions dissolved into laughter, as meanwhile, Jonathan's teeth clenched together. He'd been about to spin on his heel and go elsewhere in the club, uninterested in hearing any more of Stanfield's story, which was seemingly about another man's illicit tryst. Yet the name stopped him in his tracks. *Felix.* The detestable earl's equally detestable and blackmailing brother, as he'd come to learn. Suddenly, Jonathan found himself half-concealed behind the door, unable to look away.

"I don't know what it is about Sophie that makes him unable to part with her. I suppose it's the fact that she's well-endowed." Stanfield made a crude gesture toward his chest, which resulted in another round of chortles. "If you ask me, no chit has assets ample enough to be worth that sort of risk. Naughton may be an old coot, but he's also an excellent shot, and he protects what belongs to him like a dog with a bone. And here's his little minx of a wife, telling Felix that if he doesn't attend to her every whim, she'll go to Naughton with news of the affair herself."

He drained the remaining contents of his glass, then stood up, reaching for the crystal decanter at the opposite end of the table. "Ah, well, there's no talking him away from her. He keeps insisting he'll be able to keep Sophie content once he gets his hands on the Prescott chit's dowry, although the old spinster seems to be giving him a hard time of it—"

Jonathan lunged forward, propelled by a wave of blind fury. He shoved the door out of the way, not caring about hiding, not caring about anything, until he slammed into the

Earl of Stanfield, pushing him against the nearest wall and pinning him in place with a forearm to his throat. "You keep her name out of your goddamn mouth," he hissed.

Stanfield shook his head wildly, blinking as he took in the source of the sudden assault. "Astley?" For a few seconds, his mouth drooped wide before he quickly schooled it into a characteristic sneer. "Oh, I got that wrong. You're a d-d-d-d-duke now, aren't you? One who lurks around corners listening to private conversations, apparently."

Jonathan leaned in, using his elbow to deliver another stab of pressure to the man's neck. "It's hardly a private conversation when you hold it in a public place. And as it turns out, you said something of interest to me."

Stanfield's face began to redden, and he made a strangled noise in his throat. His eyes darted around, shooting pleading glances toward his companions. However, while the other men may enjoy flocking after him as if he were still the leader of their gang of Eton schoolboys, neither of them moved from their seats at the table. As for the only other patrons in the room—a duo of elderly gentlemen who'd fallen asleep, newspapers spread across their laps, in adjacent wing chairs—they didn't so much as stir.

Stanfield's arms shot up in surrender, and Jonathan eased off enough to let him take several great, gulping breaths. As tempting as it was to tear the blackguard apart, Stanfield would do him little good if he became incoherent.

"Devil take it, B-B-Branscombe." Stanfield cleared his throat with a scowl, apparently unable to resist a jibe even when finding himself jammed against the wall with his air supply in peril. "Forget you ever heard me utter a word about her, then. Really, though, why should it matter to you what I say? You should mind your own business and turn your attention to someone who actually has an interest in associating with you."

"*You* don't matter to me at all," Jonathan snapped. And at long last, it was true. Rather than penetrate, the insults rolled right off his shoulders. At present, he had something far more pressing on which to focus. "Your brother Felix is the one with whom I have business. *You* are useful only in your ability to tell me where to find him."

"Felix?" Stanfield blinked again, his brow furrowing in annoyance. "I can hardly be expected to keep track of his whereabouts. And even if I did know, why would I share that information with you?"

"Because." Jonathan shoved his arm forward again, not so much as to obstruct Stanfield's airway but enough to remind him of the looming possibility. "If you don't, I'll have to go looking for him myself, and I believe I'll start at a certain viscount's town house. Lord Naughton, I think you said the name was? It sounds like even if Felix is there, he'd have to keep himself hidden, so I'd be unable to speak with him. Nonetheless, I'm sure Naughton would be interested in hearing about my discoveries regarding the goings on under his roof. And when Felix at last comes crawling out of the clothespress, I can't imagine that ending well for him."

"Why in blazes would you do that? Are you mad?" Stanfield's pale eyes blazed with indignation, but at the same time, there was a worried twist to his mouth.

"Not at all." Jonathan flashed his teeth in a semblance of an even, dangerous smile. "On the contrary, this is all very simple, but I'll explain it to you in case anything remains unclear. I have a pressing need to speak with your brother Felix. If you help me find him, and if he, too, is amenable to cooperating, the information I just overheard need go no farther than this room, and you can spare yourself the duty of being named as his second in a duel he's unlikely to win. Given that *your* idle tongue put him in the predicament, it's the least you can do, don't you think?"

Stanfield's body jerked against the wall, much like an incensed bull confined to a pen. A position that he was used to inflicting on others, no doubt, but hadn't experienced himself. Yet, after a moment, he stilled, his face fixed in a resigned glower. It would seem, finally, that he was beginning to understand the meaning of defeat.

"You'd best release me, then, Branscombe," he said at last, his gaze shooting down to the elbow at his throat. "I'll take you to his apartments."

Jonathan eased away, not taking his eyes off the repugnant man for an instant. Fortunately, Stanfield remained docile, smoothing down his disheveled coat and going to retrieve the top hat he'd left beside his chair.

His companions, still planted in their seats, eyed him hesitantly, one of them reaching for his walking stick and making a tentative motion to rise.

"Oh, go to hell," Stanfield muttered, pausing just long enough to take a swig from the brandy decanter. Then, he strode toward the door, turning back to see if Jonathan followed.

Which he did. Without missing a beat, he caught up to Stanfield, making it so their strides matched. He straightened his own coat as they walked back into the entrance. Uncurled his fists. It occurred to him that his heart was pounding and his breaths were coming fast.

Yet he'd succeeded. He hadn't shied away, powerless and trembling, from Stanfield. He couldn't say *what* had happened, exactly, only that something had compelled him to power forward without relenting. Was it the moment of perfect clarity when the earl's careless words about Felix Egerton made him realize that a blackmailer could become the blackmailed? Or was it the disdain in Stanfield's voice as he spoke of the *Prescott chit*? Maybe it was the combination of the two, creating a surge of simultaneous triumph and outrage too potent to be stopped.

Whatever the case, he'd done it. He'd turned the tables and gained control over Stanfield.

And with that, he may just have the key for setting Amelia's troubles right, too.

23

The Symonds House ballroom was packed wall to wall with a conglomeration of society's finest. However, of all the sets of eyes that glanced up as a footman announced the Duke of Branscombe's arrival, none belonged to the only person Jonathan wished to see.

He pushed his way through the crowd and the muggy, perfumed heat, vaguely aware that if he kept peering about, analyzing each face, while simultaneously ignoring the trail of voices that called out his name in greeting, he would earn a reputation of being an even bigger ingrate than his uncle. However, he couldn't let that stop him right now. If she was here, he had to find her.

Clusters of guests danced, chatted, and sipped on glasses of ratafia and lemonade. Except he made it to the other end of the room, and still, none of them were her. Had she possibly decided not to come after all? Should he work his way back through the sea of people and instead make his way to Rockliffe House in hopes he'd be permitted an audience?

In front of him, though, was a set of double doors leading to the terrace, not much in use due to the foggy mist that had settled into the night air. Not much in use, but it warranted a look nonetheless, for didn't they usually find each other in gardens?

He slipped outside, closing the door carefully behind him despite how it would be impossible for the soft snick to draw attention amidst the din of music and conversation.

And there, at the opposite end of the terrace, leaning against the balustrade, was a figure. A lone, slender figure facing away from him, looking out into the garden beyond. Her short, red-gold curls were styled with a bandeau, while a dress of light blue silk, overlaid with a filmy skirt embroidered with silver threads that caught the torch light, clung to her body and pooled at her feet around the terrace stones.

She was resplendent, the sight of her making his breath catch in his throat. Yet he managed to take a few silent steps forward, to utter her name as a low murmur into the darkness. "Amelia."

She turned instantly, her face pallid and drawn. Except then, recognition set in, and her blue eyes softened. Her rosebud mouth formed a small *o*. And all at once, she was running toward him, colliding with his chest, burying her face against his shoulder.

His arms shot out to encircle her, desperate for the feel of her soft warmth, while he rested his chin against her hair, inhaling the apple blossom fragrance. Things he'd thought he may never have the pleasure of experiencing again, which made their return that much sweeter.

"Jonathan," she murmured, still nestled against his shoulder, and although her voice was muffled by his coat, it was impossible to miss the strain. "This is the night. The night when Felix Egerton said he was going to tell everyone my secret. I didn't give in to his demands. I made up my mind to endure whatever gossip ensues. However, the *waiting*—the uncertainty—is worse than anything. I haven't laid eyes on him since I got here, but I keep thinking he'll appear at any second and shout out what he knows, or that maybe, the information has already begun circulating, and the ladies whispering behind their fans are talking about *me*. I swore I would be brave and face it all, yet I just had to get away from the ballroom for a while. Resolve, unfortunately, doesn't seem to negate fear."

"It's all right. I know." And he truly did, having had cause to experience the same sentiment numerous times of late. He tightened his grip around her waist with one arm while his other hand went up to stroke her hair in a series of soothing motions, coaxing her breaths to stop coming so rapidly. "You *are* brave, Amelia. Never doubt that. But at the moment, you can rest easy. Felix Egerton isn't coming."

"What?" Abruptly, her head lifted from his shoulder, and she peered at him, her dew-dotted brows drawing together.

He glanced back at the terrace doors and the couples twirling about the dance floor who appeared behind the panes of glass. Separated from them, but still too close for comfort. "Will you walk into the garden with me? I have a great deal to tell you, and I don't want to risk anyone coming out and overhearing."

She untangled her body from his without hesitation, instead letting him hold her arm and lead her down the stone steps and into the garden beyond. Despite the drizzle, Lady Symonds had prepared for the possibility that guests would want to take the air, for a few scattered torches lit their path, keeping it from being a total abyss. They traveled around a row of hedges filled with new, tiny leaves, eventually coming to a marble bench sequestered in a quiet corner of the garden.

A bench not so different from the one he'd sat upon the first time he saw her and his world—his heart—became forever changed. It was fitting, in a way, that this conversation would take place in such a location. Because now, whatever else passed between them, maybe he could change a little of her world for the better, too.

He swept his coat sleeve along the seat to rid it of dampness, and they lowered themselves in unison. Sitting close, but not too close. Her fingers twisted in the delicate fabric of her skirts as she stared at him, her pale face dotted with tiny beads of water.

He didn't make her wait a second longer. He told her everything. Of the overheard conversation at Brooks's. Of sitting with Stanfield outside a middling set of bachelor's apartments until the swine he awaited staggered in just before dinnertime, tipsy with drink. Of sending Stanfield away and having a *very* thorough—and graphic—conversation with Egerton, in which he described exactly what would happen should he attempt to share the information he'd learned about Lady Lockheart.

"Ultimately, Egerton decided to leave London," Jonathan explained. "It's hard to say who poses a bigger danger to him: Viscount Naughton or the viscountess herself. Regardless, I think he came to see the wisdom in not showing his face again for a very long time. And as long as he has the threat of the Naughtons' wrath falling upon him, he, in turn, poses no threat to you."

Amelia had stayed stock-still the entire time he spoke, but now, her gloved hand went to her mouth, covering her lips. He didn't need to see her mouth, though, to discern the moment when her stony-faced shock changed to a smile, for her eyes lit up, glimmering in the darkness with a joy that made them crinkle at the corners. There was a sound from behind her hand. The best sound. A crisp, bell-like peal of laughter.

And then, her lips were hidden no more but upon his, pulling him into an ardent kiss, as her hands went up to clutch his nape.

He responded at once, returning the pressure of her lips,

cupping the slender line of her jaw. Not too long a period had passed since they'd last shared an embrace, but at the same time, it felt like an eternity. So many long hours where he'd grappled with the possibility that he may never know her this way again. Now that he had her back, he wanted to relearn every facet of her. The sweetness of her mouth. The softness of her skin. Every little curve and indentation. His tongue swept over hers, teasing, caressing, each stroke bringing them closer together. Giving him more and more reason to hope ...

Her body was against his now, their thighs pressing together, their arms holding each other tight. So much nearer than he could have imagined when they'd set out from the terrace, and still, not near enough to keep up with his increasing desire.

As if she could read his thoughts, she pivoted her body so she came to sit atop his lap, bending her knees so she straddled him. He bit back a groan as her breasts settled against his chest, and the pliant heat near the center of her brushed against his increasing arousal.

"Jonathan, please." She breathed out his name, and again, the sensation went straight to his groin. No more *Your Grace*. No more distance. She pulled her gloves off, and her hand came to his cravat. She pushed it out of the way so she could undo the top few buttons of his shirt and slip inside, resting her fingers over his pounding heart. Skin against skin. The light rain had permeated her gloves, giving her fingers a slight chill. The touch seared him nonetheless.

Amelia deserved a roaring fire, silk sheets, a sprawling bed where he could undress her, lay her out, and worship every inch of her. However, all they had was the stone bench, and the need in her voice—her eyes—suggested she didn't want to wait for anything beyond that.

God knew he didn't, either. The desire she'd once shied away from had sparked to life, emboldening her to ask for what she wanted, and all he could think of was *more* and *yes* and *now*.

He kissed her lips again. Her throat. His fingers found the hooks at the back of her gown, and he slipped them from the eyelets so the bodice sagged. The gown was beautiful, but what lay underneath was even more exquisite.

He tugged down her stays and shift, bringing his mouth to the gentle slope of her breast, to the nipple that was just a shadow in the darkness. She threw her head back with a whimper, and as he laved and sucked one hardened point and then the other, he studied her face. The eyelids that drifted closed and the dewy, fluttering eyelashes. The lips that parted in pleasure.

He watched every twitch, took in each of her breathy sounds. All while growing blatantly aware that she'd begun wriggling, dragging herself against his erection, and suddenly, it became more than he could bear. He let out another groan, his mouth breaking away. "Will you lift your skirts for me?" he said, his voice cracking, just as the rest of him felt ready to shatter with the weight of his yearning.

For the briefest moment, he had the presence of mind to wonder if he'd asked too much of her, here on a marble bench in the misty darkness. But in the next instant, she was raising herself on her knees, grabbing fistfuls of fabric, sliding them upward, past stockings and garters and the first bit of skin. Peering at him, her pupils wide with desire. "Will you unfasten your fall?"

His cock strained against his breeches, and his fingers trembled as he reached for the buttons, slipping them from the holes until the fall dropped down and his arousal sprang free.

"My Amelia," he murmured, his world reduced to nothing but need and pleasure and the woman hovering above him. He reached for her, needing to claim her mouth again, and as their lips connected, she took him in hand, a gesture that sucked the air from his lungs.

She broke the kiss, tracing her tongue over her top lip in a way that nearly unmanned him. "This position ..." Her gaze went from his cock to her own body situated above it and back again. "Can we?"

"Yes." It was a wonder he could form a coherent word. "God, yes."

In one swift motion, she sank down until he was buried deep within her, the contact eliciting a moan from them both. Just as he remembered, her sex was lusciously wet and hot. Except this time, somehow, the sensation was even better.

"Like this." He grasped her hips, guiding them upward and letting them plunge back down again, sending another fiery blast shooting through his veins. "Does this feel good?"

"Yes." She braced her hands on his shoulders and completed the motion of her own accord, her assertion sounding more like a cry. "So good, Jonathan."

She developed a rhythm quickly, up and down, creating friction that nearly drove him out of his head. He was so close, his body winding tighter, aching for release. Not, however, until she had hers as well.

His finger went to that secret place between her legs where he'd showed her how to chase her pleasure, circling the swollen nub. "And this?" Continuing the motion, he brought his other hand to her breast, taking the nipple between his thumb and forefinger. "Do you like this, too?"

"I ..." she panted. "Yes, I—"

Any further words dissolved, her movements too frantic to allow for speech. Her body was rigid, quivering, then shattering into pieces, her intimate muscles clenching him tight as they spasmed.

He thrust his hips upward once, twice, hurtling into a climax along with her. The waves of ecstasy shook him to the core, hitting a place deeper than he'd ever realized existed. He couldn't think straight, only knew that she was warm and snug around him, and the scent of apple blossoms mixed with arousal wafted into his nose while the heat of her hurried breaths fell against his neck.

Eventually—when the waves of pleasure at last faded away, and she, too, grew still—he managed to focus on his surroundings enough to recognize that Amelia's hair had become limp from the dampness, and her bare skin was coated with little beads of rain. He shrugged out of his coat, wrapping it securely about her shoulders so she could dry off the raindrops. Coat or not, the weather would soon necessitate them returning indoors.

His body was sated, his mind remaining hazy with the aftereffects of desire. Still, he recognized, with an increasing sense of urgency, that he couldn't let their encounter end like this. Yes, he'd delivered the vital news about Egerton's departure, but what of everything else? Hope continued to swirl within him, stronger than ever, giving little flashes of a future where all his nights ended like this. Yet she still hadn't said the words.

With a final kiss, she shifted back onto the bench beside him, the hem of her skirts floating to the ground. His body protested the loss of contact, wanting her back, wanting her on his lap in the garden all night long, rain be damned. However, he couldn't become distracted by that thought. Instead, he needed to determine the right thing to say to find out, with absolute certainty, where matters stood between them. With his head racing, he silently worked to refasten his fall, as meanwhile, Amelia straightened her shift, pulling it into place.

That's when he saw it: the folded piece of paper he'd somehow missed before that was tucked between the laces of her stays. He knew that paper. Her name, scrawled across the front, had been written by his hand.

She glanced up, catching him in the midst of staring, and gave a wry smile. "This time, I refused to let your letter out of my care for even an instant."

She removed it from between the laces carefully, setting it in her lap while she finished righting her gown. "I saved it. I thought my life was going to erupt into scandal tonight, and I wanted to have the letter ... well, for after." Her fingers traced over the page in a featherlight motion. "That didn't happen, thanks to you. I'd still like to read it tonight, though. May I?"

He swallowed, his mind going back to the day in his study when he'd put the sentiments that had followed him around the world and back to the Great North Road in England all upon the page. That was all he wanted: for her to know the truth, to have no doubt about what was in his heart.

And to find out if, maybe ... despite his flaws, despite the years of separation, despite his mistakes ... maybe, she could feel the same.

He cleared his throat. Nodded, as his future seemed to dangle on a precipice. This was the moment. "Yes."

24

Amelia's damp fingers quivered as she unfolded the sheet of paper within her grasp. Truthfully, she hadn't yet recovered from the other events of the evening. The anxiety of feeling like Felix Egerton was about to jump out and expose her at every turn. The surprise of encountering Jonathan instead, the overwhelming surge of relief as she discovered what he'd done. The passion that had consumed her, the need to be close to him, the release that had made her replete down to her soul.

And then, the realization that they were back where they'd started: a pair on a bench in a dark garden. Except now, there was a letter between them. One she could read and *know* it contained his true sentiments. And maybe the key to their future.

Yes, the night had already been filled with enough life-altering events. Regardless, the timing—here on a bench, with him beside her—felt right. She didn't want to wait any longer.

She smoothed the creases from the page she'd kept folded for days, making each handwritten word—valued because they were really his—appear before her. The first line jumped out at once, making her smile before she continued with the rest.

My Dear Lady Lockheart,

At the age of nineteen, I had the privilege and good fortune of meeting a woman who instantly captured my heart. I'm not sure what I did to merit her affection in return, but whatever the case, she agreed to become my wife.

I will not relay the circumstances that tore us apart, only that my role in them remains one of the greatest regrets of my life. I left England, roaming the edges of the earth, growing older, rising in station, but never forgetting. No amount of distance could erase the love for her from my heart.

I resigned myself to viewing these sentiments as futile—a sorrow I would always bear from afar. Yet more than a decade later, circumstances necessitated my return to England, and then ... I saw her again. As lovely as ever, with the same copper-gold curls that had long filled my dreams. I wasn't so bold as to think that eleven years of separation, and the regret that went along with them, could suddenly be undone, nor did I allow myself to hope for a reconciliation, no matter how much I longed for it.

We crossed paths again, nonetheless. Whether I have fate or some other power to thank, I happened upon her on the road at the exact moment she required assistance, at the exact time she needed conveyance north to a destination not so far from my own.

Our reunion, I'm afraid, didn't end happily there. The ensuing journey involved such a copious mixture of calamities that one could almost believe we'd done something to turn the world against us. From abysmal weather to derelict inns to an undutiful coachman to pistol-wielding footpads, nothing seemed to go as it should.

And still, I regret not a single second of those days on the road. Not the endless rain, or the mud, or the ramshackle carriage, or even the footpad's pistol against my chest. I regret nothing because those were moments spent with her. Moments I may have never gotten otherwise. Moments that made me fall in love with her all over again.

Our journey ended as it started: disastrously. Past misunderstandings and past mistakes, it turns out—even those from very long ago—do not always stay in the past. Nor should they, as I've come to appreciate. A relationship should always be based on honesty, and I believe that, if nothing else, she and I have reached a point where there is only truth between us.

My question, then, is whether I would be right to hope for another chance. I know I am flawed, and I know I have erred, but in one thing, I have remained constant, and that is my unyielding love for her. She is my sun and my North Star; the brightness in my world and my compass.

There are so many lost years between us to mourn, but at the same time, I find myself also envisioning a future. A future where I can imagine no greater bliss than having her by my side, where we can forge new, joyful memories and make up for all that lost time. Do you think, after everything that transpired, she could want this, too? She once accepted my marriage proposal and gave me happiness beyond what I knew existed. Were I to pose the question again, do you think it possible she would offer me the same response?

Sincerely,

Lord Lovestruck

Amelia's hand was shaking again, making the words begin to waver on the page. Although perhaps that was also due to the moisture gathering in her eyes. She dabbed at the corners, not allowing the tears to fall. She was becoming such a watering pot lately.

However, this time was different, the weightiness of

despair notably absent. Instead, her heart was just so ... *full*. Not heavy, though, but airy. Fluttering. Filled with a blossoming hope that everything she'd once dreamed of could come true.

She lifted her gaze from the page, meeting eyes that were dark and eager. Perhaps a little anxious, too. They were the same eyes she'd fallen in love with all those years ago. The same eyes that had filled her thoughts once he'd vanished and become nothing but a memory. The same eyes that had peered at her from across the carriage, had glimmered in the dark the first night they shared the same bed, had locked with hers as she collapsed in the middle of the road with the world closing in on her, letting her know that everything would be all right.

She crossed her hands over the letter to hold it securely in her lap, still not looking away from him. "I'm afraid Lady Lockheart is unable to give you a response."

His body stiffened, the lines of his throat appearing tight, and she reached for him to bestow a gentle caress, resting her palm above his thundering heart. She was going to need to explain herself better, and quickly.

"I've put a great deal of thought into the Lady Lockheart column over the past few days," she said, the rhythm of his heartbeat keeping her steady, just as it always did. "Regardless of how society may have reacted to the revelation, I found the thought of having my name associated with the column instead of Lady Lockheart's, and in such a callous manner, took away the fun of it for me, and I'd planned to put it to rest. Obviously, that no longer needs to happen. However, the more I think of it, the more I still feel it's time for Lady Lockheart to take an early retirement."

He opened his mouth, looking ready to form a protest, and she gave his coat a light squeeze, halting the words. "Not because I no longer wish to write," she continued. "On the contrary, having my work be part of *The Ladies' Spectator* over the years has given me a sense of accomplishment, and I'd like that to continue. It's just that I think Lady Lockheart wishes to adopt a new persona. She's rather hoping she might become a duchess."

For a split second longer, he remained unmoving and rigid. All until the meaning of what she'd said must have set in, and his face lit up. His shoulders relaxed, his chest sagging slightly against her palm, and although he pressed his lips together, he couldn't hide the smile that was beginning to burst free. One that elicited her own wide grin in return.

"Ask me," she whispered, feeling her eyes begin to dampen once more. Tears of the purest, most radiant joy. "Ask me the question again."

In one swift motion, he lowered himself to the ground, kneeling atop the grass beside her feet. His hands reached for hers, twining their fingers, creating a contrast of sturdy against slender that fit perfectly together.

Then, he uttered the best words. The kind that went straight to her heart.

"I have loved you for eleven long years. I will continue loving you for the rest of my years on earth. My greatest wish is to no longer do it from a distance but to remind you of it in person every day. We can build a life in England together. Travel the world together. Whatever you wish, for wherever you are is my home. And so, I most ardently ask: Lady Amelia Prescott, will you marry me?"

"Yes." Tears slid over her cheeks, and she tugged at his hands, pulling him forward and leaning down herself until their lips collided.

Without breaking the kiss, he shifted back onto the bench, and they stayed in the embrace for a long time, solidifying the betrothal. Making it feel real.

They stayed that way until the wetness on her face came from the sky, not her tears, and she at last felt ready to lift her head and speak again. To say the things she needed him to know, too.

"Yes," she repeated, a simple word that also had the power to change futures. "You weren't the only one who fell in love in a garden a long time ago. Nor were you the only one who carried that love across the years. Even when I thought your sentiments were false and wished so desperately to forget, I still couldn't get you out of my heart. Now, however, I don't want to forget. I want our love to grow and flourish. I want it to bind us for the rest of our days. You're my strength, Jonathan, and I don't regret our road trip either, for throughout that time, you helped me see myself as beautiful and worthy. *Brave*. I want to be that for you in return. A helpmate. The person who always sees the best in you, who will pick you up when you stumble. So *yes*. I can imagine no greater honor than becoming your wife."

"Amelia." His kiss fell on her forehead this time, and when he pulled away, his uninhibited smile had returned. "You have made me so deliriously happy, my love. It's only unfortunate that yet again"—he pushed a strand of hair away from her face, and for the first time, she realized it must have stuck there because of how wet it was—"the weather seems determined to interfere with our liaison."

She giggled, turning her face up to the night sky. It would take far more than rain to douse the joy coursing through her. Now that she considered it, though, he was right. The precipitation falling upon her cheeks had increased from a light mist to a steadier stream of droplets. "I suppose that means"—she blew out a breath, loath to leave behind her seat on the bench and the most wonderful moment of her life—"we should return inside."

She retrieved her crumpled gloves, tugging the damp silk over her fingers. No, she didn't want this secret, special time with him to end. But then again, this was only the beginning.

There was so much they needed to do. Arrangements to make. A future to plan.

"I should find my mother," she murmured as she bent over to smooth her hem. "Tell her of our betrothal before anyone else hears of it."

When she righted herself, she couldn't miss the way Jonathan's mouth had gone tense. "It's all right. She and I had a lengthy conversation recently, and I have reason to believe that she won't interfere with our nuptials this time." She leaned in for another kiss, staying until the set of his mouth softened, and when she drew back, she could feel her lips curving upward again. "In the event I'm mistaken, there's always Gretna Green."

His smile returned, too—when had they last done this much grinning? Not for more than a decade, surely—and he pushed to his feet, extending an arm to help her up. She accepted, coming to stand beside him. And immediately burst out laughing. Jonathan's wet shirt clung to his body, his cravat hung precariously around his neck with a single slipshod knot, and while she couldn't say for sure in the darkness, the knee of his tan breeches appeared to contain a grass stain. As for her own appearance, her bodice didn't seem to sit quite right—had she forgotten one of the hooks?—and her filmy overskirt no longer floated but stuck to the silk beneath in a lump.

"I believe we may have exchanged one scandal for another this evening." She brought a hand to her hair, where it turned out that her entire coiffure had sunk against her head in a wet mass. "What will people say when we return to the ballroom looking like this?"

Jonathan's arms came around her waist, and he spun her gently to face him. "I don't care what they say. They can whisper behind their fans. Print the shocking tale in all the gossip rags. I see no reason why I should let that stop me from going inside to share a dance with my betrothed. What do you think?"

She glanced down again at her attire. At his. People were apt to say they looked like a pair of drowned rats.

Blissfully happy drowned rats, though.

"I think a dance sounds perfect." She set her hand in his and positioned herself at his side. And then, they started back to the house. Together.

Epilogue

Six weeks later

The dining table at Rockliffe House had never contained so much food. Amelia set her wineglass down and rested against her chairback, once more taking in the vast array of roasted meats and vegetables, breads and pastries, puddings, jellies, exotic fruits, and even a five-tiered cake, decorated with intricately iced flowers. They'd all filled their plates—several times over, for some of the guests—and hardly made a dent in the spread.

Truth be told, Amelia would have rather forgone food altogether and gone straight from the church back to Branscombe House so Jonathan—her *husband*—could show her to her new bedchamber and remain with her there for the rest of the day.

However, her mother had been adamant about hosting a wedding breakfast, and while she would certainly never admit the reasoning behind her insistence, every extravagant dish upon the table spoke of the truth. The dowager marchioness intended it as a means of atonement, and of signaling her approval of the marriage.

That wasn't to say her mother had been pleased the night she and Jonathan had returned to the Symonds's ballroom soaking wet after a lengthy absence—although they *had* ensured all their clothing was properly refastened before entering. When they'd announced their betrothal, though, setting society humming, the dowager had taken it all with surprising calmness. As if everything were exactly as she wanted it, and she dared anyone to say a word of contradiction.

Her mother's desire for Amelia to have a proper church wedding and a wedding breakfast had been the only point of contention between them in the days that followed. But as much as Amelia hadn't wanted to go through all that fuss, she was glad, in the end, for the compromise they'd reached: a ceremony at St. George's and a breakfast, but with only a small guest list of Amelia and Jonathan's choosing.

As anxious as she'd been to officially become Jonathan's wife, she'd put the weeks in the interim to good use, arranging with Harding and Shipley for the publication of her new column in *The Ladies' Spectator*. A column not so different from *Lady Lockheart* but with a new name: *Dear Duchess*. The timing of the change had already elicited a few whispers from the ton. *Had Lady Lockheart truly been replaced by a real* duchess? *And if so, how funny that such a thing should happen only days before the former Lady Amelia Prescott was set to become the Duchess of Branscombe.*

Her identity was apt to become a poorly kept secret. Still a secret, though, in a sense. Something with which she could maintain an air of mystery, that she would never outright confirm or deny. With any luck, that would make people even more eager to read the duchess's column. Which was exactly the way she wanted it.

As for Jonathan, he'd kept busy over the past weeks, too. He'd begun attending sessions regularly in the House of Lords and had been developing acquaintanceships with some of the other peers. Allies, he said, who were like-minded in their political beliefs. He'd also been working on a speech about the critical need for stricter regulations pertaining to madhouses around the country. A fact Amelia knew well, for on some evenings—on the best, quiet evenings, when an invitation to a soiree or musicale didn't occupy their time—she would slip into the back garden where he awaited beneath the oak, and he would practice it with her. Carefully enunciating each word, asking her opinion on certain turns of phrase to ensure they were clear.

He planned to deliver the speech next month, once they returned from their honeymoon at the ducal seat, Edgecote Hall in Northamptonshire—a destination they would hopefully reach with less difficulty this time. While he may never fully shed his nerves when speaking to a crowd, his passion for the topic was apparent, and she had every confidence he'd do splendidly.

She slipped a glance at him—*her husband*, she reminded herself yet again—where he sat adjacent to her at the head of the table, and she couldn't help but smile. He was deep in conversation with the guests to his other side: Benedict and Alexander, her nephews.

Which was yet another reason—perhaps the greatest reason—Amelia had to be grateful for the wedding breakfast. After all the years she'd spent not knowing Samuel's family, and then having them become strangers to Rockliffe House again after Theo and the dowager's falling out last year, they'd finally made a small step toward reconciliation.

Perhaps Theo would never fully forgive the dowager. She would be well within her right not to. However, in honor of the friendship she and Amelia had forged after Samuel's death, she'd been willing to accept the wedding invitation on behalf of herself, her new husband, Jeremy, and her boys. That, to Amelia, was the best gift.

"You truly swam in the ocean with sharks? And then you saw a *real* tiger?" Alexander's animated voice rang out above the steady hum of chatter around the table, and Amelia grinned once again. Her youngest nephew had a fondness for crafting adventure stories, so his questions for Jonathan, once he'd discovered his new uncle's past as a world traveler, hadn't relented since the moment they sat down. Jonathan, in turn, was proving to be a skilled and patient storyteller.

He would make a wonderful father someday. Perhaps sooner rather than later if they spent their weeks at Edgecote Hall the way she anticipated. She straightened in her chair, squeezing her legs together against the faint stirring of heat that emerged. As soon as they stepped foot in the carriage and closed the door behind them, she had every intention of letting that desire ignite. For the time being, though, she planned to enjoy a little more of the harmony of the wedding breakfast.

Everything was as it should be. Everyone was here. Nearly, at least.

She leaned in to retrieve her wineglass, thinking to give a silent, private toast to the ones who'd once held a seat at this table and were no longer with them. However, her hand froze in midair. There were footsteps echoing through the corridor outside the dining room. The heavy, rhythmic thumping of boots.

Which was nothing remarkable. The butler, Flynt, had been rushing about all morning, as had the numerous footmen. Still, there was something that gave her pause, something about the steady beat that had an atypical air of command.

And then, she saw him.

He appeared as a figure in the doorway, tall and broad-shouldered, clad in a crumpled black coat. His jaw contained the shadow of a beard, his face etched with fatigue that didn't look like it could be cured by just a good night's rest. But despite the changes to his countenance, he still had the same blue eyes, not so different from her own. Hair tinged with the same auburn that had shown up in all the Prescott siblings to varying degrees.

"Nicholas." His name caught in her throat, and she blinked, waiting for him to disappear.

Except he didn't, and in the next instant, she was clamoring to her feet, running to the doorway. Nicholas—like their mother—didn't enjoy extravagant scenes or excessive displays of affection. However, she couldn't stop herself, for she'd just been mourning his absence, and out of nowhere, he'd appeared.

She ran until she crashed into him, flinging her arms about his neck. For a full year and a half, she'd heard nothing from him, thinking he might be as lost to her as Samuel. Yet now, he was here. Really and truly here, and instead of shrugging her off, his arm went stiffly around her back. The action of someone who almost seemed unaccustomed to a genuine caring touch.

"I've missed you. I'm so glad you're home." She extended the embrace another moment before her head popped up, and she peered behind his shoulder. "Where's Emily?"

A flutter of eagerness rippled through her as she surveyed the corridor, awaiting the light, childlike footsteps that used to flit about Rockliffe House. Not that Nicholas's daughter was truly a child anymore, having reached the age of twelve since Amelia had last laid eyes on her. But whatever changes had come about, Emily was her niece, and Amelia had missed her just as deeply as she had her brother.

"She was tired after our long journey, and I had her sent

upstairs to rest. I'm sure she'll be pleased to see you later." Nicholas took a step into the room, where a hush had fallen over the formerly bustling table, and all faces had turned in their direction. "I hear from Flynt that congratulations are in order. It seems we have much to discuss."

"Rockliffe." Before Amelia could form a response, her mother's brisk voice cut into the stillness, and the dowager pushed herself to her feet, causing the other gentlemen at the table to scramble up with her. "Might we have a private word?"

Nicholas inclined his head, as nonchalant a motion as if this were a perfectly normal Friday morning. Their mother, too, didn't gasp or swoon or indicate anything other than composure. Had it not been for her hand, quivering atop her cane as she crossed the room, Amelia would have never known how much the long-lost marquess's surprise reappearance affected her. No doubt she wanted to keep it that way, and to determine the details of his return away from the attention of their guests. As matters stood, the mere fact he'd shown up was apt to cause a stir that would be all over London by nightfall.

"We'll talk later," Amelia murmured, stepping aside to let her mother take her place beside him. She watched as they slipped from the room, as cool as ever, and when they disappeared, she sauntered back to the table almost in a daze, dropping onto her chair. Tentative streams of chatter had started amongst the guests once more, and Benedict and Alexander turned their attention to Theo, peppering her with questions about their unknown uncle. Leaving Jonathan without a monopoly on his attention, for the moment.

"I can't believe it." She reached for his hand beneath the table, giving it a squeeze. "Nicholas and Emily have really arrived home. And today, of all days."

He returned the pressure of her fingers, shifting his leg so it brushed against hers, concealed by the crisp linen tablecloth. "I'm so happy for you, my love. I know how much their absence worried you."

"Thank you. I'm so happy, too. Although I don't know what it is about Prescotts. We seem to have a talent for doing things dramatically, without even meaning to, and then attracting gossip." She glanced back toward the doorway, where the vision of Nicholas suddenly emerging there continued to flash through her mind. The figure had been her brother, unquestionably, but also different from before. In the time since they'd last seen each other, he'd traveled a great distance. Experienced betrayal. Become a widower. It was no wonder that in addition to his usual somber reserve, he seemed to have an added weight upon his shoulders. A weariness that went bone deep.

But that could change. She'd been given another chance, and he could, too. With time, and the right person, perhaps he could become as blissfully happy as she was with Jonathan.

"Ah, well." She settled their joined hands upon Jonathan's leg, the surface warm and solid through his wool breeches. "I suppose that's not entirely a bad thing. Were it not for the threat of gossip, I wouldn't have found myself on the Great North Road in need of assistance at the moment when a certain, um, *not*-so-ducal carriage drove past. As it turns out, that carriage stopping was the most fortunate circumstance of my life."

"Mine, too, without a doubt." He leaned in to press a soft kiss upon the bridge of her nose, gossip-spreaders' opinions about the display be hanged.

She grinned, feeling a pleasant heat spread across her face. This really had been the perfect morning.

She had her family about her, bits and pieces of it she'd thought forever fragmented now gathered as a whole.

And best of all, she had him. Her heart, once fragmented as well, had been put back together.

Yes, their vows had taken place a full eleven years after they'd planned. But what they'd lost in the past, they now served to gain as part of a bright, promising, wonderful future.

~

THE END

Bonus Content

Sign up for Jane's monthly newsletter to get access to free bonus content, including a subscriber-exclusive prologue for *A Duke Once Lost*. You will also be the first to know about new releases, giveaways, special promotions, and more.
Join now at: www.janemaguireauthor.com/newsletter

About the Author

Jane Maguire is a Canadian author whose lifelong passions for history, writing, and love stories inevitably led her to begin penning historical romance novels. While her love of historical fiction spans all eras, she focuses her writing on high society in the regency period. She enjoys crafting stories with lots of angst, which makes giving her characters their happily ever afters all the more satisfying.

When she isn't at her computer writing and researching, you can find her vacationing in the Rocky Mountains, playing classical music on the piano, or simply curling up with a cup of tea and a good book. She lives with her husband, two kids, and a very floofy cat.

You can find Jane online at www.janemaguireauthor.com.

www.ingramcontent.com/pod-product-compliance
Lightning Source LLC
Chambersburg PA
CBHW061657190726

48289CB00006B/1918